A NOVEL

Ella's Will

A NOVEL

JESSILYN STEWART
PEASLEE

Sweetwater Books
An Imprint of Cedar Fort, Inc.
Springville, Utah

© 2016 Jessilyn Stewart Peaslee

All rights reserved.

No part of this book may be reproduced in any form whatsoever, whether by graphic, visual, electronic, film, microfilm, tape recording, or any other means, without prior written permission of the publisher, except in the case of brief passages embodied in critical reviews and articles.

This is a work of fiction. The characters, names, incidents, places, and dialogue are products of the author's imagination and are not to be construed as real. The opinions and views expressed herein belong solely to the author and do not necessarily represent the opinions or views of Cedar Fort, Inc. Permission for the use of sources, graphics, and photos is also solely the responsibility of the author.

ISBN 13: 978-1-4621-1908-0

Published by Sweetwater Books, an imprint of Cedar Fort, Inc.
2373 W. 700 S., Springville, UT 84663
Distributed by Cedar Fort, Inc., www.cedarfort.com

LIBRARY OF CONGRESS CATALOGING-IN-PUBLICATION DATA

Names: Peaslee, Jessilyn Stewart, 1979- author.
Title: Ella's Will / Jessilyn Stewart Peaslee.
Other titles: Adaptation of (work): Cinderella.
Description: Springville, Utah : Sweetwater Books, an imprint of Cedar Fort, Inc., [2016]
Identifiers: LCCN 2016025759 (print) | LCCN 2016027381 (ebook) | ISBN 9781462119080 (perfect bound : alk. paper) | ISBN 9781462126873 (epub, pdf, and mobi)
Subjects: LCSH: Stablehands--Fiction. | Cinderella (Tale)--Adaptations. | LCGFT: Novels. | Romance fiction. | Fairy tales.
Classification: LCC PS3616.E2665 E44 2016 (print) | LCC PS3616.E2665 (ebook)
| DDC 813/.6--dc23
LC record available at https://lccn.loc.gov/2016025759

Cover design by Rebecca J. Greenwood
Cover design © 2016 by Cedar Fort, Inc.
Edited and typeset by Jessica Romrell

Printed in the United States of America

10 9 8 7 6 5 4 3 2 1

Printed on acid-free paper

To those who wait.

The best things *will* come.

"Revisiting the years, but ultimately the one fateful week, when Ella and Will fell in love, made my heart happy. Not only does the reader get to re-experience all of their favorite moments, but they get introduced to a whole new cast of characters and see how it all played out from Will's perspective. Ella's Will transports the reader to a kingdom far away, one is able to fall in love all over again; with Will, with Ella, with the idea of courage and kindness, and best of all, with love."

—Tara Creel, Deseret News Reviewer and Editor at Month9Books

"The question of how to be a great man is one that has been asked throughout time. Through the eyes, heart, and hands of Will Hawkins, the reader will be enveloped with the delicate answer. Ella's Will is a story of sacrifice, selflessness, courage, and the truest of true love. Your heart will be touched over and over again by Will and his Ella."

—Mandy Al-Bjaly, author (or should it say blogger) of ablisscomplete.com.

"If you loved Jessilyn's first story "Ella," you will love this remake told from Will's perspective. I couldn't put it down. A perfect companion story!"

—Emily Barton, blogger of "Emmy Mom—One Day at a Time, www.emmymom2.com

"No great wisdom can be reached without sacrifice."

—C. S. Lewis

Prologue

NO ONE HAD BOTHERED TO WIND THE CLOCK. THE HOUR hand and the minute hand hung lifeless at the six. Merciless fingers of smoldering heat reached out of the fireplace even though the late afternoon sunshine still filtered in through the lace curtains, splattering the room with random spots of light.

Will Hawkins sat on the chair next to the bed where Henry Blakeley lay shivering under three thick quilts. Through blurred eyes, Will noticed the sheen of moisture on Henry's forehead, the hollowness of his cheeks, and the feebleness of his hands. Mr. Blakeley's once work-roughened and sun-darkened hands now appeared fragile and strangely frightening, like they belonged to some stranger. Trembling, Mr. Blakeley reached out one of those unfamiliar hands and clasped Will's hand with a startling strength.

"Will, I need you to know that I love you like a son," he whispered, his glimmering gray eyes staring straight into the younger boy's. Will shifted in his chair under Mr. Blakeley's piercing gaze; but at those words, a wave of joy mingled with despair constricted Will's chest and his breath came in shallow, quiet gasps. Mr. Blakeley's form began to look less substantial through the tears that clouded Will's vision. After days of fighting against it, Will acknowledged that soon Mr. Blakeley would be fading from this life . . . and from his own.

His chin trembled and he balled his free hand into a fist to force himself to gain control. He wanted to be strong, to be a man—not to cry and be weak like a lost child. At the same time, Will needed to tell Mr. Blakeley that he loved him, too, that he loved him like a father, and that since his own father's death, Mr. Blakeley truly had become his father. He wanted to tell him that he hoped to be just like him—he wanted to help people and raise horses and have a family. But all he could do was swallow and blink furiously and fight the ache that seemed too heavy for his fourteen-year-old heart.

The window was open across the room, the curtains lightly fluttering in the friendly breeze of late summer. Will took a deep breath and it helped to steady his emotions. The slanting sunlight streamed across Mr. Blakeley's bed and lit up his face. He smiled at Will with tears in his eyes.

"I always wanted a son," Henry continued. "I love my Ella. There are no words to tell you how much I love my Ella. But if Eleanor had lived, I like to think that we would have had a son and that he would have been just like you."

Nodding and pursing his lips, Will clenched his fist even tighter. Though he never wanted to leave Mr. Blakeley, he also felt the almost overpowering urge to run from the room and find a corner where he could bury his head in his hands.

"Will?" He couldn't look up. He couldn't let Mr. Blakeley see the weakness and fear in his eyes. "You're going to be a great man, son. You're already well on your way."

The gloom lifted for a moment as a comforting sense of purpose eased the ache in Will's chest. His head shot up and his eyes searched Henry's face.

"How can I be a great man?" His voice was rough and quiet, but tinged with an urgency that seemed to bring some life back into him.

Henry chuckled weakly. "I'm still trying to figure that out, son."

Will scooted forward on his chair. "You *are* a great man, sir. Please, tell me."

His arms shaking from the effort, Henry pushed himself up a little higher on the pillows. He opened his mouth to speak when Ella's laughter floated up to them through the open window. Henry turned away from Will and toward the direction of the sound and smiled. But soon, Ella's laughter faded, and Henry's smile with it.

His gaze still fixed on the window, Henry spoke, though he seemed to be talking to the breeze. "She doesn't know how much her life is going to change. How am I going to tell her?" He fell silent for a moment. When he spoke again, his soft voice trembled. "How am I going to leave her?"

The servants had been instructed not to tell Ella how ill her father was—that he would tell her in his own way and time. They obeyed, though some had wondered if it would soon be too late.

With his free hand, Henry reached for the violin that sat on the other side of the bed and, grasping it by the top of the scroll, he stood it upright and began spinning it slowly around and around with his fingers. Will saw that on the back of the violin, on the lower bout near the chin rest, Henry Blakeley's name had been engraved. Henry sighed and laid the violin back down, still resting his hand on it.

Henry's eyes became more unfocused, his grip easing on Will's hand. Not wanting to intrude on whatever had brought this expression of quiet contemplation to Henry's face, Will started to pull his hand out of Henry's. But Henry turned back to him with that same penetrating gaze and grasped Will's hand tighter.

"Will, some people think that men have to be strong all the time, that they have to be tough and unyielding, that they have to be in charge and make things happen. Those are all admirable qualities under the right circumstances; but sometimes I think we, as men, take them too far and hurt those around us. Instead of being leaders, we can become tyrants."

Will nodded. He couldn't be certain, but he thought Henry may have been talking about Will's father. Mr. Blakeley had been well enough acquainted with the now deceased Mr. Hawkins to know that he had been a tyrant. Will couldn't remember his father ever speaking a kind word, when he had actually been home. And though many of Will's brothers had followed down the same path as their father, he wondered if there was still hope for himself. Having the good fortune of working for Mr. Blakeley since his father's death had opened Will's eyes to a different kind of life, a different way of living. In those four short years, Will felt the hopelessness he had become accustomed to as a child begin to transform into a sense of purpose. He was determined not to live the way his father had, he just wasn't sure how.

"Will, sometimes admitting that we are weak can be a strength. Sometimes acknowledging we don't know something is wise. Sometimes the poorest of men are the richest of men. Sometimes courage looks like cowardice to the people who don't understand. Sometimes sacrificing our own happiness for the benefit of others brings us joy." He released Will's hand and reached up to gently squeeze his shoulder. "Do you understand, son? Being a man—a great man—doesn't always mean being the boldest and toughest. It's simply knowing when to use your strength for the benefit of those around you. Often, a situation calls for boldness and force, but sometimes, gentleness and meekness are needed. A great man knows when to use both." He sighed. "Yes, I am still trying to figure it out." He smiled and let his hand drop from Will's shoulder and onto the bed.

Ella laughed again and it was as if it were the sound of her voice, untroubled and brimming with the charms of childhood, that made the curtains flutter again. Henry turned back toward the open window and closed his eyes. His unshaven chin trembled and he lifted his hand off his violin and placed it on his chest, as if trying to hold the sound of her laughter within him.

Gathering his courage, Will took a deep breath and scooted forward on his chair. "Mr. Blakeley?" he whispered, the heaviness in his chest making it nearly impossible to breathe as the image of Mr. Blakeley became so blurred he could barely see him.

Henry looked back at Will, a perceptive smile on his dry lips.

"I-I love you, Mr. Blakeley. I love you like you were my very own father. I hope that someday I'll be a great man like you." The tears had started flowing down Will's cheeks, clearing his vision. For the first time since his own father's death, he felt a weight lift off his shoulders. Hope filled his heart even in the midst of his sorrow.

"You already are, son," Henry whispered, his own tears on his cheeks.

Chapter 1

Ella Blakeley sat on the chopping block, a dead chicken dangling from her fingers. Her other hand deftly plucked the feathers that landed on her lap and fell to the ground in fluffy white puffs around her bare feet. Her golden hair fell loose across her shoulders and on either side of her face, her expression calm yet focused. The quick plucking motions she made indicated this was definitely not the first time she had performed such a task.

I stood in the middle of the road, watching the perplexing scene in front of me, my eyes wide in disbelief. Without actually making the decision to do so, I moved closer to her—and closer to the house where I had started working as a mourning ten-year-old boy. It had been six years since Henry Blakeley had died and I hadn't set foot inside the house since. Today I had decided to take the road on my way home from work, instead of cutting through the forest as I usually did, trying to avoid all the mud from the recent rains.

As I drew closer, my head moved slowly back and forth in bewilderment. Ella hadn't seen me yet and she continued in her lowly work. I tried to make my mind grasp what my eyes were seeing. Her cheeks were smudged with dirt and what looked like flour. The last time I had seen her, her cheeks were streaked with tears at her father's passing, but she had at least been clean and well-dressed, loved and cared-for. Her hair had been curled in the childhood ringlets of a ten-year-old girl and her feet shod in the most fashionable shoes with silver buckles. I knew her shoes because I had been the one to shorten her stirrups when she went riding with her father.

But today, despite the onset of an early winter, her pink feet were bare. Her breath came in puffs of frosty clouds, her cheeks and nose rosy from the cold. I stared at her tiny bare feet in the mud, surrounded by feathers. My eyes moistened at the sight. She was cold, though she didn't shiver. She was hungry. I could tell by the gauntness in her face and the exaggerated roundness of her eyes.

How could this be the daughter of Henry Blakeley?

I stepped even closer—close enough that I could see tired, dark circles under her eyes. Close enough that I could see the pale slimness of her laboring hands—hands that had once worn soft leather gloves when she held horse reins to protect her skin from calluses and blisters; hands that had once been warmed in her father's big, warm hands if hers were ever too cold.

Ella sat in the one patch of sunlight there was in the yard, which also happened to be the one spot I could see her from the road. The heavy clouds from the latest storm and the tall trees that surrounded the house blocked out most of the light and all of the warmth.

The chill of the approaching darkness was in the air, but I hadn't really felt it until that moment.

"Miss Blakeley?" I whispered, as I risked a tentative step onto the yard.

Her hands froze, her fingers covered with down. Her eyes shot up and met mine and were not just filled with surprise or embarrassment as I might have expected, but with a wild and uncontrollable fear. Holding up my hands and stepping back a few paces, I hoped to show her I meant her no harm, though I was startled by the terror in her wide eyes and in her tense, motionless body. For a moment, I wondered if this truly was Ella Blakeley, or if I had mistaken her for a servant. Before I could look any closer, she suddenly stood and dropped the chicken in the pile of feathers at her feet, grabbed her skirts, and fled to the back of the house.

Standing helpless and utterly dazed, I took a moment to decide what I should do. I knew I had frightened her, and I knew that by following her I would probably scare her into fits of hysteria. But I couldn't leave her this way. I decided to follow after her, knowing it was probably foolish, but also knowing that I had to learn what had become of this girl—the daughter of the man I had loved like a father; the girl who should be the lady of this grand house, not the one who plucked dead chickens outside in her cold, bare feet.

As I strode to the back of the house, I saw the barn door swing closed, but it didn't latch completely. At least she had run inside the barn and not inside the house. I couldn't very well go knock on the door of a house I hadn't been to in years, demanding to know what had happened in Ella's life to make her this way. I was a stranger here, and the thought brought me overwhelming sadness. It was here that I had learned who I was and what I wanted to be. I had cleaned out every stall in the barn I was now walking toward. I had fixed the gate that I now passed by. I had groomed the horses in the stable off to my left, which now stood empty, its door hanging open crookedly on one rusty hinge.

No sound came from anywhere in the barn, but I pulled the door open, ignoring the practical part of my mind that told me I was being irrational. The door creaked closed behind me and I stood in the empty barn. I had hoped that it would be slightly warmer once I was inside, but I was mistaken. The expectation of warmth made the coldness feel even colder. A chill shivered down my neck, though just moments before on my walk home I had removed my jacket, a whistle on my lips, enjoying the crispness of early evening and the memory of my walk with Jane Emerson.

My eyes adjusted to the darkness. Soon I saw little puffs of quick breaths in the back corner indicating where Ella was hiding, but I stayed where I was.

"Miss Blakeley, it's me. It's William Hawkins. Are you all right?" It was a ridiculous question to which I knew the answer, but I hoped it told her I was only there to see how she was doing and not to harm or scare her . . . at least not any more than I already had.

She didn't answer so I glanced around the barn while I waited. I was pleased to see that there were two cows in the stalls and that they looked well-fed. I also noted that the barn was immaculate and in good repair. I wondered how many servants were still here at Ashfield, helping Ella. But why, if she had help, was she doing any of this work at all? I knew that when Victoria, Henry's new wife, had sold all the horses soon after his death, we stable workers were all forced to find new work. I wondered if the house servants had suffered a similar fate as I realized that I never saw anyone who worked at Ashfield any more.

Looking back at the clouds of breath, I noticed that they had now slowed to a normal rhythm.

"Please, Miss Blakeley. I just need to know that you're all right. Can I speak with you for a minute?"

There was a moment of hesitation, then a rustling in the hay, and soon Ella emerged from the shadows. The previous terror in her eyes had quieted and she seemed more peaceful. She clasped her hands under her chin and she started to shiver, almost as if she just realized she was freezing.

"I thought it was you," she murmured, a whisper of a smile on her lips and a hint of tenderness in her eyes.

"You remember me?" I grinned at her, though her gaze was now fixed on the floor.

"You were Papa's favorite." She lifted her eyes to mine for a fleeting moment, and then toward the house, almost as if her father were still inside and she might be able to see him there.

"Well, besides you," I said. Her smile grew warmer and the hollow expression in her eyes softened. "Miss Blakeley, please forgive me, but why were you plucking a chicken? Why are you barefoot? And why are you not inside keeping warm on a day like today? I just don't understand. Is everything all right here?"

The panic from earlier returned to her face and her eyes darted back in the direction of the house. She faced me again and her expression became pleading.

"Please don't tell anyone, Mr. Hawkins. I-I was careless. No one is supposed to see—" She closed her mouth so quickly I heard her teeth snap together. "I was only so close to the road so that I could be in the sunlight. The sun was behind the trees and it was so cold. . . . Forgive me for complaining. It was a thoughtless mistake. I'll be more careful in the future."

Understanding was beginning to dawn on me, and with it came a wave of outrage that burned away the chill in the air. Her fearful, unnecessary apologies. Her nervousness. Her eyes that darted toward the house every few seconds. The charming, cheerful little girl who had everyone's heart in her hands was gone. In her place was a sixteen-year-old young woman who, instead of being concerned with nothing but romance and courting and schooling, stood barefoot—freezing, and obviously starving.

Someone had sucked the life out of her, and I had an idea of who it was.

"Has . . . *she* done this to you?" I couldn't even say Victoria's name, but it seemed I didn't need to. Ella didn't need any clarification. She didn't say anything, but her mouth opened, then closed, and her frantic eyes kept shifting from me and back at the house. I had my answer.

The only interaction I had had with the new Mrs. Blakeley before Henry's death was when he brought her out to the stables to introduce us to our new mistress, and the two or three times when she went out riding with him. She detested the horses and was not good at hiding it, at least when Mr. Blakeley wasn't looking. She would subtly, but forcefully, push the horses' heads away from her if they got too close and scrunch up her face if they even breathed in her direction.

She wasn't fond of us either. She'd refused to let us touch her with our dirty hands to help her up into the saddle. Instead, she insisted on using the mounting stool on her own, which would sometimes elicit quiet chuckles from the grooms as we watched her. And after Mr. Blakeley's death, the only interaction I had had with her was when she came out to the stables and callously told us all to leave because we were no longer needed.

In the years since Henry's death, I started to notice her whenever I saw her in town or at church. I wondered what kind of woman she was. I couldn't help wondering if Henry had truly known her. As soon as the socially acceptable amount of time had passed after his death, Victoria was always at every gathering, always the center of attention, always the most sought-after in any crowd. I had never been fooled by her, though. There was a coldness in her eyes that hinted at something more sinister underneath her dynamic and alluring personality. There was a hungriness about her that seemed to feed on adoration. She seemed to revel in the power that her popularity had given her.

I had always been annoyed and puzzled by Victoria Blakeley, but now I hated her with such a passion I didn't know I was capable of. In my anger, I stepped closer to Ella—too quickly and too deliberately—and she jumped back like a frightened cat.

"Miss Blakeley, I can't leave you here. You must come with me. I'll never forgive myself if I leave you here." I tried to think of where I could take her. I couldn't take her to my one-room, drafty cabin, but I was sure the town doctor would know of a place, if he didn't even take her in himself. Dr. Clayton had at least five daughters, from what I could count anyway. There had to be room for one more.

I held out my hand and took a cautious step forward. Her eyes gleamed as her gaze fell from my face to my outstretched hand. She stared at it as if it were something beautiful. She looked back into my eyes, the pleading expression back from before, almost asking for my permission to escape.

"Please," I whispered. "You're cold. You're hungry. You need someone to take care of you."

At those words, something seemed to snap inside of her. She blinked and took a deliberate step back.

"Take care . . . ," she whispered to herself.

"Yes, you need someone to take care of you." Why was she backing away?

She shook her head back and forth, while still gazing at my hand.

"I promised . . ." Her voice trailed off and I waited. "I'm not going anywhere," she ended abruptly and almost boldly.

Stunned, I breathed out an exasperated breath.

"You promised . . . what? Who?"

Her eyes became resolute and almost piercing in their determination. "I'm staying here."

"No. This is absurd. What if your father knew you were living like this? You must come with me. I'll never forgive myself if I leave you here, and neither would he." I stepped closer and she met my eyes steadily. Her previous pleading had now passed to me and she became the stubborn one.

She studied my face, and for a moment her eyes were neither timid nor fearful. In response to whatever she saw on my face, the stubborn set of her jaw relaxed, her lips turned up in a gentle smile, and her eyes softened into compassion.

"Mr. Hawkins, I can't tell you how much I appreciate your concern. I honestly can't remember the last time I really spoke to . . . anyone. Years." A shadow darkened her expression for a moment, but she deliberately brightened. "I'm sorry I reacted so . . . nonsensically when I saw you. I was just surprised, that's all." A subtle change had come over her. She stood up straighter. Her smile, though thin, was sincere and warm, her gaze more direct. "You reminded me why I'm here, and for that I thank you. I have had a difficult few days and was feeling the strain, but now I feel much better."

I could see it. In just a few minutes, her whole countenance had illuminated and the way she looked back at me now made me feel like I was the sun that had brought her that light. It was suddenly hard to breathe. Her unexpected resoluteness, though encouraging considering her utter lack of life just a few minutes earlier, was also frustrating. She really was refusing to accept my help. As baffled as I was, I could see how her making the choice to stay had lifted her spirits, though I couldn't understand why. What had I said to make her feel and look this way? What was this promise I had reminded her of that made her smile so beautifully and infuriatingly?

Perhaps, I hoped without truly believing it, her life wasn't as harsh as I had feared. Perhaps she did have more help than I had imagined. Perhaps, I tried to tell myself, she happened to enjoy plucking chickens . . . in the cold . . . in her bare feet. Whatever the reason for this inexplicable expression of contentment, her smile grew, and it was my turn to feel like she was the sun. She radiated warmth and kindness, and for the first time since I saw her plucking that chicken, I could see a little bit of her father in her.

Unfortunately, that also meant that I had lost. Her determination had overpowered my pleadings.

"Miss Blakeley, will you please tell me if you need anything? I still live on the property my family has owned for as long as I can remember, only now I live in a little cabin on the southwest corner of our property. It's just a little back from the road, but you can see it if you head east. I can't leave until I know that you're all right."

"I'm better than all right," she said sincerely. "I have a friend in the world."

"Yes, you do have a friend, Miss Blakeley."

"Please, call me Ella."

"Will. I mean . . . *I* will." I smiled. "And please call me Will," I finished lamely.

"Will." She was kind enough not to laugh at my awkwardness, though I would have loved to hear it. She nodded and walked past me into the fading blush of sunset, the heavy clouds quickly chasing away the last slivers of light. The chill crept back into my fingers and toes and the back of my neck. I grimaced at her bare feet.

She paused as she entered the yard and turned back to me. "Please don't mention what you saw here today to anyone. I beg of you."

"Why not?" I had planned to go straight to the doctor's house after I left.

"She won't like it, and it won't solve anything."

My powerlessness was maddening, but the solemnity in her eyes forced me to admit she was probably right. "Only if you promise to tell me, or anyone, if you need anything." I ducked my head, ashamed that I was actually going to leave her here. I stuffed my hands in my pockets to keep me from grabbing hers and taking her away before she could protest.

"I promise." She turned around and continued toward the front of the house.

Catching up so I could walk next to her as she returned to her abandoned chicken, I was unable to keep myself from glancing down at her every few steps, though she kept her grave eyes straight ahead. When we reached the chopping block, she bent over, picked up the chicken, and nodded to me in farewell. She returned to the back of the house and into the freezing shadows, obviously unwilling to risk being seen by any other passersby.

Once she was out of sight, I hurried home and went straight to my woodpile on the side of my cabin. I gathered as many logs as I could, tied them together with a rope, and loaded them onto Charlie, my horse. I searched through my box of extra tools and odds and ends, found a hinge, and put it in my pack along with a few nails and my hammer. When I returned to Ashfield, all the lights were out. Quietly, I replaced the rusty, broken hinge on the stable door with the new one. I then replenished Ella's woodpile, wondering if it was also she who had cut the wood. As strange as seeing her pluck a chicken was, I couldn't imagine her splitting logs. But, it was safe to assume, though I had rebelled against the thought, that Ella was the sole servant left in her house and it was most likely she who did all the chores. I growled to myself in fury, forcing myself to respect her wishes and not go charging in to take her with me . . . somewhere.

When I walked out my door the next morning, there was a loaf of warm bread on my doorstep.

Chapter 2

Life continued on as normal. Mostly normal. For a while. I stopped cutting through the woods on my way to and from work. Instead, I took the road past Ashfield. Ella was never there, never plucking a chicken or chopping wood. Sometimes I even wondered if seeing her sitting on that chopping block had been a dream. Or a nightmare.

But I knew it was real. Something inside me had changed.

Whenever I walked with Jane, I was distracted, earning me some pouts and an occasional stomped foot. Soon, our walks came to an end and with that came a relief I hadn't anticipated even a week before. My relief was mingled with her father's, who wished I had never shown an interest in his daughter in the first place. When I saw Jane in town, her sorrowful eyes followed me, but I had no desire to return her glances. I wished her sorrow would simply fade into indifference, but instead it ripened into jealousy. Her glances soon became glares if I ever spoke to anyone in front of her. All that did was make me grateful it had ended when it did. She knew I was preoccupied and uninterested, though she didn't know why. I could barely explain it myself.

All day, every day, while I worked at the palace, my thoughts kept turning to Ella—wondering what she was doing, if she was all right.

Prince Kenton even noticed.

"I know that look," he said from the open stable doors one day. He chuckled good-naturedly though I had failed to notice him standing there waiting for a horse.

I jumped, dropping the bridle I had been absentmindedly oiling. "Forgive me, Your Highness." I hurried to his favorite horse and tossed a saddle on its back.

"I wish there was someone out there to make me so oblivious to the world." He laughed again as I led the horse to him. I smiled at him apologetically, ignoring his insinuation. "You wouldn't be willing to share, would you?" His eyes were mischievous as usual.

"She's not royalty, Your Majesty," I replied as I adjusted his stirrups. "Besides, it's not what you think. I'm just concerned about an old acquaintance. That's all."

"Royal or not, your *concern* about this *acquaintance*," he said dryly, an ironic grin on his face, "is making me envious."

"Of me?" I finally had to laugh, grateful for a moment of levity after so many days of worrying.

"You'd be surprised." I didn't detect any note of sarcasm in his statement, but he had kicked the horse's flank and was behind the hill before I could respond.

The only time I saw Ella was at church. I supposed I had seen her there for years but never really noticed her. Now I could understand why. She walked in, not speaking to anyone, her head held down. She didn't flirt with any of the boys. She didn't try to get attention in any way. Her quietness was overshadowed by Victoria and her daughters. I wanted to talk to Ella now that I saw her, but I didn't even know what to say to her. I barely even got to see her face. She stayed right next to her stepfamily, standing a little back, while Victoria made people laugh out on the lawn after services ended.

Weeks went by and just as I was beginning to truly believe I had imagined the whole thing, I saw her again. It was early in the morning and though it was winter, it was warmer than it had been in a month. I was closer to Ashfield than I was to my own home, having found a perfect fishing spot where the ice had melted and the fish had pooled together. Though I had just been appointed head groom, I wasn't needed at the palace stables that day. Prince Kenton was on another one of his trips and the king and queen didn't need the horses.

It was so quiet at the pond, I could almost hear the fish's fins swaying underneath the water. Just as the sun rose and brought a little more warmth to the wintry morning, there was a slight rustling of leaves in the distance and then an unmistakable cracking of branches. Soon, the rustling and cracking was accompanied by something I had never heard in the woods before—the sound of a woman humming. Soft and sweet, the humming echoed off the trees and traveled over the stillness of the pond.

Instead of disturbing the silence of the dormant forest, the humming complemented it, making everything feel more alive. Abandoning my fish and rod for a moment, I stood and walked closer to the sound. Just across the pond, hidden behind some trees, I saw Ella Blakeley. She was pulling the low, thin branches off a sapling and bundling them on the ground. I didn't know if she needed the wood for kindling or to make a broom, but it was the second menial task I had seen her perform with remarkable, though bewildering, skill.

The transformation I saw in her compared to a few weeks ago took my breath away. Her hair was braided and her heavy, dark blue dress was clean. She seemed warmer, not just because of what she wore, but from the inside. Her once pale cheeks were now rosy, tinged with pink from the cold, but also with vitality. She was still just as thin, but I could see that she was strong. She had a small, dull hatchet that she used to chop the branches that were too thick for her to snap off. Her lips turned up in a natural smile and her song continued to melt in with her surroundings.

Once again, I found myself moving toward her. When my boot stepped onto the boards of the bridge, Ella gasped and turned toward me. I smiled at her, but didn't stop walking.

"Good morning, Miss . . . Ella." It felt inappropriate, yet comfortable at the same time, addressing her by her first name. I wondered if her father would have approved.

"Will! You startled me!" she gasped, placing a hand over her heart.

Once I crossed the bridge, I risked walking even closer to her. She took a small step back, but didn't run away. She was real, even more real than she had been that first day I saw her. That day, she had been almost a shell of someone actually living. I remembered how she looked before she had noticed me in the road—human, but not really alive—performing a necessary task with mechanical coldness. Her eyes had been remote, her movements lifeless. But now, though she still had her defenses up and there was hesitation in her eyes, there was life in her.

She ducked her head. "What is it?" she said, suddenly inspecting the sticks in her arms.

"Oh, I'm staring aren't I?" I chuckled. "Forgive me, but you almost seem like a different person today than . . . last time." Abruptly, I felt very foolish for how I had acted—following her into the barn, begging her to leave with me, even though I was practically a stranger to her.

She sighed, but the sound was light and almost wistful. "I *feel* like a different person. I feel lighter and happier, though nothing has changed. I think I have you to thank for that."

She spoke so sincerely, yet her eyes only glanced up at mine once as she spoke. Her gaze was mostly fixed on the trees or at her pile of branches on the ground.

"And I have you to thank for the most delicious loaf of bread I have ever had in my life." I laughed, once again astonished by her. She ducked her head again, but looked back up at me with a hint of rebuke in her timid smile. "Will, you didn't *have* to restock my wood pile or fix the hinge."

"And you didn't *have* to bring me the bread." We paused and smiled.

"It was my pleasure," we said together.

Her eyes shot up and met mine. "Then it must be true," she whispered, her eyes swimming with tears that never spilled. She sounded so much like her father, my own ache set in. He would say that when two people said something at the same time. The first time I remember him saying it was soon after I started working for him. In fact, it was about Ella. Henry was talking to one of the gardeners when Ella walked by, holding a baby chick. The men stopped what they were saying to watch her.

Then, they both said, "So much like her mother," and Henry had said, "Then it must be true," with a tender smile. I only heard him say it a couple of other times, since we weren't all running around saying the same thing at the same time, but hearing it from Ella's lips showed me that she and I may have many shared memories I hadn't even considered.

It seemed we were both silently reminiscing—my thoughts wandering and Ella's eyes looking far away—when abruptly, Ella turned away from me and in the direction of Ashfield.

"I have to be getting back." A strange mask fell over her eyes then, blocking out any light that had been shining in them. She didn't become cold or angry—just lifeless. She more closely resembled the frightened, empty girl I had first seen from the road.

"Wait. What are your sticks for? Can I help you?"

"Oh, I just have to repair the chicken coop. I bundle the sticks with mud and string. It's nothing."

Now she was building chicken coops out of branches and mud and string. But, it was nothing, of course. I shook my head in amazement, a smile on my face. I suddenly felt very inept next to this resourceful and humble girl.

She bent over to gather the rest of her sticks. "Let me help you," I said, leaning over to help her.

She gathered more quickly. "No, please. It's a miracle she didn't see you in the yard the other day. If she saw me accepting help . . ." She didn't finish her sentence, but collected all the sticks before I could grab any.

"Ella, I'm just a friend helping a friend."

"She doesn't see it that way. She'll think I asked for help and that you know that we're . . . poor. She can barely admit it herself, much less allow anyone else to."

"Even a poor stable worker?" My eyebrow raised and I scoffed at the idea.

She stood, her arms full of sticks, and met my eyes evenly. "Even a poor stable worker." She didn't say good-bye, just spun away from me and hurried toward home.

She didn't have the skip in her step of other sixteen-year-old girls, and as she drew closer to home, her stride became a little bit heavier, her head held a little bit lower. And my heart broke to watch it.

I soon discovered that she went down to the pond almost every morning, at least when the weather was good. I stood out in the rain and even the snow enough times to learn that for myself the hard way. After a few weeks, there were nights that I could barely sleep, knowing that I would get to see Ella in the morning. She became my morning.

As the years passed, I had the privilege of watching Ella slowly come back to something that resembled living, at least for a few minutes every morning. First came the smiles—evolving from tight-lipped grins to stunning beams of warmth that lit her face. Then, slowly, her laughter came back. On more than one occasion, I couldn't laugh along with her because my breath was taken away by the sound of hers. Her laughs were never loud or carefree; they were never coy or flirtatious. But they were genuine, even if they were a little hesitant. She still hadn't allowed herself to truly open up, but I had those glimpses into how much she wanted to, even if she didn't quite know how to yet.

Though her smiles and laughs increased over the years, her wardrobe diminished to just one gray dress. Her chickens were reduced to just two, and her two cows to one. She grew into a woman, with no one to show her how. But, as everyone had always said when she was a child, she had inherited a natural grace and charm from her mother, and a pleasant and generous disposition from her father. She somehow allowed these to become her most obvious traits, even amidst her poverty and the harsh physical and emotional demands placed upon her. She kept her goodness, though she had very few examples of it. She kept her kindness, though she was very rarely shown any. Instead of becoming hardened in her situation, she became even more humble.

Her smiles and laughter were enough to make me love her, but when she started to blush, it was as if I, too, were coming back to life when I hadn't realized I wasn't fully living. To see her cheeks warm when our eyes met made me wonder if she might be feeling something, too. My adoration grew deeper every day, but I learned very early that if I moved too quickly toward her, literally or figuratively, she would take an instinctive step back. I understood in those moments how very fragile she was. When she was with me, smiling and seeming so light and unburdened, it was easy to forget the life that she would have to go home to—the coldness, the distance, the anger, and the harsh punishments inflicted upon her by Victoria.

I gave up trying to convince Ella to leave one day—the day she finally told me about her promise she had referred to in the barn. We were sitting at the pond; she was giving my horse, Charlie, a good brushing and I was repairing the crank on her butter churner. She hummed quietly and contentedly to the rhythm of the brush strokes.

"Do you always hum while you work?" I asked, breaking the comfortable silence.

She glanced up, apprehension in her eyes. "I'm sorry. Does it bother you?"

I laughed. "I can't even tell you how much it *doesn't* bother me." I looked down at my work so she could relax. "I love it."

After a moment, I glanced up at her and I saw that her lips were pursed into a small smile. She didn't blush yet. That didn't come for a little while longer. "No, I don't always sing when I work. Only where she can't hear me."

"She doesn't like it?" I asked. We both knew who "she" was.

Ella shook her head. She bit her lip, seeming to debate over something.

"I'm sorry. I didn't mean to pry."

"No, it's not that. It's just that I think I . . . that it reminds her of my father."

"I would think that would make her happy."

"I would, too. But . . ." She hesitated again. "Either she didn't love him, or she loved him more than I know. I don't think I'll ever be sure."

Once again I was absolutely perplexed as to why she stayed at Ashfield with that woman. Ella couldn't sing in her own home. I didn't even want to think of what had happened to Ella that taught her how Victoria felt about her singing.

"Ella, I must ask, just once more. Why don't you leave?"

She smiled. It was as if she knew the question had been coming for a long time.

"I don't know if anyone will ever really understand, but I think you, of all people, might. First, I love my home." Her voice caught unexpectedly. She blinked rapidly and continued. "I was born there. My father was born there. My mother died there. All the happiness of my childhood is held within those walls. A million happy memories are there to greet me whenever I'm having a hard time. It reminds me of who I am . . . or who I once was." She barely whispered the last few words. She sat silently for a moment, and then continued, her voice strong. "Secondly, and most important, I made a promise to my father on his deathbed that I would take care of his new family."

I opened my mouth to speak and she held up her hand. "I know what you're going to say, that he never meant for me to take care of them like this." She did know exactly what I was going to say. "But to me it doesn't matter. I promised. They depend on me. If I left, they would starve." She made it sound like that would be a bad thing. "They would never ask for help, or even admit they needed it. The house would become desolate and in disrepair. I would never forgive myself." She echoed my same words from when I spoke to her in the barn. "Father never intended for this to happen, but that doesn't change what it is. I don't know if things will ever change, but I have decided, and I'm not going anywhere."

I had never heard her be so candid or speak so confidently. She knew exactly what she was doing. She wasn't always thinking of some way for her to escape, like I had been. She had no intention of leaving. When I offered to take her away that day in the barn, she might have been tempted for a moment because it had been her first real opportunity to escape, but she had not given in.

I knew then that I would never be able to persuade her to leave. That was the day I knew that if she ever left it would have to be her choice.

It did get easier, as unlikely as I had ever thought that possibility could be. She was never bursting with confidence, but she did carry with her a quiet peace that helped me know that she had no regrets. I felt my own peace from hoping that perhaps I helped make her burden a little lighter.

Of course, I wasn't always satisfied with her decision to stay, even if I understood why she did. Some days I just couldn't bear to see her pain and I became gloomy and angry, which didn't help anything. On the days I felt powerless, I discovered that if I helped her—anonymously and quietly—it helped ease the pain. If I saw her avoid my eyes because she had become so guarded to protect herself, later, when she was asleep, I would silently place a few extra logs on her woodpile—just enough to help, but not so much that she would notice. When I worried about the dark circles under her eyes from working too late into the night, I would quietly go and tighten the hinges on the doors of the barn, or pull a few weeds from the garden. They all had to be subtle jobs, nothing too obvious—just things that would help her life be a little easier, and things that would bring me peace . . . as I waited.

Her smiles and laughs and her timid blushes continued to give me hope. There were times when she met my eyes and the expression on her face made me forget where I was. She never met my eyes for very long, and it was usually from a few feet away—I doubted if she even knew what color my eyes were—but those little looks let me know that she was happy to be with me, that she might even look forward to our little early morning meetings as much as I did, that she might gain the same strength from them that sustained me through each day.

I gradually learned that Ella didn't need to be saved—she needed to be understood. She didn't need a rescuer—she needed a friend. And being Ella's friend was the greatest privilege of my life.

Chapter 3

Four years after that first fateful meeting with Ella, I found myself in Lytton, leaning against the wood rail fence, watching Mr. Harris smile at his new horse.

"She's a beauty! Are you sure you can part with her?"

I chuckled. I had asked myself that question a thousand times, but I knew the answer.

"Very sure. Right now, I need the money more than I need the horse."

"Got big plans, eh?" Mr. Harris said as he latched the gate.

"Yes, sir." I couldn't contain the huge grin that spread across my face.

Mr. Harris laughed. "I have a good idea what those plans might be. Only a woman could bring on a smile like that. You bring the little lady back here the next time we do business, understand?"

"You have my word, sir." My grin widened and my heart pounded at the prospect.

"Twenty-four years old. That's a good age to settle down. That's how old I was, actually. Not too young, not too old. Don't wait too long, though. We can't have you becoming a menace to society. Take Prince Kenton. He should be married by now."

"Oh, he'll find someone, Mr. Harris. I expect an announcement any day, actually." I laughed. "But imagine how miserable it would be trying to find a wife among a bunch of spoiled princesses."

"That doesn't sound all that bad." He winked. "I hope your young lady knows how lucky she is to have caught your eye."

"No, sir. I'm the lucky one. Or, at least I hope I'll be." My stomach immediately twisted into a knot. Ella wasn't exactly "my young lady" yet.

He chuckled as we walked away from the pen. "Don't we all?"

With one last look at the foal, I parted with Mr. Harris at the stable where Charlie was waiting. As I shook hands with Mr. Harris, it was reminiscent of when Henry Blakeley had given me Charlie. But he had given me much more than that. He had given me knowledge, a purpose, and a dream. I smiled with satisfaction. Now I was selling a horse I had raised, with a promising future ahead of me.

Charlie and I headed toward my sister's house so I could have my last meal before going home the next morning. I walked up the front steps and as I pushed the door open, six little nieces and nephews jumped on me and pulled me to the ground.

"Uncle Will! Did you sell your horse?"

"Can I see the money?"

"Are you going to buy me a present?"

"Can I *touch* the money?"

Tiny, excited voices filled the room and mingled with the quiet laughter of my sister, Margaret, and her husband, Jonathan. My mother stood in the corner and watched, smiling, as I pretended to lose the six-to-one wrestling match.

After a few minutes, I was comforting the child who got kicked in the eye by her brother as Margaret muttered something about "it's all fun and games." Once everyone was happy again, I plodded over to the kitchen table, a child hanging from each arm, one wrapped around each leg, and one sitting on my shoulders, her fingers covering my eyes as she giggled. Margaret held the youngest, though he pouted at the injustice of being left out of the fun. We crammed in around the table, and I ate as best I could with a niece on one knee and a nephew on the other.

"Can't you stay for one more day, Uncle Will? You just got here yesterday." Billy whined through a mouthful of food.

Margaret sighed exasperatingly. "Billy, don't talk with your mouth full."

"So much like his mother," I mumbled with a grin. As a child, it seemed like Margaret had actually made a point of waiting to speak until she had food in her mouth. She glared at me and then stifled a laugh. Mother smiled knowingly. I turned to Billy, whose bottom lip jutted out. "I'm sorry, Billy. I really need to get back to work. But I'll be back soon."

"And next time he may bring someone with him." Margaret smiled and winked at me and exchanged a shrewd smile with my mother. Mother's smile was warm and affectionate and she reached over to pat my arm. I loved seeing how happy she was here, even though it had been a hard transition leaving the home she had raised us all in.

Her smile was contagious, though I wished I had kept my plans about Ella secret. It was hard enough not getting my own hopes up without the not-so-subtle hints from everyone in my family. Their hopes were as high as mine were . . . almost.

"Uncle Will, why are your cheeks so red?"

"Oh my goodness, he's blushing! He's actually blushing!" Jonathan roared with laughter as he leaned back in his chair and slapped his knee. I shoved another bite of stew into my mouth.

I tried not to think about the possibility of one day bringing Ella here to visit my family. It seemed too good to be true. There were too many factors to consider before it even became a possibility, but I was ready to consider them together with her.

I hugged and kissed my nieces and nephews good night, knowing that it would also be good-bye, at least for a little while. I gave the youngest his very own shoulder ride to his crib and he hugged my neck so tightly I could hear his little teeth clenching. Once every child got their last hug and story and was asleep, I rolled out a blanket onto the floor, forced myself to not think about the next day, and tried to get some sleep.

It felt like my eyes had only been closed for two minutes when it was time to leave. Racing against the dawn, I dressed, wrapped some bread and apples in a cloth, and silently opened the door. I tried to be as quiet as possible, but as I was saddling up Charlie, my mother and sister poked their heads out the door, their hands clasping their nightgowns at their necks.

"Give our love to Ella!" My mother called quietly.

"Yes, and give her *yours,* too." Margaret added. My mother blew me a kiss and they closed the door, giggling.

***

Our kingdom of Claire wasn't a large one. The three main town squares of Maycott, Lytton, and Milton were all deliberately situated relatively near to each other for trading purposes. Lytton's sprawling hills were ideal for raising sheep, horses, and cattle and provided much of the kingdom's meat and wool. Milton was the sea-bordering village. I hadn't been there since I was a child, but I remember licking my lips and tasting salt. There were people from all over the world, speaking languages I had never heard before, dressed in brightly colored clothing. Crates of fish preserved in salt lined the bustling streets, waiting to be shipped and traded. The rich soil of Maycott, nestled in the mountains and adorned with streams, lakes, and forests, provided the kingdom with much of its produce. The planting, growing, and harvesting seasons were comparatively shorter than the other villages because of our elevation, but the quality more than made up for it.

The palace was also located in Maycott. We had an almost constant flow of visitors—royal and common. But we also had the families that had been here for generations. I was the last of my family living in Maycott, but I had no plans to leave.

By the time I crossed from the outskirts of Lytton to the outskirts of Maycott, the sun was skimming the tips of the sycamores. I had let Charlie pace himself, knowing we had a long trip ahead of us, but as we rode along the familiar roads, I nudged him into a quick trot.

I couldn't wait one more day to ask Ella to marry me. I had already delayed for years, saving every penny, working later and longer than anyone else in the king's stables so that I could finally have something to offer her. I hoped to ask her before dark. I kicked Charlie into a gallop.

"Oh, W-i-i-ll!" a sing-songy voice called. I glanced toward that voice I knew too well just as Jane Emerson crossed her yard and reached the picket fence. She waved at me, a wave that wasn't just a greeting but an invitation to stop. I sighed and slowed Charlie's pace. I was in a hurry, but I didn't want to be rude.

I came to a stop in front of her house and she beamed up at me, but I remained on the saddle. I could stop to say hello, but that didn't mean I could stay for tea.

"It looks like you've had a long journey. Can you stay for tea?"

I laughed quietly. "Thank you, Miss Emerson," she scowled at my formality, "but I really must be on my way." She planted a smile back on her face.

"Where are you coming from?"

"Lytton." I saw the curtains flutter in an upstairs window and I knew what would be coming soon.

"Oh, I just adore Lytton. Were you there for the wildflower festival?" Jane asked with a hopeful grin.

Wildflowers? "No, I actually had some business there."

"Oh, I guess it is a little late in the season. How silly of me." She giggled.

Jane was a nice enough girl, and prettier than most, but she had a knack for being completely unaware of what was going on around her. Sometimes it was amusing, and other times—like this one—it was exasperating.

"Miss Emerson, it's been nice seeing you, but I really must be going." I touched the brim of my hat and turned to face the road.

"Are you going to visit . . . someone else?" The false pleasantries now abandoned, Jane's eyes misted and she crossed her arms.

"Jane," I said softly, "I have had a long journey today and I am on my way home."

"Will . . ." She was going to start pleading. I could feel it. Just then, Jane's father opened the front door. He didn't need to say anything. Jane knew she was in trouble for talking to me . . . again.

I nodded politely to Mr. Emerson. He was actually one of my favorite men in the village—almost always jovial and friendly . . . to everyone else but me. It seemed I would never be able to atone for the innocent, meaningless flirtation I shared with his daughter years before. Jane obeyed her father's silent command to come inside and I smiled at them both. Mr. Emerson slammed the door once Jane was safely in the house. I shook my head and chuckled quietly. If only they both knew how absolutely unlikely it was that Jane and I would ever be together. I had told her years ago that nothing would ever happen between us, but that hadn't deterred her, even with her father's repeated warnings that she could have nothing to do with a poor stable worker. True, I worked at the palace, so that made me one step up from working in an ordinary man's stables. But still, I was a stable worker. And horses were horses, work was work, sweat was sweat, and dirt was dirt. Not that I minded that, but Mr. Emerson most certainly did. But whether he approved of me or not, or Jane loved me or not, I knew that my future didn't involve either one of them. A part of me had to admire her determination, but at the same time, it was borderline obstinacy. I had decided long ago that the only way she would stop was if someone better came along, and it was only a matter of time.

After we left the Emerson's, I steered Charlie toward the shortcut through the forest. He knew we were close to home and quickened his pace on his own. I leaned farther down in the saddle, closer to his neck, hoping to provide less resistance so we could get home that much faster.

"Hey, Charlie!" another familiar voice called out as we passed by main street and its dozens of shops. "Oh, Will. Hello! I didn't see you there," Corbin chuckled at one of his favorite jokes.

I slowed Charlie to a stop next to my friend. "Corbin! What are you doing out here alone? Shouldn't you be picking out flowers for the wedding? Or at least talking about flowers with someone somewhere?"

Corbin rolled his eyes and sighed, then lowered his voice. "You don't know how true that is. If you *ever* decide to get married, elope. Just elope. You'll thank me later." Corbin glanced behind his shoulder to make sure no one heard him.

I laughed. "I'll remember that. So when's the day, again?" He knew that I knew. I was his best man, after all. I just wanted to hear his countdown.

"Next Friday. One week, one day, fifteen hours . . ."

"Please don't tell me the minutes. I might lose my lunch."

He laughed with me. I wasn't going to tell him I knew exactly how he felt.

A soprano voice floated over the crowded square. "Corbin. There you are, you handsome man, you! We have to decide on the flowers!" Corbin's fiancée, Francine, emerged out of the dress shop, ran up to him, threw her arms around his neck, and kissed him multiple times on the cheek, ending with one on the lips. She pulled away, but kept both hands in one of his. Corbin looked down and dug the toe of his shoe in the dirt, but he couldn't quite contain the smile from spreading across his face.

I grinned. "I think that's my cue. See you in one week, one day, and fifteen hours!" I turned to Francine. "I'll be sure to bathe that day."

Francine pulled her eyes away from Corbin's red face long enough to glower at me. She could never take a joke.

I finally made it home a little before dusk. Once I put Charlie away with my other two horses and quickly fed and watered them, I opened the door to my little cabin I had built eight years earlier. Through the single window on the west side of the cottage, I could still see the top of the grand house I grew up in above the trees in the distance, though it didn't feel like home to me anymore. We had once belonged to Maycott's upper class—my siblings and I had been educated at the best schools and welcomed into the best homes. But a few months after my father's death, we learned that he had accumulated an incredible amount of debt through gambling. I started working at the Blakeley's stables soon after and my mother and sisters took in sewing. Unfortunately, our wages were not enough to sustain us, not to mention pay Father's debts. We had to sell our house and property and Mother moved in with Margaret. I was sixteen by then and was able to purchase a small corner of our land from the new owners and build a one-room cabin. The roof leaked and wind constantly howled through the window I hadn't made time to fix. Besides, it was just me who lived there and it didn't bother me too much. It was small and drafty and I slept on a mat on the floor, but it was home.

I pulled off my dirty clothes and quickly washed and shaved. A man can't propose with whiskers and dirty hands. Ella and I had never kissed, or even held hands, and there were good reasons for that. But if all went as planned, tonight might change that . . . I hoped. We were always so careful around each other. We had been friends for years, but nothing had ever happened between us. I worried that this proposal might even send her into shock.

I changed into a clean set of clothes, ran my fingers through my hair, and bolted out the front door to the road that led to Ashfield.

"Will!" yet another voice stopped me in my tracks and I sighed. This voice would only come to my home if it were an emergency. Last time, one of the king's horses was lame and had to be put down. Another time, one had escaped and we had to search all night to find her.

"Hello, Grant. What's wrong?" I kept moving in the direction of Ella's house, though a little bit more slowly.

"Prince Kenton is coming back tonight," he panted. Grant had come on horseback, but it sounded as if he had personally run the whole way.

"Why is he coming back so early?" I asked, too preoccupied to care much what the answer would be as I continued to walk. The prince was the most unpredictable person I knew. We thought we still had weeks to prepare for his homecoming.

"It didn't work out with that princess. They're not getting married after all." Though he was breathless and a little frantic, the corner of Grant's mouth twitched as he fought a smile. The princess he was referring to was Princess Rose of Laurel and she had come to visit the palace a year earlier. I thought Ella's stepsisters were bad, but this girl made even the horseflies quiver with fear.

I couldn't help chuckling at the memory of the haughtiest woman I had ever met. She had demanded to ride the most spirited horse the king owned, after being told repeatedly that it was too dangerous. It had bucked her off into the mud after only a few seconds. She had actually thrown herself on the ground, kicking and screaming. She even flung mud in the prince's face, and mine, for good measure, and then stormed back to the castle. For some inexplicable reason, the prince had wasted a year of his life chasing after that woman. I hadn't cared much, except that he was a decent enough fellow and she was an absolute terror. We affectionately referred to her as The Beast. I couldn't help feeling sorry for the prince. Pickings must be slim in the royal world.

"Will, they sent a rider ahead to let us know that his whole entourage will be arriving at the palace any minute. All the horses need to be attended to."

"Grant, you know I want to help. Normally, I would come without hesitation, but I have something important to do right now. There are plenty of you up there."

"That's not all." he said.

"They're having a royal procession . . . tomorrow."

It wasn't until he said those words that I stopped walking. I gazed in the direction of Ella's house, closed my eyes, sighed, and nodded. A royal procession meant every saddle and every bridle had to be oiled, every stirrup adjusted for every rider. Every carriage polished and shined. Every horse brushed, every mane combed. It wasn't often that the royals had a procession, but when they did, we usually had a week to prepare. Not one night.

The smoke from Ella's kitchen chimney rose gently above the trees. She must be cooking supper for her stepmother and stepsisters. Soon, it would be time for nightly chores. The sun was now a dimming, thin beam in the distance. I had missed my chance.

Tomorrow, I told myself. Tomorrow morning I would propose. It didn't matter if I was scruffy or smelled like horses. I would meet her at the pond, like I did every morning, but this time I would ask her to be my wife.

Tomorrow.

"All right. Let me go get Charlie. I'll meet you on the road in five minutes."

Chapter 4

Grant and I reached the wide iron gates of the palace and the two guards swung them open for us, the hinges screeching piercingly.

"Good evening Simon, Hugh," Grant said as we passed.

"Will. Grant." Simon answered stoically, his eyes drooping. I tossed Simon and Hugh each an apple from my bag, which I hadn't emptied from my journey. I laughed as they tried unsuccessfully to hide their grins of gratitude.

Once the gates clanged shut behind us, our pace quickened into a trot, then a gallop, then into a run, which quickly turned into a race. Charlie wasn't a racehorse; he was built to work and pull, but his strength made him fast, and we easily beat Grant and the palace horse he'd borrowed.

"Cheater," Grant gasped.

I laughed and lightly punched his shoulder. "Maybe next time . . . or maybe not."

That earned me a much harder punch on the shoulder than I had given him, but it was worth it. We put the horses away and noticed with relief that the prince and his entourage hadn't arrived yet.

"Maybe they'll be too tired for the procession tomorrow," I said hopefully.

"Don't plan on it," Grant mumbled.

Just then, the rumbling of horses' hooves and carriage wheels echoed through the darkness. The dust they kicked up hovered in the early evening air. Before we saw the actual riders, we saw the flags emerge from behind the hill, followed by carriages and drivers. The prince appeared on his white horse, leading the company, and was followed by dozens of courtiers on horses and in carriages. Some of the grooms stood at attention in a straight line in front of the palace as horse after horse after carriage stopped at the front steps. The ladies emerged from the carriages, and some alighted from their horses and followed. But many of the royals who rode on horses, including the prince, chose to take them down to the stables themselves, where the remainder of the grooms waited. When the royals arrived, we helped the ladies down, careful not to look into their eyes, or we would be accused of assaulting them.

I couldn't help comparing these ladies to Ella. These women had to force themselves to be graceful. Ella had a natural grace that I think would make most women cry with jealousy. These women needed fancy, expensive clothes to make them beautiful. Ella wore the same plain, gray dress every day and her beauty was breathtaking. These women's smiles were fake and insincere, even when they were smiling at their fellow royals, and not just at us. Ella almost always had a content smile on her face, even when she was hurting.

There was one lady who wasn't arrogant like the rest of them. Lady Gwen. She seemed sincere when she thanked us and didn't cringe when we placed our hands on her waist to help her down. But she was definitely out of our class, though Grant could never seem to accept that.

As always, I did my best to make sure Grant was the one to help Lady Gwen, otherwise he'd be sure to trip me in the mud or "accidently" throw a brush at my head later. I nudged him lightly with my elbow as he pushed past me, but his eyes remained fixed on Lady Gwen. He raised his arms and his hands encircled her waist. He couldn't fight his smile.

"Thank you, Grant, dear," Gwen said as she placed her hands on his shoulders. The words *Grant* and *dear* were always blended together to form one word, which the other grooms teased Grant mercilessly for.

"Not at all, Lady Gwen." Grant lifted her down from the saddle to place her safely on the ground. A small twinge of jealousy twisted in my stomach. It wasn't that I wanted to help Lady Gwen. It was that I wanted to help Ella. I wanted to be closer to her. I wasn't feeling self-pity, just restlessness. I wanted things to change. But change would have to wait another day.

Once Lady Gwen was on the ground, she squeezed Grant's arm in an uncharacteristically intimate show of thanks before rejoining her group. I looked over at Grant and he couldn't wipe the stunned smile off his face. I wasn't the only one who noticed.

"Why, *Grantdear*, that blush looks lovely on you in the moonlight," Paul joked under his breath once Lady Gwen was out of sight. This remark was followed closely by a grunt of pain and chortles from the other grooms. Paul was always willing to risk a beating to get a snide comment in. I had already been punched that night, so I left the teasing up to him.

The royal party lingered by the stables to talk and laugh together in the dim light of the stable lanterns.

"Thank you, young man," Sir Thomas said as he handed me his horse's reins. I led the horse into the stable and saw Prince Kenton standing in the doorway.

"Hawkins! Good to see you. How is everything?" he said, looking up from his gloves he was pulling off.

"Very well, Your Majesty. Two foals were born while you were away, though we did have to put down Chocolate Truffle." I wished they let me name some of the horses. I secretly called Chocolate Truffle 'Tom.'

"What a shame. I loved that old horse."

"I'm sorry, Prince Kenton. I know he was a favorite of yours. Though he is Vanilla Custard's sire, so a part of him lives on," I said soberly with a hint of a smile.

Prince Kenton chuckled lightly. "Where do these names come from?"

"Don't look at me, Your Majesty."

We both glanced in the direction of the palace, where the queen—the infamous horse-namer—waited for her son's return. Prince Kenton laughed. I only smiled, not wanting to appear disrespectful.

"Well, I'm sure you took excellent care of him, Hawkins. I'm most grateful. And hungry, come to think of it."

He grinned and went back to removing his gloves, so I bowed and resumed my duties. It didn't occur to me until after I was finished speaking with the prince that he didn't look like a man whose wedding had just been called off. Princess Rose wasn't exactly pleasant company, but they had been engaged for over a year and he didn't seem heartbroken. Or anxious. He was running out of time to be married, according to the law. But now, he appeared to be starting over. I shrugged; it was none of my concern.

Once I was back inside the stable, Grant and I unsaddled and brushed the horses while the other grooms tended to the carriages. Sir Thomas and Prince Kenton remained in the stable and I tried to be invisible as I walked right behind them to grab a bucket of oats. Grant and I continued working silently as we unintentionally eavesdropped on their conversation. I normally had absolutely no interest in what the royals talked about, but I was unable to escape this conversation.

"So, I will be at the ball, looking for the girl who could be the next queen. Correct? And the whole kingdom is invited this time? Even the commoners?" Sir Thomas asked, not seeming to be concerned with who heard him.

Invite the commoners to a ball? Had I heard that right?

"Correct," Prince Kenton answered. He looked a little older, now that I saw him in the lamplight. He was about my age, but I wondered just how boisterous life had been for him this past year away from the palace. He looked weary, and not just physically. It seemed that courting The Beast had taken a lot out of him. Prince Kenton continued, "She must be beautiful, refined, graceful, elegant . . . but mostly beautiful," he added with a laugh.

Sir Thomas didn't laugh. He was taking his job very seriously. "And, she can be from any walk of life, Your Majesty? A commoner, even?" If the prince noticed how Sir Thomas dropped his eyes in disapproval, he made no indication.

Prince Kenton was nodding even before Sir Thomas was finished speaking. "Yes, any walk of life. And, I would actually prefer if she were a commoner. I need something refreshing in my life." He lowered his voice so no one, well, no other royals could hear. "If I have to listen to one more woman talk about who her stylist is and where to buy the best silk and how to tie the fanciest bow, I'm going to throw myself from the nearest balcony."

Sir Thomas smiled sympathetically at this comment. "So, Your Majesty, you'd rather hear about milking cows, washing dishes, and plucking chickens?" Sir Thomas laughed quietly.

"More than you know, my good man. More than you know. And if all goes well, we could even be married that very night. The ball could become a wedding with the whole kingdom already invited." Prince Kenton flung his arm around Sir Thomas's shoulders and they were both still laughing as they went back to rejoin their party.

I had been standing absolutely still, holding a bucket of oats to Sir Thomas's horse, not even pretending I wasn't listening to every word. Grant had been brushing the prince's horse with particular care, though he seemed a little more nonchalant.

"Does this mean . . . ," Grant began.

I waved my hand and shook my head. Prince Kenton and Sir Thomas could be right outside the doors and it wouldn't be very prudent to talk about their conversation we had meticulously listened to. But, that wasn't the only reason I motioned for Grant to stop talking. I simply didn't want to talk about the conversation at all. My hands shook as I hung up the bridles and got out the oil to treat the leather.

I fought the fear that was growing inside of me. The prince wanted to marry a commoner. She needed to be refined, elegant, graceful, beautiful. Every new way he found to describe what he was looking for brought a fresh vision of Ella's face to my mind.

He could take Ella away from me. I knew it. If he saw her, I knew he would choose her. And not just because I was biased. I loved her and saw all the beautiful things she was, but so could everyone else, if they were ever able to see her. She was everything the prince told Sir Thomas to look for. If she went to that ball, she would never come home. The prince, once he saw her, wouldn't let her go.

Chapter 5

IT TOOK ALL THE GROOMS WORKING THROUGH THE NIGHT to ready the horses and carriages for the procession. We learned that while he was riding in this procession, the prince planned to make an announcement. Of course, the villagers wouldn't know what the announcement was—that the prince was holding a ball and that at the ball he would choose his future bride from among his subjects. I wouldn't even know that much if the prince hadn't chosen to speak about it in the stable. But, simply knowing that the prince was coming and that he had something to say would be enough to get every single person into town tomorrow.

Except, perhaps, one person.

As I treated the leather on each saddle and bridle, I hoped that somehow Ella wouldn't hear about the announcement. She rarely ever went to town, unless she needed something she couldn't make on her own. She didn't really talk to anyone, besides me. And her stepfamily, if they needed her to do something for them. And occasionally Jane Emerson, but only *about* Jane Emerson and what was interesting in Jane's life. And even if Ella's stepfamily heard about the announcement between now and the afternoon, I was sure they wouldn't even tell her about it.

I thought about all of this as we brushed, combed, oiled, and polished. I worked in absolute silence as everyone around me laughed, joked, and teased.

The only time I spoke was after the royals left and Grant tried again to talk about what we had overheard.

"Will, he's going to try to marry one of . . . *us*?" he asked, his eyebrows raised so high they disappeared underneath his hair.

"*You*, maybe. Not me," I joked, though my jaw was tight and my smile forced.

Grant shook his head, not laughing at my half-hearted retort. "You know what I mean. A commoner. One of *us*. Just a regular person."

"Sounds like it," I muttered.

"S-so," Grant stammered. "Who's the girl you're worried about losing?"

My head snapped up. I couldn't remember ever saying anything about Ella to Grant.

"I can see what's happening. You've looked miserable ever since we heard the prince talking. I'm not an idiot."

"Yes, you are," I mumbled. I didn't want to talk about this . . . ever.

"I don't know who it is, but I know there's someone. You've become a totally different person in the last few minutes. I've never seen you like this."

I was at least four years older than Grant and suddenly I felt like a child who had been caught in a lie.

The horse I was brushing was going to have a bald spot if I didn't move. I put down the brush and started polishing a buckle on a bridle.

Grant continued, apparently not picking up on my not-so-subtle cues. "Will, I've looked up to you like the big brother I wish I had, and . . ."

"You have an older brother," I interrupted.

"Yes, but you're the older brother I *wish* I had. I'm only saying if I had a girl I loved, I would go and claim her before anyone else does." He continued with a falsely innocent expression.

"Especially if that person was an outrageously rich prince. And I'm no expert, but he isn't exactly what most women would call ugly or anything."

I knew it was true. I couldn't stop the prince from loving Ella once he saw her, and I couldn't stop Ella from loving the prince once she saw him. I had never told her how I felt. I had missed my chance to ask her to marry me, and now I wasn't sure if I would get a chance before the announcement. Everything I'd ever hoped for was slipping through my fingers.

Grant bent over and picked up the bridle I had just dropped and placed a hand on my shoulder, obviously not knowing what else to say, for which I was grateful. I shook his hand off and he went back to work with a sigh, sounding like an old man whose wise advice had just been rejected.

Claim Ella. That was what Grant had said. I was supposed to walk up to her, tell her how I felt, kiss her, and claim her before the prince could.

Could I do that? Would she want me to?

"All right, men," I called when I noticed that many of the grooms had fallen asleep in the stables, and the rest were moving so slowly nothing was really getting accomplished. "I think we've done all we can for tonight. Get some rest and be back first thing in the morning."

The men's grateful groans echoed loudly in the dark and quieted the soft chirping of the crickets. They yawned and stretched as they walked to the bunkhouse, and I went to the stable to get Charlie so we could ride home. I didn't live in the bunkhouse with the rest of the men, though it would have made sense. I would have food and shelter and a never-ending supply of firewood if I lived on the palace grounds, but I wouldn't be near Ella. Besides, I liked having a break from the palace at the end of each day. The men stopped asking why I preferred to ride miles home every night to a leaky, drafty cabin all alone, and just assumed that I was odd. That was perfectly fine with me.

"Come on, boy. Let's go home," I said once Charlie was saddled up. Too exhausted to even put my foot in the stirrup, I grabbed hold of Charlie's reins and led him away from the palace.

We plodded through town and onto the road that would lead us home. The road would also bring us past Ella's house. Maybe it wasn't too late. Maybe she would still be awake. She was up late quite often, finishing up some sewing or some other project, though I knew she wanted to do nothing more than sleep. But tonight, it was closer to morning than evening.

I trudged on, knowing I was being ridiculous for going so slowly. The last time I had slept, I was in another village, and even then it was on the floor of my sister's front room. My body was weary, but my mind was completely alert as I rounded the bend in front of Ashfield. I let go of Charlie's reins and let him graze in the grass by the trees. I looked for any sign of life, but every window was dark and every chimney void of smoke. Maybe, I hoped, Ella had let the fire go out, but was working by candlelight in the kitchen.

I stepped closer to the house, my heart racing. If I proposed now I wouldn't have to worry about it anymore. Ella would be mine, ball or no ball. I moved forward, tentatively, every crunch of my boots on the dirt shattering the stillness. But then, I stopped. I knew I was fooling myself. I knew Ella was asleep. Besides, I couldn't just go knocking on her back door in the middle of the night. I knew she slept on the hearth when the weather started to cool as it had in the past few weeks. I even knew that if I glanced in through the windows that I would see her there, sleeping on the hearth, trying to soak up just enough heat to keep her warm and sleeping.

I couldn't propose. Not tonight. I would wait until morning.

Perhaps we could even be married before the end of the week and we wouldn't even have to worry about the ball. I comforted myself with that thought and pushed the uneasiness I felt out of my mind and walked home.

Chapter 6

I THINK I SLEPT, BUT IT WAS ONLY FOR AN HOUR OR TWO IF I did. I got out of bed, cleaned myself up, and tended to Charlie and my other two horses. With my fishing rod resting over my shoulder, I headed to the pond. Some fish were swimming close to shore and I stopped to catch them before I reached my favorite spot. The boys who lived in the bunkhouse were provided with food from the palace, but they preferred plain fish to what they were given there, when I could bring it.

I would give Ella all the fish I caught, if she had been allowed to accept help. I gave her fish to take home one time a few years ago. She was so grateful. Ella hadn't told Victoria where she had gotten the fish, but Victoria knew that Ella hadn't caught them. Ella learned very quickly that accepting help from anyone was worthy of ten lashings at the very least. So, I learned that if I wanted to help Ella, I had to do it in more subtle ways so that Victoria wouldn't find out.

My anger at the injustice of it all gave me more resolve than ever to carry out my plan of proposing and "claiming" Ella. My line of fish was almost full when I stood up and started walking to my usual spot.

Today was September first—ten years to the day since Henry Blakeley had died. For a couple of years, this day had been painful and lonely. I felt like I had lost the only real father I had ever known. But over the years it grew into a day of reflection. I would remember the faith he had in me and how he saw my potential, even when I was a quiet ten-year-old boy. I often wondered—if he were still here—if he would be proud of me, if I had become what he saw in me. I knew very profoundly that Ella was a most beloved daughter of a wonderful and revered man. She deserved the very best. Was I what he had in mind? Or would he glare at me in disgust, like Mr. Emerson, every time I came near his daughter?

I was about to ask Ella to marry me. My hands shook, though it had nothing to do with the cold.

Ella had arrived at the pond before I did. I noiselessly sat on the opposite bank, against a tree, lowered my line into the water, and waited.

Her bare feet dangled in the pond and she sat in the mud, leaning back on her hands, her long hair covering her like a threadbare blanket. The dim morning light reflected off the pond and onto her face and I could see the glisten of tears on her cheeks. Ella never cried; well, rarely. And if she ever did, she had a good reason. She wept quietly, as soft as a whisper, but I didn't need to hear it to have it tear at my heart.

She opened her eyes and met mine across the pond. Quickly raising one of her hands she had been resting on, she wiped the tears from her face. It hurt me to know that she was hurting, that she felt alone in her grief, and that she thought she needed to hide it, even from me. She waved, her fingers fluttering, and I smiled at her, my heart beginning to race. She smiled back and it was like the sun had decided to rise a few minutes early.

"Any luck this morning?" she said quietly. I could hear the tears in her voice, though she tried to sound cheerful.

"Of course!" I answered in a regular volume. I didn't want her to worry about scaring the fish away. I had plenty for the boys at the stables. "But I wouldn't call this luck. This is expertise."

"Of course," she said, mimicking me. Her gaze returned to the pond and I saw that she now wore her familiar, contented smile. As always, I was pleasantly surprised to see how much she had come alive since I first saw her four years ago. A light had crept back into her eyes. I knew it still wasn't as bright as it could be, but it was there, and it was growing brighter every day.

I took a deep breath, gathered up my fishing gear, and walked over to the rickety little bridge that connected the two sides of the pond. My heart leapt with each step I took. As I crossed the bridge, Ella washed her hands in the water and stuffed her long hair into her scarf. No one had hair like Ella. It was thick and golden and it fell in waves all the way down to her knees. She picked up some baskets off the ground and came to meet me at the bridge.

This was the closest I ever was to her—standing an arm's length apart. We had spoken almost every day for the past four years, but we had never closed that gap. A part of me knew that if we were ever going to get any closer, Ella would have to take the next step.

I glanced down at the two baskets she held in her hands. There was a cloth covering them both, but I could see that underneath they were filled to the brim with berries.

"When did you get up this morning? This must have taken hours!" I said. I tried to sound nonchalant, but I watched her, searching for the expression that gave me a little glimpse into how she felt, or could feel.

She nodded slowly, wearily. "Yes, it was an early morning." She made a sad little sound in her throat and pursed her lips to keep them from trembling.

"Ten years," I whispered. She blinked against the tears that threatened to spill over. Her eyes looked especially soft and suddenly my chest felt achingly hollow, but heavy at the same time. As much as I hated to see her tears, I was strangely grateful for them. In order to protect herself from Victoria, Ella had become numb to the pains and injustices she endured daily and had instead opted for the shield of detachment. Though her tears would most likely be dry by the time she returned home, the fact that she allowed herself to shed them was no small miracle. It opened the gates for other feelings that she might not even know she was suppressing.

"I'm so sorry, Ella" was all I could say. Though my own grief at Henry Blakeley's death had evolved into something less sharp and painful, Ella's grief had never had the chance to ease or transform. Her life had been pulled out from under her, and she was left without anyone to guide her through her sadness and loss. Her grief gripped her mercilessly. How different her life would be if someone had been there to comfort her instead of turn her away when her father died. I had tried my best to be that person, but I had done all I could do from this distance.

Ella blinked and a pearl of a teardrop slipped down her cheek. I slowly lifted my hand to brush the tear away, but as always, I felt the invisible barrier go up between us and I knew I couldn't cross it. Not now. I felt weak and powerless. Suddenly, I heard the words of Henry Blakeley in my mind, "Sometimes admitting that we are weak can be a strength." I wondered if my restraint was a weakness or a strength, if my holding back was helping Ella or hurting her.

She looked at me with an expression close to pity. My helplessness must have been plain on my face. "These are for you," she said, very cheerful all of a sudden. Too cheerful. She placed one of the baskets in my awkwardly outstretched hand and my fingers closed around the handle mechanically. Our fingers almost touched and some of her warmth transferred to me.

"Thank you, Ella." I tried to smile, but her attempt to hide her pain only made it more obvious. "You always pick the best ones."

"This is for you, too." She reached over to the basket she had placed in my hand and pulled back the cloth to reveal a small, tin pitcher.

"Cream?" I could already taste it.

She nodded, a bright smile on her face.

"I'm going to eat like a king! You spoil me, Ella. You don't have to do all this . . . but I'm also very grateful you did." I laughed.

"You're very welcome. It's refreshing and enjoyable doing something for someone who actually knows how to say thank you. I think I would fall over dead if I ever heard those words at my house."

"Let's hope they never say it." I laughed again and she joined in, her laugh sounding like a song.

"How was your trip? How is your mother?" she asked.

"They are doing very well. Margaret just had another baby and my mother is healthy as a horse." I smiled. I knew it was a pathetic joke, but it reminded me that I had sold another horse and I was finally in a financial position, albeit a pitiful one, to ask Ella to marry me.

"What is it?" she asked with a sly grin.

"Well, I sold the foal while I was in Lytton. I got more than what I asked for her." I smiled in satisfaction.

"Will, that's wonderful!" In her excitement, Ella raised her hand and grasped my arm. My heart beat almost painfully and the pounding in my ears made it nearly impossible to hear. She had never intentionally touched me before. I couldn't quite make sense of what she was saying, but it sounded like, "Your dream is coming true!"

She stopped talking and turned a lovely shade of crimson. In all the years that I had seen her blush, she had never blushed so deeply. Her eyes widened and she looked down at her hand holding onto my arm, her mouth falling open in disbelief. I couldn't remember her ever being spontaneous and I had to add it onto the list of things I loved about her, even if it was the first time it had ever, ever happened. She dropped her hand quickly, but I could still feel the warmth of her hand through my sleeve. I couldn't imagine her doing anything like that even one month ago.

I spoke before she fainted from embarrassment. "Well, not quite, but I hope I'm headed in the right direction."

Unfortunately, the talk of horses, mingled with the brightening sky, reminded me that I had to be at the palace—and soon. But there was still something very important I needed to say. I had spent so much time talking about berries and horses, trying to work up my nerve, but the moment just hadn't been right. She had blushed and smiled, she had touched my arm, but she had barely looked into my eyes. I still had no clear sign about how she might feel about the words that hadn't been able to escape my mouth.

I looked toward the sunrise and saw that the sun was now a blinding golden sliver behind the distant hills. My mouth went dry, but I opened it and tried to form her name. At that moment, she made a little cry of surprise and ran to the pond. At first I was afraid that she had somehow read my mind and was running away from the words that I was about to say.

But those thoughts fled as soon as Ella bent over the pond.

Suddenly, I couldn't even remember what I had been about to say to her. All that mattered in that moment was that as Ella had her back to me, I could see every rib through the thin fabric of her only dress. Fury almost blinded me and the ground swayed under my feet.

Ella was starving; starving as she fed those arrogant, despicable people she lived with. They weren't large people, by any means; they might not even eat more than Ella did, at least when they weren't eating at someone else's house. But they absolutely did not work more than she did, or at all. I never hated them more than I did at that moment. But, if I was being honest, I included myself in that hatred because I felt that I had allowed this to happen.

Unclenching my teeth, I forced my thoughts on what had alarmed Ella. "What's wrong?"

"I'm covered in dirt and you've just been standing there looking at me not saying anything!" The most gorgeous smile was slowly spreading across her lips, accompanied by a hint of timidity in her downcast eyes. She cared what I thought about her. How could I notice dirt?

"Oh, I'm sorry. I didn't notice," I said honestly.

She was so good, too good for me. Here she was, missing her father so much, not to mention the life she once lived, and she was out picking berries for me—always thinking about other people.

"You're a good friend," we said at the same time, and then we laughed together.

"Then it must be true," she said. We exchanged a tender smile at those words that meant something to both of us.

The sun was rising. I would have to leave soon. And I knew I had to act immediately, or I would miss my chance . . . again.

But the words wouldn't come. I was growing more and more frustrated with myself. Why couldn't I ask the question I was dying to ask?

"Are you going into town today?" A different question than I had planned came out before I could stop it, or really understand why I asked it.

"I don't think so. I have so much to do at home." I watched as her thoughts became much too old for someone so young. The worries. The fatigue. But, selfishly, I breathed a sigh of relief. She would be at home today. "Why? Is anything important happening?" She asked, her eyebrow raised quizzically.

"You know I don't pay any attention to what they talk about inside the palace. It's just a lot of tedious royal blather." In my mind, I punched myself in the mouth. If a carriage had been driving by, I would have jumped in front of it. What was wrong with me? Why had I mentioned the palace? So much for discretion.

I hung my head in rebuke and told myself to stop stalling and muster some courage. With my head hanging down, I saw Ella's little toes poking out from under the hem of her dress. I couldn't remember the last time I saw her wear shoes, but for some reason, the sad sight of her bare feet bothered me more than it ever had.

"Ella, where are your shoes?"

She looked down and smiled for the tiniest instant, but then the smile faded. She sighed like she was a hundred years old. "I have to save my shoes for when I really need them. They're almost worn through. Besides, I can feel every pebble and twig through the soles anyway, so why bother putting them on?"

The unease that had been building up inside me was now almost overwhelming. For years, I had seen Ella's bare feet, her ragged dress, and her infrequent, though no less heart-wrenching, tears. But today, the sight of them was too much. My thoughts were chaotic, and just as I was beginning to grasp at them, a shrill voice pierced through the stillness.

"Ella!"

I glared in the direction of that ugly voice and my whole body started to shake. I couldn't look at Ella. Somehow, I couldn't hide my loathing and fury this time. I hated that I had to turn away from her as she entered into the lions' den where the lions' mouths were wide open.

I could feel Ella's wide, frightened eyes on my face and I knew she saw my expression. I didn't know if she would see it as hatred. I didn't think she even knew that emotion. She knew anger. She knew hurt. She knew fear. She knew despair. But, there were things she would never allow herself to feel, and hatred was one of them.

But I could.

And I did.

Without a backward glance, her head held high, Ella walked toward that voice. I turned away, unable to watch this time. My heart was empty, and my hands were empty. I had come with every intention of "claiming" Ella, and now I was walking away . . . again.

A few images kept flashing through my mind as I trudged home. Each time I saw them, I hurt a little deeper, though my thoughts became a little clearer. Ella's bare feet, her ribs through the worn fabric of her dress, the terror in her eyes when Victoria called for her. This was the day I had hoped to free her from all that. And yet, I hadn't.

Because I wasn't the one who could do it.

Chapter 7

By the time I arrived at my small stable and was saddling up Charlie, my agitation had quieted and my thoughts were finally beginning to make sense. That didn't mean they were easy to grasp, or that I wanted to agree with them. But they were sensible and I had to see the truth that was staring me in the face.

Ella couldn't stay there. Not for another winter. Not for another week. And if I could have gotten her out today, I would have.

If it had been the right thing.

I desperately wanted to be the one to rescue her, but I had learned years ago that Ella would not be rescued. She was a fighter; she endured. She didn't run from her problems. She did what needed to be done, patiently and with incredible strength.

The truth was that Ella needed a chance at a better life, even if it wasn't with me. I had no right to take that away from her. I had gone there, as Grant had instructed, to claim Ella—I wasn't going to *allow* her to marry anyone else. I had foolishly thought that she belonged to me, and that no one else could have her. But, remembering those ribs showing through the fabric of her dress, and her tiny bare feet standing in the mud, I knew she deserved, more than anyone, the chance to be with the prince.

I waited for the self-pity. I was, after all, giving Ella the chance to marry someone else. And not just *any* someone else—the prince. But the pity didn't come. The feeling that this was the right thing prevented it.

But, the pain did come though, and I had to clutch the frame of the stable door to steady myself. I prayed that I could fight that pain and remember why I was doing this during what could be a very long week.

By the time I arrived at the palace and to the stables, the first of the grooms were just arriving. The royals had hours before they would be fed and dressed and ready to ride in the procession. We sat around the fire on tree stumps and ate our breakfast of fish. When they were finished, most of the grooms went to ready the carriages and Grant and I stayed behind to polish up the last of the stirrups and bits.

"So, did you take my advice?" Grant asked, dipping his cloth into the polish.

"What advice?" I could tell he was feeling very grown up, but I wasn't going to let him.

"You know exactly what advice! My very mature and wise advice about how we need to claim the women we love before the prince swoops in and steals them from us." He made the whole sentence sound like one, long word.

"Oh, yes. That advice. As mature and wise as you are, you have no idea what you're talking about." I chuckled at his defeated expression. I was taking away his moment. "Grant, that might work for some people, but my situation is . . . complicated." He opened his mouth to argue, but I continued. "I don't want to talk about it. We have a lot to do today."

"Will, you know how I feel about Lady Gwen. Well, every time she's with the prince, I worry about how he feels about her and if he would ever pursue her. They're in the same class—well, closer than most—and I think it would just kill me if he did. I don't know why you can't just—"

"Grant, this is the opposite of *not* talking about my situation. The prince hasn't chosen the woman I love. He hasn't even *seen* her. She doesn't even know about the ball. I think we should just take it one day at a time." I stopped, but then a thought hit me. This was the perfect opportunity to take the subject off of me—hopefully forever. "But if the prince is willing to marry a commoner, maybe all these class distinctions will vanish and Lady Gwen won't be so unattainable . . . as far as you're concerned."

Grant froze, his hand hovering above the stirrup he was polishing. He gaped at me like he'd never seen me before, like he'd never seen the sunrise before. It was comical and encouraging at the same time. I needed that expression of hope today.

"You're a good man, Will Hawkins," Grant muttered, still a little dazed.

***

Once they were all brushed, the horses' coats gleamed so brightly in the sunlight that my eyes watered. The procession wasn't for another couple of hours, and our supply of oats was far too low to feed all these horses, especially since they would all need to eat when they returned. The boys decided they would be fine to make the rest of the preparations without me. Besides that, none of them wanted to load all the heavy bags into the wagon.

Charlie and I rode home and hitched up the wagon. It was warmer today than yesterday, but there was the hint of autumn in the air. The sun shone brightly, yet a crispness mingled in with the heat and made everything feel clean.

As I drove past Ashfield, it looked the same as it always did. There was no sign to tell me if Ella was there or not, or if she had heard about the announcement in town, if she was excited about it, or if she had already forgotten all about me. I gripped the reins and told myself to calm down.

All thoughts of calming down fled when I saw the unmistakably tiny figure of Ella just up the road. She was walking behind Victoria and her daughters, who seemed to be in quite a rush, their quick footsteps kicking up as much dust as Charlie's hooves. If Victoria hadn't sold their carriage to pay off debts, they wouldn't have to be racing toward town on foot down a dusty road in the afternoon sun.

"Whoa, Charlie Horse!" I called as I approached Ella. I chuckled, suddenly nostalgic, remembering the comical look on Henry Blakeley's face when I named my horse as a ten-year-old boy. Ella looked over at Charlie with such fondness it reminded me that she loved Charlie as much as I did, and for the same reasons. He reminded her of her father.

Seeing the two of them together for the first time in longer than I could remember reminded me of when Henry Blakeley had given me Charlie—had given me a purpose.

Henry had stood next to me just outside the horse pen with his hand on my shoulder.

"See how his head is held high?" Henry had said. "How his back is straight and his legs are sturdy? But look at his eyes. See how they are open, calm, and kind? That's how you can tell he's a good horse. It's all in the eyes."

I'd smiled up at the older man. I had only been working for Mr. Blakeley for a few months, but he spoke to me with respect and even admiration, though I was still a child.

The foal trotted around his pen, occasionally walking with his mother; then returned to exploring.

"Step inside and say hello," Henry said, smiling. He was almost always smiling, but he had looked especially happy that day. He gave me an encouraging pat on the back and I ducked under the rails and into the pen.

The foal had been grazing on some grass, but when he saw that I had entered his pen, he walked toward me, curious and friendly. I held out my hand and the foal nickered softly, then he stepped closer and nuzzled my hand. I turned back to look at Henry who was grinning widely in approval. I slid my hand down the foal's neck, and patted his back, which was level with my waist.

"Do you like him?" Henry had asked.

"He's the most amazing horse I've ever seen."

"I agree," Henry said. "You have a great eye for horses, young man. And I have a feeling this horse has taken a strong liking to you." He smiled down at me. "He's yours."

I paused for a moment, my hand frozen on the foal's smooth coat. I blinked hard and shook my head, thinking I must have imagined those words.

"He's . . ."

"Yours, my boy!" Henry had said, chuckling. "I know you'll take excellent care of this horse. And it will give you great experience, should you want to raise horses of your own one day. I've heard you mention it once or twice." He winked. I had talked about nothing else; I just didn't think anyone was really listening.

"Mr. Blakeley, sir, I . . . I don't know what to say."

"Say, 'Deal!'" Henry stuck out his hand.

I walked away from the little horse and gripped Henry's hand tightly. I shook his hand as manly as a ten-year-old boy could. I'd tried to make my face look as serious as possible, hoping to show Henry that I understood the importance of the task. I looked over at the foal that was now mine. He had gone back to grazing and his gray coat glistened in the sunshine. I looked back up at the man who had so much faith in me and I saw the tender twinkle in his eye and an expression that felt like he looked on me as a son. My chin started to tremble and tears filled my eyes, and then I flung my arms around him.

Henry wrapped his strong arms around me, ruffled my hair, and patted my back.

"Thank you, Mr. Blakeley," I had managed to say.

"You're welcome, son. Very welcome."

I pulled away and we watched the foal while the reality slowly sunk in that the horse was really mine.

"What are you going to name him, son?" Henry said.

I smiled. I already knew. "Charlie. Charlie Horse."

Henry had laughed out loud and clapped me on the back. "A perfect name, for this horse and coming from a ten-year-old boy!" He walked away, laughing softly. He stopped abruptly and turned. "If you love this horse and give him room to grow, he'll love you forever." Then he spun back around and headed toward the stables.

Now, fourteen years later, I sat on the wagon seat and watched as Ella reached into her basket and pulled out a carrot—a precious carrot that she could have sold for maybe one button or an ounce of flour—and held it up for Charlie to eat. She laughed quietly to herself and it fascinated me. Was he tickling her hand? Was she remembering something amusing?

"May I offer you lovely ladies a ride?" I asked, pulling my eyes away from Ella. Victoria, and her daughters, Mabel and Cecelia, turned to glower at me. I detested them, but they amused me sometimes. They were all tired and sweaty and clearly wanted to get into town. I assumed it was because they had heard about the announcement. At this realization, the desire to rush Ella back home and safe out of the prince's sight almost overwhelmed me, but I ignored it.

"Did you get off work early?" Ella asked, breaking the uncomfortable and laughable silence.

"Not exactly," I replied. "I need to pick up some more oats for the horses." I wished it were just Ella and me and that we could continue talking, but three sets of eyes were glaring at us. I turned to them. "So, do you want a quick ride into town, or would you rather enjoy the anticipation while you walk?"

"Yes." The word came from the stepmother, though I wouldn't have even known if I hadn't been looking directly at her when she spoke. Her expressionless face looked back at me, awkwardness permeating the silence. I hesitated, wondering if I had actually heard correctly, then hopped down from the driver's seat and hurried to the back of the wagon. I stood there, smiling, with my hand outstretched trying to be as pleasant as possible. Without another word, she sauntered over to the back of the wagon, eyeing the bales of hay with an expression worse than abhorrence, and held out her hand.

I would have to touch her; there was no way around it. I grasped her hand and fortunately she had gloves, so I didn't have to touch her bare skin. I lifted her up and soon discovered that she was lighter than I had supposed because I practically threw her up into the air and onto the wagon bed. I felt a little guilty about that. But, then she sat haughtily onto a hay bale like it was a throne and my disgust returned.

Next were the wicked twins. Actually, I didn't think they were real twins, but they were interchangeable to me. I think Mabel was older . . . or was that one Cecelia? I didn't know. They were both equally awful.

I helped them each into the wagon. They were heavier than their mother so I didn't throw them in, but I thought a little collision with a hay bale would do these girls some good. They settled themselves down on their hay and stared in opposite directions at nothing.

Suddenly Ella was there and she was the only person in the world. She stood so sweetly with her little basket. She was at least five inches shorter than her wardens. I had always known she was small compared to me, but I had never realized how small she was compared to other women.

"So, you *are* going to town today, then?" I murmured. There was no way to avoid it now; she was going to town, she was going to find out about the ball and everything was going to change. I kept telling myself that this was what I wanted and how it had to be, but it didn't change the fact that I wasn't very excited about it. Her gaze was perceptive as I watched her put my words and actions together and I knew she suspected something.

I forgot my disappointment when I realized I was about to help Ella into the wagon. This had seemed like an impossible situation just hours earlier, and here I stood, on a dusty road, moments away from touching her.

I held out my hand and she placed hers in mine and it was as if I held a drop of sunlight in my hand. The sensation was short-lived, however, because almost immediately she withdrew her hand with a quiet gasp. As she hid her hands behind her back, I saw the angry red lines from a whipping she must have received sometime that morning. Her lip trembled and her eyes filled with tears, but she kept them from spilling over.

A wave of too many emotions than I was ever used to crashed down on me. I had just basically thrown Victoria into the wagon and I was seconds away from throwing her out. But that was in the background of my thoughts. My stronger emotion was to snatch up Ella into my arms and take her away with me. But, I forced myself to stay still and my arms felt like iron rods hanging helplessly at my side.

Quickly—as long as it took me to take a deep breath—I calmed down and looked up. Ella's eyes were pleading for my discretion knowing what the consequences would be if I said anything or showed any of the outrage I was feeling. If I knew I could confront Victoria, but keep Ella from facing the consequences of my actions, I would have. But I knew from experience that Ella would not be able to avoid being punished, and things would be worse for her than before.

The knowledge that Ella had to go to the ball was overwhelming. This wasn't about me. This was about who could help Ella more—me or the prince—and based on the last four years of my pathetic attempts to help Ella in my own abysmal ways answered that question. But for right now, I had to figure out a way to nonchalantly get Ella into the wagon without drawing attention to what just happened.

Only a few seconds had passed, but I knew I had to act before Victoria noticed the delay. Thankfully, she still seemed bored, not upset. I looked down at Ella's waist and felt terrible for being so happy over what I was about to do. Without asking permission, I wrapped my hands around her waist. This was different than helping any royal lady onto or off of a horse. When I helped those ladies onto their horses, I didn't have to force myself from taking every one of them into my arms. But I did this time. It was easier than I ever imagined to lift Ella off the ground, and when I had placed her on the wagon, it was harder than I ever imagined to let her go.

Ella stared after me with a beautifully dazed expression and pink cheeks. I turned away as quickly as I could, climbed onto the wagon, and snapped the reins.

Chapter 8

When we reached the outskirts of town, I heard Victoria mumble something to Mabel . . . or was it to Cecelia?

"Drop us off here," whoever-it-was said.

I pulled Charlie to a stop, climbed down, and helped the three women out of the wagon bed. They hurried off without a backwards glance and I was just fine with that. I didn't need their thanks. Their absence was good enough for me.

Once they were gone, I turned back to help Ella down. She seemed to be doing a little dance by herself in the back of the wagon. I couldn't help smiling. She was obviously trying to figure out some way out of the wagon without my help. She looked like she was contemplating climbing down herself, by either climbing over the seat, or somehow sneaking past me in the back, but she must have figured out as she skirted back and forth that it was useless.

I might have been hurt that she didn't want me to touch her, but I knew her better. She was worried about her hands and that I would say something about them now that the other three were gone. Another reason, I suspected, was that she didn't know what to do with this new Will who just grabbed her whenever he wanted to. I tried to feel guilty about that. I failed.

I smiled as I reached out my arms for her and she very compliantly placed herself into them. She didn't hold onto my arms to steady herself, possibly because it would cause her pain, possibly because she was too self-conscious, so she sort of clasped her hands under her chin as I lowered her down. I didn't want to make her feel any more uncomfortable than she already was, so I let go of her as soon as she was steady on her feet. She trembled.

"Thank you for the ride, Will," Ella said quickly. "That was very kind of you, and besides that, I needed a good laugh today." She then told me how ridiculous Victoria looked in the back of the wagon—how entertaining it had been watching Victoria attempt to look regal while sitting on a hay bale in a wagon. Ella told the story to the air in front of her, avoiding my eyes, indicating how nervous she really was despite her smile. As she told her story, I grinned down at her and soon her words slowed and she looked up into my face.

"I would have given anything to see her face sitting back there." I laughed. But, my smile faded. The reason for Ella's nervousness and fear was because of that woman. The reason Ella was in pain was because of that woman. The reason Ella was so unaccustomed to anyone being close to her in any way was because of that woman. "The way they treat you infuriates me." I looked down at her hands, and then away again.

"I know, Will. But we both know that confronting them only makes things worse."

She was right, and that was another one of the reasons I hadn't been able to do anything about Ella's situation. Yes, Ella had promised to stay and take care of them, but another reason I hadn't been able to persuade Ella to escape was because Victoria had a strange, intimidating, manipulative power over Ella that I had never been able to understand. Victoria punished Ella by whipping her hands, or occasionally the nape of her neck or even her back. But the real scars went deeper than Ella's skin.

I learned this lesson about two years after I had found Ella plucking the chicken. I had watched her slowly come back to life, only to be pushed back down again and again into her world of solitude and fear by Victoria.

"It's so nice to be in the sunlight. It feels especially bright after I've been out of it for so long. Almost painful," Ella had said one day.

I'd looked closer at her then and observed that she did indeed look pale and dark circles shadowed her eyes.

"Have you been ill?" I had asked.

She pursed her lips, almost in remorse, but for what I didn't know. Why should she feel guilty for being sick?

She had sighed and looked down at the road. "Victoria thought I stole a necklace from her. My father had given it to her and she thought I wanted to keep it for myself. She accused me of being selfish and hiding it from her when we needed the money so badly. She locked me in the cellar . . . for a while."

Ella didn't cry. She didn't ask for pity. She simply answered my question. She kept her eyes on the road while her fingers played with the braid that draped over her shoulder.

"How long?" I had asked.

She had only ducked her head.

"How long?" I forced my voice to be gentle, though the muscle in my jaw tightened. I knew that all the anger I felt was manifest in my eyes and I tried to calm down so I didn't scare her.

"Two days," she had whispered. When she said how long, I knew the only reason it hadn't been longer was because they needed Ella to cook and clean for them.

I couldn't speak. I couldn't stand this another minute. I didn't ask Ella's permission. I left her at the pond and marched right through the front doors of Ashfield. I barged into the house, not bothering to knock. Victoria was sitting on a chair in the drawing room; they'd still had some furniture then.

I can't even remember what I said. All I remember was that she listened. I would have thought that maybe she was being taught her lesson and she was too afraid to argue, if it weren't for the devious smile on her lips.

I didn't even think to stay and make sure that Ella wasn't harmed. I had said what I had come to say and I was young and arrogant enough to think that Victoria had listened to me, and might even fear me. I found out later that Victoria had thrown Ella into the cellar for another two days.

If Victoria had yelled at me, I would have been angry, but I could have taken that. But, she had gotten back at me in a way I could never forget. She had hurt Ella—to teach me a lesson. I had never encountered anyone who could punish someone so effectively. It was as if she knew exactly how I felt about Ella and knew precisely how to use that against both of us.

I had been angry at Victoria. I hated her for locking Ella in the cellar, but I hated myself more for making it happen. Victoria was masterfully conniving, and that knowledge was the only reason I could remain silent when I saw that Ella had been mistreated. It was also the reason that Ella was silent when she had been hurt. Ella was better at hiding it than I was. Over the years, Ella had become almost as masterful in her ability to avoid Victoria's wrath as Victoria was in executing it. Ella simply kept her head down, did what was ordered of her, and showed no anger or resentment. Eventually, she got to the point that she didn't, or couldn't, even feel them anymore.

I pushed the memory of how I had inadvertently caused Ella pain out of my mind and raised my eyes to look at her. Ella had become calm again as we stood next to the wagon. The fear that had been in her eyes had transformed into pity and understanding as she looked up at me. She knew I hated to see her pain . . . but she still didn't know how much it hurt me, or why.

"There's nothing we can do. Life is difficult and that's just the way it is," Ella said. "But thank you for caring, Will. You're such a good friend to me."

I nodded, but couldn't speak. I wanted to tell her that life didn't need to be difficult all the time; that it could be enjoyable and beautiful. But she had forgotten that kind of life, and so far, I hadn't been able to remind her.

Chapter 9

As I climbed back up onto the driver's seat, I saw Ella straighten her back, square her shoulders, and smooth her dress and hair as she walked into town alone. It made me proud and sad at the same time. She rejoined Victoria and her daughters and I drove the wagon around to the mill at the other end of Main Street. The sacks of grain and oats were stored in an adjacent warehouse that stood behind the other shops. There was no sign of Mr. Lawrence, the mill owner, so I decided to take care of other things while I waited for him.

Apparently, every person in town had heard about the announcement. There were so many people crammed into the streets and walkways it felt like there was barely enough air to go around. A choking cloud of dust hovered, enveloping the square in a dream-like yet chaotic haze. I hurried over to the blacksmith shop to escape the crowds.

The doors closed behind me and my eyes adjusted to the darkness in Corbin's shop. An orange fire dimly glowed in the corner and a red hot horseshoe lay on the anvil, waiting to be shaped.

"Hello, Corbin! Are you busy?" Corbin emerged from the shadows across the room, a cross peen hammer in his hand. He pulled off one of his heavy leather gloves and his skin shone black from working over the forge.

"No, I just like to dress like this so I look hardworking and important." He laughed and pulled his other glove off and shook my hand with the strong grip of a blacksmith. "What can I do for you?"

"Charlie's overdue for new shoes. I came to see if you would have time today, or if I should try later in the week."

"I would love to do it today, but Old Man Emerson just dropped off five horses. Let's try for early next week." He paused, a grin spreading across his soot-blackened face. "Better make it the week after, if that's all right. I'll be on my wedding trip next week." He turned away, his grin never fading, and held the horseshoe steady with some tongs and pounded it with the hammer. Sparks flew with every blow.

"Well, if you think wedding trips are more important than shoeing horses, I suppose I can accommodate your schedule," I joked. A chisel and file were lying on the bench next to me, so I picked them up and slowly scraped the chisel across the file to sharpen it. "Are you going to be able to get away for the announcement?" My stomach dropped. I suddenly felt like I should warn him what the announcement would be, but decided against it. He was engaged to a girl who was shamelessly in love with him, as I had been forced to witness on too many occasions. Corbin didn't have any reason to worry.

"Sure I'll be there! I even wore my best set of clothes to greet the Prince in." There wasn't a spot on him that wasn't covered in smoke, soot, and burns. I couldn't imagine anyone in town standing in sharper contrast to the Prince than Corbin. I laughed and then coughed, smoke filling my lungs.

"Is Francine in town today?" I couldn't shake my concern.

"Hands off, Hawkins," Corbin warned with a grin, and then held up the horseshoe to inspect it before another round of hammering. I held up my hands in mock innocence, the chisel in one hand and the file in the other, then returned to sharpening. "She's with her mother at the dress shop. Her wedding dress is finished and they're picking it up. I'm not allowed to see. Honestly, I'm really excited about it. I guess I'm one of those grooms who wants to wait to see what his bride will look like until the wedding day. She's going to look like an angel."

"That's the last thing I would expect you to say when you look like the very devil." I laughed at his grimy grin, his white teeth gleaming in contrast. "I'll be there to catch you in case you faint."

"Thanks, Will!" Corbin placed the hammer on the anvil and clapped me on the shoulder with a black, burn-scarred hand. Holding the horseshoe with the tongs, he dipped it into the quenching bucket with a satisfying sizzle.

I placed the file and chisel back on the bench and walked to the doors. I pulled one of them open and before the door closed behind me, I heard Corbin start to whistle to himself and I couldn't help smiling. I hoped Francine knew how lucky she was. She was the eldest daughter of one of the richest families in Maycott. But she had fallen for the illiterate, unrefined blacksmith, much to the despair of her parents. After months of whining, begging, and even threatening, Francine had convinced them to let her marry him. It was all anyone talked about for weeks—the upper-class McClure girl marrying the town blacksmith. Some people claimed that Corbin had lured her in, hoping to improve his social status. Others said that Francine fell for Corbin in a surge of post-adolescent rebellion. If Corbin heard the rumors, he never commented on them. He was too in love to notice or care.

Just outside the blacksmith shop stood a large group of men laughing boisterously under a thick cloud of cigar smoke. I didn't hear exactly what they were saying—just bits and pieces—but I didn't have to. They were watching each of the ladies as they walked by, making rude comments to each other and then congratulating whoever came up with the crudest remark. I tried to tune them out and get as far away as possible, though the dense crowd made it difficult. But the name "Blakeley" made me stop as if someone punched me in the stomach. I turned back to them and balled my hands into fists, ready to defend Ella from their vile remarks.

Immediately, I learned that they were not talking about that particular Blakeley.

"Yes, two of the Blakeley sisters came with their mother to visit me this morning," one of the men said. He had a close-clipped mustache and fine clothing, his diamond cuff links sparkling in the sunlight. "I hadn't even gotten out of bed when they arrived, and there were two more ladies in line after them." He sniffed and flicked the ashes off his cigar in what looked like an irritated gesture. "Ella Blakeley hasn't come to visit yet, but she will." I tensed, ready to strike. "I took dance lessons with her when we were children, you know. Her father was quite fond of me. And richer than any man in Maycott. I'd take any of the Blakeley girls. I'd settle for that Emerson girl, but I'd prefer a Blakeley. Ella in particular. She actually has his blood in her veins." He took a long draw on his cigar. "I'm telling you, I just can't keep up with all these women. But," the man grasped onto his lapels and took a deep breath, a wicked smile curling his lips, "I guess I'll just have to try."

He then went into detail of what each woman wore and how beautiful or ugly he thought her to be and why. The other drunkards listened in awe, their eyes dazed and watery. I realized then that the man must be Roger Wallace, recently returned from his travels. I cringed, assuming that if Henry Blakeley were still alive and if Ella were still in the high-class circles of society, Roger would have been a potential suitor for her.

I had been ready to punch his foul mouth if he said anything rude about Ella. He was more pathetic than offensive, though, and I chose to leave him to his dreams of winning one of the "affluent" Blakeley girls. I smirked as I walked away.

I spied Mr. Lawrence walking into his shop and I hurried over to meet him. After I paid for the oats and grain, I walked over to the warehouse next door, climbed up a stack of oats, grabbed the top bag, hefted it up onto my shoulder, and climbed back down. I flung it into the wagon bed where Charlie was waiting just outside the warehouse and returned for the others.

By the time I returned to the wagon with the third sack, a small group of girls had gathered. They giggled and whispered as I lifted the sack on top of the other ones in the wagon, and one girl actually placed a hand over her heart and pretended to swoon. I rolled my eyes, hoping they would take the hint, but my little audience stayed until I was done with the job.

Once the sacks were all loaded, I drove the wagon to the back of the warehouse, out of the way of all the shoppers and crowds of people. I gave Charlie a few handfuls of oats and hitched him by the watering trough. There was nothing left to do but wait. I couldn't see where Ella was in this mass of people and I wondered if she had heard about the announcement yet.

As I wandered through the swarms of people, I saw that Mr. Wilde had come back into town. He was a traveling salesman who sold used items on a little cart that he pulled from village to village. Most of his things were worthless—a shoe without a match, a broken locket, spoiled fruits and vegetables, or a potion promised to cure any ailment, though it was most likely only sugar water. As always, I walked past his cart, not exactly stopping, but quickly looking over the items in his cart for something I had been searching for for years.

"No violin today, Mr. Hawkins," Mr. Wilde said out of habit as he rearranged some vegetables in a crate.

I nodded, smiled, and strode away quickly before he could try to sell me anything. I scanned the crowd and found Ella almost immediately, her face acting like a beacon for my eyes.

She was standing against a pillar by the shoe shop, looking horrified at something. I followed her gaze and saw that Roger Wallace was approaching her from across the road, slowly and with a distinctive drunken swagger. Without even thinking, I began pushing my way through the crowd, almost rudely, as I tried to quickly get to Ella so I could protect her from that revolting man.

Roger made it to Ella before I did and my stomach turned as he appraised her slowly, starting at the worn shoes on her tiny feet and making his way up to the top of her uncovered head. His ugly thoughts were reflected on his bloated face. My heart pounded in my ears with the fury that coursed through my veins and I did become rude then, pushing roughly against people, moving them out of my way, my eyes constantly on the scene in front of me. But then I witnessed something that made me smile and my heart beat proudly; my rage melted away into wonder. Ella lifted her chin and met Roger's eyes evenly. She spoke only a few words, but her eyes sparkled and there was a note of quiet dignity in her air. Once I saw that Ella could take care of herself, I stood back and watched with a grin on my face.

I couldn't hear what was being said, but it seemed that Ella had offended Roger—who had most likely hoped to charm her—the only Blakeley who actually had the blood of the late, once-rich Mr. Blakeley running through her veins. Like everyone else, Roger obviously didn't know about the "once-rich" part.

If his objective was to charm her, it appeared that Roger had utterly failed. After Ella spoke, Roger's face flushed and his eyes tightened and I wanted nothing more than to know what she had said to him. Then, he leaned closer to her, his unclean lips almost at her ear and an unrecognizable wave of some nauseating emotion paralyzed me right in the middle of the road.

In response to whatever Roger said, a change occurred in

Ella. She kept her head up, but her countenance fell. Roger sauntered away, rolling his cigar in his mouth, and hiccupped. My eyes darted back to Ella. She stared at the ground, deep in thought and awash in sorrow. Ella hadn't been offended, she had been hurt and that was unacceptable. I felt torn, not knowing if I should go and comfort her somehow, or confront Roger.

Then, I saw Ella do what I had seen her do a thousand times. She sighed, straightened her shoulders, smiled, and turned to Jane Emerson who I hadn't seen until that moment. Ella had a friend to turn to. And though I wanted to comfort her and quiet the sadness that had crept into her eyes, I admitted to myself that Ella had all the strength she needed to combat whatever pain Roger had inflicted on her all by herself. She had had enough practice dismissing unpleasant things to know exactly how to do it.

Ella was able to fight her own battles. I had been taught this over and over again, but no matter how many times I saw it, I still had the overpowering urge to shield her from those battles. And if I had been unable to shield her, I would at least attempt to take some of the pain away. I liked to think that at times I had done just that, even if Ella didn't realize it . . . and that was exactly how it should be.

Chapter 10

Once I was sure that Ella was going to be all right, I marched in the direction Roger had gone. I chastised myself for not hitting him earlier as a warning against the way he spoke about the women in town. I could have prevented Ella's pain. By the time I reached him, Roger had rejoined his group of cronies, and my guilt and fury almost blinded me. I could imagine the satisfaction I would feel when my fist came into contact with his vulgar face. He was laughing, obviously retelling the story that had just happened, but I didn't even wait to hear his words. I grabbed the collar of his suit coat and spun him around, my other hand clenched into a fist. He looked at me in surprise, his bloodshot eyes having trouble focusing on my face. I had acted so quickly, his friends didn't even seem to realize what was going on.

"You may be welcome in town, but your filthy remarks aren't," I said through my teeth. Roger was just beginning to understand what was happening, and his confusion gave way to outrage. I raised my fist but just before it flew forward, I was distracted by the sudden, though not unexpected, sound of blaring trumpets. The already dense crowd moved as one body in the direction of the sound, knocking me off balance and separating Roger from my grasp on his coat. The throng moved us farther apart and soon we were standing on opposite sides of the square. He gave me a look that told me he wouldn't forget about this. I wouldn't either. With one more blare of trumpets followed by a surge in the crowd, Roger was out of sight.

Reluctantly, I looked to where the sound was coming from and I could make out the first of the flags waving above the crowd. I looked away, not excited for what was coming next. My eyes found Ella who stood directly across the square from me. She was almost completely swallowed up in the mass of people around her, but her face was the only one I could see.

Her eyes were absolutely enormous and her mouth gaped. I laughed, unable to fight the amusement that stole over me even in the midst of the unpleasant situation. She was obviously surprised by the spectacle and it seemed she somehow hadn't found out about the procession. No one actually knew what the announcement would be, and would most likely be beside themselves with excitement and dreams of living a royal life, but it was Ella's reaction I had to see. There was no precedent for this. She had never been offered the chance to escape her present miserable condition for a much better life and I wondered how eager she would be for the opportunity.

The procession came to a stop and the dust slowly settled. I was more than a little dismayed that the royal carriage came to a stop directly in front of Ella. It not only blocked my view of her, but it also put her in prime position to be noticed by the prince, and for her to notice him. He was an outrageous flirt, and what many, if not all, women would call charming. He was also an entertainer and knew how to put on a good show.

The king's spokesman, Sir Fitzpatrick, waited for the crowd to quiet down, and stood up from where he sat on the driver's seat. He unrolled his scroll, and announced in his nasal voice the return of Prince Kenton who had been away for more than a year. *And practically his whole life before that*, I added to myself.

As I repositioned myself so I could get a better look at Ella's reaction, Prince Kenton climbed out of his carriage, leaving the king and queen inside alone. I caught a glimpse of their reaction, and just as I suspected, they were absolutely distraught over the whole thing. The king and queen were the most traditional our kingdom had ever had and I couldn't imagine the strain this was putting on them. But Prince Kenton was his own man, and now that he was back and would also be the next ruler of the kingdom, things were definitely going to be done differently.

Kenton jogged down the road a few feet and jumped up onto the fountain that sat in the middle of the town's square. He was even closer to Ella than he had been before. In fact, she was the closest woman to him. And next to her stood Jane Emerson. Both women had their faces upturned toward the prince, and not toward the spokesman. They had found the more interesting subject.

Once Sir Fitzpatrick had finished speaking, Kenton began his own introduction. "Let me introduce myself formally to you all. I am your prince. I have been away for many years, traveling the world, meeting fascinating people, and seeing magnificent things. I have been in the company of princes and kings, sultans and czars, emperors and rajahs. But," he paused for the perfect amount of time to build up the perfect amount of anticipation, "I have come home. And now I would like to spend some time with butchers, bakers, and candlestick makers."

Prince Kenton laughed at his own joke, which I didn't think anyone understood but him. He seemed to think they knew all about the ball and that they were invited, but since they didn't, his remark made absolutely no sense. It didn't matter much, though. He could get away with not being very articulate, even a bit impulsive. He was the prince, and his quirks just made him that much more interesting, and even fascinating.

"And so," he raised his arms out as if to embrace everyone in the crowd, "We are going to have a ball! And you are all invited!"

A girl next to me jumped so high, her elbow hit me in the face and her squeal pierced my brain. I looked down and saw that it was Francine, Corbin's fiancée. For a moment, I forgot all about my pain and how it could grow exponentially this week, and instead focused on Corbin's potential pain. Francine was not acting like a girl who was about to marry one of the best, most decent men in the kingdom. She was behaving like a childish schoolgirl. I hoped Corbin couldn't see her, wherever he was. I wanted to move away from her, but then I wouldn't be able to see Ella. And it didn't really matter where I moved; every other girl was acting the same way. Except for one.

Ella didn't scream. She didn't jump. She didn't elbow anyone in the face. Her formerly stunned and even fascinated face had become serene. She stood quietly, a small smile on her lips.

"As you may know," Kenton continued, "I am almost twenty-five years old, and as is our custom—our law—I am to be married before my twenty-fifth birthday. I have seen all I want to see of the world. I have met everyone I want to meet. I am ready to settle down—to marry the girl who shall one day be our queen."

A courteous, subdued cheer followed this announcement. It seemed to be an obviously anticlimactic declaration. We already knew he was to be married. That was pretty much his whole reason for existing. I, of course, knew there was more to it, but he was the consummate performer. He had the crowd exactly where he wanted them.

"And, it has also been our custom that royalty has always married royalty," the prince continued. "But, my dear father and mother and I," he gestured to the unmistakably displeased king and queen seated in the carriage behind him, "have found that this custom is simply that—a custom. This is *not* a law.

So, in conclusion . . . I may marry anyone I wish." He paused. "And it may be one of you."

My eyes were riveted on Ella, until an unexpected weight knocked me to the side. Francine had fainted, her face ghostly pale, her eyes closed. I reached out to catch her before she hit the ground. This was no small feat, considering I was being bumped and punched and kicked by every hand and foot and body of every person around me. Every girl had tears streaming down her face. How could they cry so instantaneously?

There was nowhere I could safely deposit Francine's limp body so I held her in my arms while I waited for the excitement to die down. I searched frantically for Ella, but the crowd was in complete chaos. I shifted Francine's weight so her head wasn't flopping backwards unsupported. Finally, my eyes found Ella's face in the crowd. She was, once again, absolutely serene, but this time her face was turned upward. She had a smile on her face and a blush that was unmistakable even across the square; the blush that belonged to me—the blush that I had made reappear after so many years of pale impassiveness. I followed her gaze and immediately felt a peculiar sensation, like I was trying to stay upright as some strong current rushed past me. Ella was staring directly into the face of the prince, and though he was turned away from me, it looked as if he was staring straight back at her.

If I thought I had felt jealousy before, it was nothing compared to this—this nauseating dizziness that made me feel like I was being swallowed up into a dark pit of agony. Ella finally lowered her eyes and the tumultuous crowd had calmed down enough that the prince was able to continue.

"The ball will be held one week from tonight," Kenton said, facing my side of the crowd. Then, he very deliberately turned and looked in Ella's direction. In a voice that could only be described as seductive, he said, "Let's all get to know each other a little better."

Ella's smile was deliberate and infuriatingly stunning. *What was she trying to do?* I knew the answer to that question instantly. Nothing. She was just being herself, smiling because she felt like smiling, not trying to lure in anyone. I just hated that she felt like smiling so exquisitely and that the prince was there to see that smile.

Kenton jumped down from the fountain's edge and practically skipped back to his carriage as he waved at the crowd. I was once again bumped and pushed out of the way by all the girls waving and blowing kisses at the prince, hoping that their kisses would somehow fly through the air and land on his royal lips. I looked down and saw that my formerly unconscious cargo had awoken and was vaguely waving and smiling. The prince climbed back into his carriage and the procession moved on to the next village.

One week. I knew the ball was going to be held in one week, but the significance of the day hadn't hit me until right then, when I looked down at Francine in my arms. She was apparently too delirious with excitement to notice that, first of all, she was most inappropriately being held in my arms in the middle of the village square with no intention of using her own legs to support her; and second of all, the ball was to be held on the day of her wedding.

A tap on my shoulder forced me to slowly turn and face the person I least wanted to have to see Francine in my arms. Corbin was there, his hands out, ready for me to place his fiancée in his arms. I recognized his expression at once. It was like I was looking in a mirror. He was defeated.

HERE, CORBIN. I THINK SHE SAW A RAT AND FAINTED." I weakly laughed at my pathetic joke, hoping he would lighten up a little bit. Even after I transferred Francine into Corbin's arms, her eyes still followed in the direction the Prince's entourage had driven out of town.

Corbin shook his head slowly. He couldn't say it right then, but I knew with that one look he had seen the whole thing. He had been watching Francine the way I had been watching Ella. I turned away from both of them, leaving Corbin to deal with his disappointment while I dealt with mine. I wondered how many other fiancées the prince would woo before the end of the day.

Suddenly, I wanted nothing more than to be out of town. The dust from hundreds—thousands—of feet was choking. The giggling, sighing, daydreaming girls were taking up every foot of space and sapping my sanity. I couldn't breathe. I couldn't think. But at the moment, I didn't want to do either. I just wanted to escape.

I looked back to where Ella still stood across the square. She hadn't joined in with the other girls who were blowing kisses at the prince, but she did seem more tranquil than she had before. Like me, she might have felt a little exhausted now that the excitement had died down.

I walked over to her, passing the fountain Prince Kenton had stood on. Her head was bowed down and just as I reached her, she walked forward right into me. The packages she had been holding fell to the ground and she stumbled backward. Quickly, I reached out and grabbed her arms before she fell over, then dropped my hands once she was steady. Her eyes seemed troubled, and it looked to me like she wanted to escape town as desperately as I did.

Hoping she wouldn't mind, I took it upon myself to see her home. I gathered up her packages and she followed me to where the wagon was still waiting behind the warehouses. Apparently, she didn't want to join in the dozens of circles of girls talking about what they were going to wear to the ball.

"I'm going to wear my pink silk gown," one girl was saying. "I heard that pink is Prince Kenton's favorite color." I didn't know where she had heard that, but she was going to be terribly disappointed.

Ella's stepfamily was in one of those circles. When we reached them, Ella motioned to the wagon, indicating that we were leaving. I chuckled a little when Victoria's only answer was to scrunch up her face at the wagon and turn back to her friends.

Ella shrugged and allowed me to help her up onto the driver's seat. When I placed my hands on her waist, I was pleased that I could still make a blush rise to her cheeks, even though she had just been in the presence of an obnoxiously charming prince.

"No hay this time?" she said almost playfully. It seemed that taking her home was the right decision. She already looked happier. I joined her on the bench and snapped the reins, leaving the chaos behind us.

As we drove along, we didn't talk much. I looked at the road, even though I had it memorized, and tried not to think—not about the ball, or about Ella's smiles at the prince; not about how much he seemed to favor her already; and especially not about how much I loved her and how much it would hurt to let her go. I failed miserably.

"Will, did you keep the announcement from me because you were worried I wouldn't have anything to wear to the ball?" I hoped she didn't notice me jump as I snapped out of my unwelcome reverie.

I looked over at Ella, remembering my blunder from earlier when I had mentioned the palace, and that I had asked if she was going to be in town today. She hadn't been fooled. She knew that I had known about the announcement. I couldn't admit to why I didn't tell her—that I had been about to propose, but wanted her to be free to marry the prince. This was about her, not me.

Glancing down at her worn shoes and her gray dress she wore every day, it actually did occur to me that she might not have anything to wear to the ball.

"Yes, that's it." It was true, even if it wasn't the reason I didn't tell her about the ball.

"Oh, you don't have to worry about that. You're so nice to be concerned about me."

I smiled down at her, though I did feel guilty for not being completely truthful. I was always concerned about her, of course, but it had very little to do with fashion.

We reached the fork in the road that would either lead to Ashfield or back to the palace. Ella insisted that she could walk the rest of the way.

I hopped down from the wagon, hurried to her side, and held out my hands for her. She smiled timidly, and let me help her down. As her feet touched the ground, I was filled with the dreadful reality that this could be the last time I ever touched her. I had never been able to justify touching her before today, and the chances of this happening ever again were very remote. Besides that, the ball was a week away and I was quite confident that I would most likely see very little of Ella after that day. The realization of that possibility was going to make letting go a near impossibility.

I tried to force myself away from her, to drop my hands from her waist, but I could smell the sunshine in her hair and could see the way her eyelashes brushed against her cheeks. She gazed down at the ground and I knew she was uncomfortable and unaccustomed to all this closeness. For a tiny instant, she glimpsed up at me, as if to see if I had any intention of ever letting go of her. Then her eyes returned to look at the ground and she bit her lip nervously.

I probably shouldn't have considered kissing her at that moment, and I was angry for allowing myself to feel closer to her, instead of keeping our usual, safe distance. Now was not the time to pull her closer to me. She needed to be as free as she possibly could be. Resisting the urge to sigh pitifully, I slid my hands away from her waist and stepped back. I unloaded the packages, making sure one more time that she really wanted to walk the rest of the way.

"Don't be silly. I can see Ashfield from here," she said, taking the packages from my hands. I climbed up into the wagon. "Thank you, Will!" I heard her call as I rounded the bend. I wanted to turn around, to look at her one more time, but all I could manage to do was wave in farewell.

Chapter 12

ONCE I REACHED THE PALACE STABLES, I STARTED unloading the sacks of grain into a corner of one of the smaller stables. It was strangely quiet, knowing that everyone should still be at work. All the horses were still gone, being ridden and pulling carriages from village to village today. But since the major towns were close together; the carriages would be back before it was too dark. I heard someone snoring as I walked around the far end of the last row of stables. I looked around the corner and saw that all the men had fallen asleep, and they lay scattered all over the ground. They thought they were getting out of the more difficult job by not going into town, but it appeared that staying behind had been more strenuous than they had anticipated.

I chuckled to myself and stretched out on the grass. The warmth of the sun lightly prickled my skin and my eyes drooped. With the tumult of the last two days finally stilled, my mind was able to grasp what had happened. I hadn't proposed to Ella. She had to have her chance to marry the prince. Ignoring the heaviness in my chest and trying to focus on my hopes for her, I put my hat over my face to block out the sun, and fell asleep.

I didn't know the procession was about to return until Paul kicked me in the ribs to wake me. The sun had fallen behind the trees and there was a definite chill in the air. I had barely gotten to my feet when the first of the horses started filing in.

The king and queen were dropped off at the palace, but Prince Kenton continued on to the stables. Occasionally, he liked to put his own horse away and brush her after a long day. Normally, I would admire this about him, but today it irritated me to the point of committing treason. I had had enough of him for one day.

"Why have I allowed myself to be away for so long? Why didn't anyone tell me there were enough pretty girls in my own kingdom to fill a hundred thrones?" Kenton was laughing with some of the guards who had ridden alongside his carriage.

"Any village in particular?" one guard asked. He seemed very pleased that the prince was paying attention to him.

"Maycott. No doubt about it!" Kenton replied. "I wished we'd saved it for last. I didn't even want to go to any other villages after that one."

My hands shook as I unharnessed the horses from the carriages. I couldn't be sure, but it was safe to assume that he was referring to Ella, considering he had practically spoken directly to her the whole time. Or maybe Jane. That thought comforted me considerably.

The prince didn't go into any more details, and I was grateful. I couldn't bear to think or hear about it anymore. I was just glad it was over. Ella knew now, so that worry was gone. She was excited about the ball, so I didn't have to wonder about her reaction anymore. But there were too many disappointments mingled with these reliefs for me to feel any real peace.

The horses were brushed, fed, and watered, and all the carriages and supplies put away a couple hours later. All the grooms looked like they would gladly sleep in the stable instead of walking the hundred yards to the bunkhouse, and some actually did. It was tempting for me as well, but I had to get back home to take care of my own stable and horses.

And waking up at home ensured that I would be closer to being with Ella in the morning.

***

I WOKE UP EARLY, MY BODY NOT RESTED BUT MY MIND alert. It was Saturday, and after the many miles they traveled the day before, the palace horses would most likely get a rest today. I had collapsed into bed late after taking care of my chores, but woke up as soon as it was light enough to find my boots. Ella was an early riser and I didn't want to miss this opportunity to see her.

Quickly, I took care of things at home, and decided that when I saw Ella, I would offer her a ride to the ball. Corbin's wedding was scheduled for just after dinner on Friday, and I could take Ella to the ball when the wedding was over. With Victoria selling the Blakeley's carriage to pay off . . . I couldn't even remember what . . . Ella had no way of getting to the ball. Yes, she could walk, but it would take hours, and that would be absurd. By taking Ella to the ball, I would feel like I was a little more in control; that I was helping her to have this once-in-a-lifetime experience. If I saw her looking happy and excited, it might ease the sting a little bit. Or, maybe it would make it worse, but I would deal with that when the time came.

When I arrived at the pond, Ella was sitting at the edge of the water. The hem of her dress was soaking wet and she had a pile of cattails lying in her lap. I silently crossed the bridge to her side, and she didn't stir. I was about to say hello to let her know I was there, but she spoke first.

"Good morning, Will." She didn't even turn around. I could hear the smile in her voice and it put a smile on my face.

"Good morning," I said. I walked forward to be closer to her, but remained standing. I decided not to delay saying what I had come to say. I had learned that much from the last twenty-four hours. "So, you mentioned yesterday that I shouldn't worry that you don't have anything to wear to the ball, so I won't," I said, smiling. I wondered if I was at all convincing that I had been worried about what she would wear, and not about her leaving me to become the princess.

Suddenly, the same debilitating fear I had felt the day before paralyzed me, and I couldn't make any more words come out of my mouth. I felt ridiculous. Yesterday I had actually thought I could ask her to marry me, when today I couldn't even ask her to let me take her to the ball. I realized that this would be the first time I had asked to take her to any kind of social function, and it just happened to be the very function where the prince could propose to her. But, even without all of that, it was still the first time I was asking to escort her somewhere, and I felt a trickle of dread when I imagined her saying no. I swallowed hard and continued as lightly as I could.

". . . But have you figured out how you plan on getting there? You don't have a carriage, and I doubt you would want to go on horseback or even cow back, though Lucy loves you enough I'm sure she'd be willing. So, I was wondering if you . . ." I forced myself to stop rambling absurdly. She wasn't laughing. I was obviously joking, but there wasn't even a hint of a smile on her face.

"I'm not going." She tried to sound nonchalant, but there was an edge to her voice.

"What? Why aren't you going? I was only joking! You won't have to ride a cow!" I smiled a little, but then became serious. "Isn't this every girl's dream? To be chased after by some ridiculously charming prince and live happily ever after?" I decided to apologize again, hoping that it wasn't me who had made her reconsider going to the ball. "I'm sorry I kept it from you yesterday, but I really think you need to go."

"I am not going and I don't want to talk about it." There was that spark of fire again—adorable and encouraging, but under the circumstances, very confusing.

"I don't understand."

"Will, look at me." She held up the corner of her apron and watched me like I should be interpreting something from this mystifying clue.

"What? What's wrong?" She looked perfect to me.

"Do I look like princess material to you?" She was more than princess material; she was queen material. She was angel material. She was so perfect, she barely even belonged in this world. I wanted to tell her this, only I couldn't imagine a world without her, so I couldn't say it. "Will, I'm not going to waltz into the palace surrounded by people who are supposed to be there and pretend that I belong. I don't belong anywhere that isn't a barn or a kitchen, and putting on a fancy dress isn't going to change that."

She crossed her arms and turned away from me. She was trying to gain control, her arms seeming to hold her emotions tightly inside of her.

"I don't want to be late again in case they've decided to become early risers." She smiled pitifully at her little joke. "Please don't worry about me. It will be all right, Will."

She spun away, perhaps trying to escape before I could try to convince her she was wrong. But the words wouldn't come. I knew what I wanted to say, but I couldn't find the right way to say it.

Just before she was too far away from me, I reached out for her. My hand caught and encircled her wrist and it felt like the most natural thing in the world. She stopped immediately and my hand slid down to rest in hers for a moment. Her hand was so cold and small, but so strong at the same time. Almost unconsciously, her fingers gently curved around mine. I didn't want to let go. Slowly, I let my hand fall to my side and she turned to face me. I was more resolved than ever.

"You have to go to the ball," I said. I truly meant it.

"Will, I told you I would feel like a fraud. Besides, why

would I care about some silly ball when I can barely keep food on the table and my house is falling apart and—"

"That's why you need to go," I said quietly, but earnestly. "You need to get away from all of that, even if it's just for a night."

"But what about after the ball is over? Why would I go, only to return to the same problems I had before?"

That was the question I dreaded most to answer. But, I answered honestly.

"Maybe the same problems won't be there." I tried to sound detached and practical.

"So if I go to a ball, all my troubles will be over?" Uncharacteristic sarcasm darkened her tone.

I sighed. She still wasn't seeing it, not *allowing* herself to see it. "You have a chance to get out of here."

"Me? Don't be absurd." She laughed, but it came out hard and bitter. "Why would I go throwing myself at a prince, hoping he'd choose me over a girl who comes from a proper family or who has a dowry, or even a second pair of shoes?" Her face crumpled and she bowed her head.

She wasn't listening. She had forgotten who she was. She had never done that, not as long as I'd known her, not since the day I found her plucking that chicken. That was the only other time I had seen her look this dejected and lost. But, since that day—the day she found she had a friend and that she was understood and thought of and cared for—she carried with her an inner peace, even when she had felt lonely, scared, and abandoned.

But not today. It was as if her strength was dwindling even as she stood there. Victoria had done this to her. She was the one who had robbed Ella of her self-confidence. She was the reason Ella couldn't imagine herself at the ball. I knew I had to find a way to make some of her despair my own, to lift some of it off her shoulders and onto mine.

I surprised us both when I suddenly grabbed the tops of her arms, pulling her close to me, the wetness of her skirt brushing against my legs, soaking through the fabric. Her eyes were wide with alarm, but not fear.

I blinked back the moisture in my own eyes, unable to tolerate the pain for one more minute.

"You need to open your eyes and see yourself more clearly. Don't forget your father and who he was—and who you are."

She tried to wrench out of my grasp, but I wouldn't let go. If I had released her then, she would return home and slink even farther down into the gloom that overshadowed her and she would be consumed. I couldn't let her leave now, when she was so discouraged. I had let her have her way for years; I hadn't forced her to escape. I had watched as she chose to return home again and again, and each time, she took a piece of my heart with her, whether she knew it or not. This time, however, I couldn't let her leave until I saw her smile return and her eyes light up again. And it wasn't just because I needed to see it—she needed to feel it.

She glared back at me with more anger than I had ever seen on her face. Her cheeks were flushed, her jaw tight, her eyes glistening with angry tears that never spilled. I wondered if this would finally be when she yelled at me, and I would welcome it.

But I watched as her eyes slowly softened into gentleness and all traces of anger and sadness faded away. Her lips turned up slightly at the corners, and I was astounded and confused by how she could so quickly gain control of herself. But, seeing the warmth and the subtle hints of happiness that played at the corners of her mouth and the twinkle in her eye made my frustration melt into relief.

"I'll think about it," she said quietly and calmly.

With the passion of the moment now faded, my closeness suddenly felt awkward. Now that we were both composed and I had no excuse to touch her, I looked down at my fingers wrapped around her arms, and slowly released them. She exhaled sharply and I realized she had been holding her breath.

"He would be proud." I smiled, knowing that Henry Blakeley never would have forgiven me if I allowed Ella to wallow in self-pity and stay home from the ball. "By the way, it doesn't matter how many pairs of shoes you have, Ella. Your plain, black shoes worn out with work and taking care of others are worth more than the queen's dainty slippers any day. If the prince can't see that, he doesn't deserve you."

She *needed* to see that she didn't need to prove herself to anyone, ball or no ball, prince or no prince. The only person who needed to see how remarkable Ella was . . . was Ella.

Chapter 13

When I arrived at the palace after seeing Ella, the grooms and horses were all still asleep, both exhausted from the last two days. There were no royals waiting to take any horses for a ride around the countryside, or even just within the palace grounds, and I was grateful to have a calm day.

I drained the old water out of the watering trough and pumped in fresh water from the newly installed well that poured the water straight into the trough. I was grateful I wouldn't have to carry the water by the bucket load, taking half the day to fill it back up. I emptied some of the oat sacks into barrels in the corner of the stable and carefully closed up each sack to keep out the mice. Then, I shoveled out the stalls of each horse. Ants had found the box of sugar cubes, so I tossed them a good distance from the stable into a little natural pond formed by recent rains. Even the flies seemed lazy today, not bothering to pester me, just hovering sluggishly in the warmth of the stable. I wouldn't miss their obnoxious presence when the weather cooled.

Once the main stable was taken care of, which housed the horses of Prince Kenton, the king and queen, and a few other royals, I moved to the lower stables, where the carriage-pulling horses were kept, and I performed the same duties. One of the Belgians was favoring a leg, bending it slightly and not putting any weight on it. Grabbing a hoof pick, I walked over to her, ran my hand down her leg to the ankle, and she lifted her foot compliantly. I ran the pick from heel to toe and a rock that had been stuck in her hoof fell to the ground. Before dropping her foot, I took salve off a low shelf to my right and rubbed some into her hoof.

With everything done and everyone seeming to take a much-deserved day off, I decided I would go home to take care of things there.

Charlie and I walked toward home through town. Mr. Wilde was there with his cart of odds and ends, and he caught my eye as I passed. I raised my eyebrows to ask the only question I ever asked him and he replied with a shake of his head, and left it at that.

We left town and walked along the road. Up ahead of us I saw a man walking, his head down and his hands in his pockets. It was Corbin.

I hadn't seen him since I placed a semi-conscious Francine in his arms and saw the defeated look in his eyes after the prince's announcement. Judging from the way he hung his head and shuffled his feet, I guessed things hadn't improved much since then. I dismounted and caught up to Corbin to walk next to him.

"Where are you headed?" I asked.

"Nowhere."

"Looks like it," I grinned, as his feet continued to take him . . . somewhere.

He kept his eyes on the road, but his cheek lifted a little as he smiled. He kept walking, his face falling again.

His moody silence prompted me to start with the small talk. He hated that. "Nice day, huh? Not too hot. Not too cold. Well, it did start out a little cool, I guess. Probably going to be a cold night. What kind of tree is that? I never did know. Do you see that bird? I think it's some kind of jay.

Look at that bush. It's very bushy, as far as bushes go . . ."

"I'm going to toss you into that bush if you don't stop," Corbin finally said, a laugh in his voice. He sighed. "Francine has barely spoken to me since yesterday."

"What happened after I left?"

"Well, you know she fainted, obviously."

"Yes, it must have been a big rat." I joked, carefully avoiding the word *prince*.

"Right, a rat. A huge, handsome rat with stupid dimples and bags of money. No one should be allowed to have dimples *and* money." He growled. I would have laughed, except I knew exactly how he felt.

"How long did she stare after him before she realized he was gone?" I asked.

"About five minutes."

"That long, huh?"

"Yes," he mumbled. "She finally snapped out of it and made up some excuse about needing to discuss gowns with her mother. She had already picked up her wedding dress from the dressmaker's. What was that supposed to mean?"

It meant that she went to go search for a ball gown.

"Corbin, don't worry about it. You know she loves you. *Everyone* knows she loves you . . . whether we want to know or not. I've never seen anyone kiss anyone as much as Francine kisses you." I laughed with an uncomfortable twinge of jealousy.

He chuckled. "Yes, yes she does," he said absently. I didn't know, nor did I *want* to know, what memory he was reliving, but I noticed that it was slowly making him more and more depressed, realizing how much things had changed between them. It was time for more small talk. I noticed the last of the wilting wildflowers growing on the side of the road.

"What kind of rose is that? I think it's a moss rose."

"Just a rose," he mumbled.

Chapter 14

Late Sunday morning I sat with the other stable workers on our usual pew. The king's grooms had sat on this pew for as long as I could remember. Most of them who sat there now were older teenaged boys who had come to work at the king's stables to get started on their futures. I was the oldest, and most of the boys looked up to me. I went to church, so they went to church, but they never complained. They got a lot more than spiritual enrichment while they were there.

Every Sunday, the boys would come home with one or two love letters each. I still got the occasional note, or perhaps a set of batted eyelashes or a coy smile. I usually nodded and smiled politely, but not encouragingly. Though there was a time when I hadn't always reacted that way. In the past, their smiles would have been received with a wink and a church-appropriate grin; the young lady would then duck her head and smile through pursed lips as her cheeks warmed. I hadn't become reacquainted with Ella until I was nearing twenty, so I had experienced my share of meaningless romances. But those days were long gone for me. I had passed the age where I was simply charmed by a pretty face. Now that Ella was in my life, I wasn't charmed, I was captivated. I knew that there were other good and beautiful girls, but I was past even wanting to find out. My heart was taken.

I loved seeing Ella at church, even if we didn't get to talk much . . . or at all. Ella usually stayed close to Victoria, having to play the role of dutiful daughter every week. But it was still nice to see her there, resting, with no work to do and an expression of tranquility on her face.

Ella hadn't arrived yet today, but as I waited, I was entertained by the boys who sat on my pew. Every time a girl walked by, they squared their shoulders and tried to look mature, which, of course, did the opposite. I smiled at them, suddenly feeling much older than I actually was.

When Jane Emerson entered the chapel, she would always try to get my attention as she walked by, much to the dismay of her father. I wondered why he still even worried. I hadn't paid Jane any real attention in years. I would usually nod in greeting, and leave it at that. But today as she entered, she practically marched past me down the aisle and plopped down rather heavily onto her pew. She didn't look very happy to be there, to say the least. I didn't care enough to wonder why. I was still waiting for Ella to come.

Finally, Ella and her stepsisters walked into the chapel. For the first time I could ever remember, Victoria was not with them. Victoria didn't come to worship; she came to socialize. Whatever the reason for her absence, it must be bad enough to keep her from being the center of attention. But because of Victoria's absence, Ella was free to sit wherever she liked. Much to my delight, she sat near the back, closer to me and separate from her stepsisters.

Mr. Grey began his sermon with a joke about how hard it must have been for everyone to come when they had a ball to plan for. There were a few chuckles, but even louder was the collective sigh from almost every young lady.

What on earth could take almost a week to prepare? If I were to go, I couldn't imagine it taking me longer than ten minutes to throw on some clothes and shoes and head out the door.

Mr. Grey stopped talking about the ball, thankfully, and went on with his sermon. I listened, mostly, but a scene caught my attention and I had to look away so I didn't burst out laughing.

Roger Wallace was sitting next to his mother, and he seemed sober, which was a Sabbath-day miracle. His mother looked up at him every few seconds and smiled. She even pinched his cheek at one point. But, that wasn't what made me laugh—well, it wasn't the only thing that made me laugh.

Roger wore a scowl on his face that would be the envy of any spoiled three-year-old who didn't get the pony they wanted. He was looking at every girl in the congregation, probably hoping for some sign of admiration, or at least acknowledgement, but they were all studiously ignoring him. He looked like he was going to cry, or scratch someone's eyes out, or throw himself on the ground in a good, old-fashioned tantrum.

I caught a glimpse of Ella and she didn't seem to be paying much attention either. To the casual observer, she would have looked thoughtful, but slightly bored. To me, I could see that she noticed something and it made her smile—or try not to.

***

The service ended and we all filed outside to the lawn where everyone liked to mingle when the weather was nice.

"Where's Widow Blakeley?" Mr. Grey said to no one in particular. "She was going to tell me about the time she met the queen of Laurel." Mr. Grey loved Victoria's stories more than anyone—always laughing the loudest and asking to hear more. Searching the dwindling crowd, he spied Ella a few feet away and jogged over to her. As he spoke to her, his eyes almost disappeared under his deeply furrowed brow.

"Give that sweet lady my best . . . ," a somber Mr. Grey said after a few minutes.

"I will. Thank you, Mr. Grey," I heard Ella reply.

After Mr. Grey left to talk to someone else, Ella lifted her hand to wave at someone, but then quickly lowered her hand. She pursed her lips in embarrassment, and perhaps hurt, then turned to walk in the direction of home. I saw an opportunity to be with her—just her—and I took it, ignoring the warning voice in my head that told me I was making things harder on myself.

"How did you like the service today?" I asked when I caught up with her.

She smiled slightly and turned a little pink, but didn't exactly answer my question. "Did you notice the girls acting strangely today?"

"I don't notice any of those girls," I said frankly.

"Of course you don't." I could almost hear her roll her eyes. "I've never seen anything like that. It was like there was a war going on right in the middle of church, but the weapons were glares and squinty eyes." She laughed quietly.

Now that she mentioned it, it all seemed so comical to me, but I supposed if I were a girl, it would have been intimidating, even frightening to know that they were all striving for the same thing—marriage to the prince. "I don't envy you, you know. Women fight a harder battle than I'll ever know."

"I don't know about that." Her brow puckered in thought. "We're all competing *for* the prince; it must be at least that difficult for the men to be competing *with* the prince."

She had said the perfect thing without even knowing it.

"There's no competition," I said so quietly she probably didn't even hear me. I didn't want to sound like the brooding child Roger Wallace was. I brightened. "So, you're saying 'we' now? Do you include yourself in that group of women fighting *for* the prince?" She was considering going to the ball. That meant she must not feel as bad as she had the day before . . . I hoped. I smiled down at her, but my lips felt tight.

She sighed, indicating her exasperation with me, but a smile played at the corner of her mouth. "I told you I would think about it. I know Father would want me to go, and if I do go, it would only be because I don't want to regret it later. I just want to see what it's like. But I am not willing, nor am I worthy, to compete with those girls,"

"Ella! You're worth one hundred . . ."

"Will, there's no competition," she interrupted. I rolled my eyes, but grinned. She *had* heard me earlier. Now she was using my argument against me.

The walk to Ashfield was far too short. We even walked especially slowly. If we had gone any slower we would have been going backward. Ella didn't seem in a rush to get home, but she had nowhere else to go. I had to go to the palace and it was the last place on earth I wanted to be.

We reached the front yard of Ashfield and I couldn't help admiring what a beautiful home it was. Yes, it needed painting and some things needed to be repaired, but Ella took impeccable care of it. It was a job for twenty servants, and she did it all herself. The rose beds were immaculate; the porch swept; the front walk free of weeds or grass. I couldn't see the backyard from where we stood, but I knew the henhouse was clean, the animals well-fed and cared for; the garden was neat and growing or already harvested. Ella's meticulous care of the house and property had to be one of the main reasons that no one suspected how much things had changed inside. There were no outward signs of the deterioration that had occurred in the souls of the people who lived here. Ella fought against it, and had mostly succeeded, but even the strongest of people had a limit to what they could stand.

I couldn't believe that even a few days before I had thought that I could take Ella away from this to marry me and live in my little hut. She loved Ashfield more than I even understood. I knew that she had promised to take care of her stepfamily, but there was so much more than that that kept her here. She could have escaped so many times, but I suspected it would have torn her apart, knowing that Ashfield might be neglected without her, which it most certainly would be.

Ashfield needed Ella and Ella needed Ashfield.

I don't know how long we stood there, staring at this grand and beautiful house we both saw every day, when Ella suddenly turned to me. She was going to say something, but she smiled instead and looked up at me with an inquiring expression. Her eyes wide and questioning, she tilted her head as if to ask me what I was thinking.

I couldn't tell her exactly what I was thinking, but I did want to tell her how extraordinary she was and how much I admired her. I had often complimented and encouraged her, but was always careful about how much I said or how I said it. I usually focused on her log-splitting skills, her delicious bread, and her gardening expertise, without putting my emotions on the line. I had been waiting for her to give me some sign that I could be more open before I took that step. I looked down at her sweet, searching face and saw what I needed to see.

It was the expression I had seen a few times in the past that told me there was something more between us than our mutual friendship and even admiration. The expression was usually accompanied by a flush in her cheek and a downcast eye. It was that same expression that had given me some hope that when I had planned to propose, her answer could be yes. I was still afraid to connect a certain word with that hope, and I realized I might never get to. For now, I could tell her a little bit of how incredible I thought she was. My heart could handle that, without taking away her freedom to choose her own path in life.

"You are a beautiful person, Ella. Do you know that? You give and give with no thought of getting. You work hard without complaint and you see the good in difficult circumstances."

She beamed up at me as I spoke, a look of absolute wonder on her face. I was pleased to see not even a hint of doubt or self-deprecation. I smiled, realizing that I not only admired Ella, I admired that we both had the same mentor. We were both trying to be the same person, only she was succeeding. "I've only known one other person like that in my life."

We both knew who I was talking about—Henry Blakeley. She blinked rapidly and her eyes shone with tears. "Thank you," she whispered.

I couldn't help myself from taking a step closer to her—closer to those eyes that smiled up at me and her golden hair that blew gently in the wind and those soft cheeks, now flushed pink. For years, I had imagined what those cheeks would feel like. I stepped even closer to her. She didn't look down this time and didn't seem overly scared or uncomfortable by my closeness. She looked right back into my eyes, with only a whisper of hesitation, as her eyes widened slightly. I raised my hand, and silently chastised myself for trembling. Her hair had blown across her face. With the tips of my fingers, I brushed it back and let it fall behind her shoulder. I placed my hand against her warm cheek. The heat burned my fingers, like she was standing next to a fire. So subtly, I wouldn't have noticed if I weren't cradling her face in my hand, she leaned into my palm.

Remembering that she wasn't mine, I forced myself to drop my hand, but I curled my fingers into my palm, trying to hold onto the sensation. She stood there, motionless and almost dazed, as I abruptly smiled and walked away.

For a moment, it had just been Ella and me. No prince, no ball, no Victoria, no chores, no fear.

Just us.

Chapter 15

I DIDN'T REALLY REMEMBER THE WALK HOME. I COULDN'T see the road or the sky or the trees, just the memory of Ella's face looking back up at mine. My feet took me to my stable while my head was preoccupied. A twinge of unease had settled upon my mind as I walked. I was feeling closer to Ella than I ever had, but remembering the open and imploring look on her face just a moment ago made me wonder if she was feeling the same. A few days ago, I would have wanted nothing more than to feel that we were growing closer together, but now, with the ball and the absolute necessity of Ella's attendance and freedom, I felt guilty. I couldn't have her feeling torn.

At the same time, I wondered if it might also be fair to let her know what she was choosing between. I was expecting her to choose when she didn't really know there was a choice. Would it be so terrible if she truly knew how I felt about her? That I didn't just pity her? That I wasn't just helping her because she was the daughter of Henry Blakeley? It was impossible to know where her best interest ended and mine began, or where my pride took over and overruled my common sense.

Once I arrived at my stable, I automatically started saddling up Charlie. The palace grooms usually rotated Sunday shifts because we weren't all required to be there, but we were told we all needed to report to the stables in preparation for the ball. I couldn't even begin to imagine why we would need to come in to work on a Sunday so that in five days people could come to the palace to dance around and eat fancy, fluffy food.

As I rode along the dirt road and contemplated what the stable workers could possibly be needed for, I heard a carriage approach me from behind. Pulling on Charlie's reins, I moved to the side of the road to get out of the way, but the carriage sounded like it was slowing down instead of passing me. I turned around to see someone, who looked a lot like Roger Wallace's mother, sticking her head out of the carriage window. It was hard to recognize her when she wasn't pinching Roger's cheek.

"Driver, halt!" she called. As her carriage slowed, I pulled Charlie to a stop, trying to imagine why this woman would want to talk to me. I even glanced up at the carriage driver to see if he could give me any clue, but his eyes stared straight forward, glazed over with boredom. I shifted in the saddle so I faced Mrs. Wallace and nodded politely, looking her straight in the eye so that she could see that she had obviously mistaken me for someone else.

"Mr. Hawkins! How lovely!"

"Mrs. Wallace, how . . ." I couldn't force the word 'lovely' out of my mouth, but I also couldn't think of any word at all to describe this encounter. I had never spoken to this woman in my life. "Awkward" might have sounded rude.

Thankfully, she started talking, saving me from more discomfort. "As you know, my dear boy, Roger, has recently returned from his travels." I knew, but didn't care . . . at all. "We are throwing a welcome-home party for him on Tuesday night and we would love for you to be there."

"Oh? Um . . ."

"I'm so sorry about the late notice. We were going to wait at least a month until he got settled, but we thought it best to help him feel more at home sooner."

What she meant was, he was the most eligible bachelor in the kingdom until the prince practically proposed to every girl, and now he had to act fast if he was going to get the wife he felt he deserved before the prince could snatch her up at the ball.

"Well, I . . ."

"You may not know this, young man, but I was dear friends with your mother once upon a time. Well, before . . ." She trailed off, not able to say that she was friends with my mother before my family came to ruin because my father had been a gambler and that he died from drinking too much. Thanks for the reminder. She continued. "I understand that you used to work for the Blakeleys. We invited the Blakeley daughters to the party, but I just wanted to make sure that Widow Blakeley knew about the party too."

"The Blakeley daughters?" I interrupted.

"Yes, dear. Mabel and Cecelia. Anyway . . ." It was infuriating that no one even acknowledged Ella's existence anymore. "I wanted to see if you could escort the girls to the party. We would love to see you all there."

She didn't even give me a chance to tell her that nothing could convince me to go to her pathetic party for her pompous, overgrown child, and that those girls would never listen to a thing I said—if I actually chose to talk to them—and that I didn't care who came her party. She drove off in her fancy carriage, her lace-draped hand waving out the open window, her rings catching the sunlight and blinding me. She must have invited the wicked twins after church; they wouldn't be interested in associating with any man who wasn't a prince. But that didn't explain why she would ask me to come.

She must have thought that I had more influence over them than I actually did. Which was absolutely none. But, the real reason was probably that I was so lowly that I wasn't real competition for her son. The Wallaces obviously couldn't invite just the women, so they invited non-threatening men to be their escorts.

I wasn't offended; I didn't care enough to be. Instead, I laughed as I rode along, imagining myself talking to Mabel, Cecelia, and Victoria; I imagined telling them that they needed to go to Roger Wallace's party and that I would be their escort. I laughed out loud again, suddenly fond of the oblivious, patronizing Mrs. Wallace for providing me with the best joke I had heard in ages.

As I got closer to the palace, I returned to my original thoughts before Mrs. Wallace had interrupted them with all her "lovely" talk. Besides driving carriages or taking care of horses, I wondered what else they would need us stable hands for.

It was worse than I ever could have imagined.

I was glad I hurried to the palace after walking Ella home because mingling outside the stables, waiting for assistance, was Prince Kenton, Sir Thomas, another royal-looking man, and a carriage driver.

"Can I help you, Your Majesty?" I asked, after galloping over and pulling Charlie to an abrupt stop.

"Yes, wonderful! I would like to take a carriage ride today, so we will need a carriage and two horses, if you don't mind," he said, patting me on the back. I could have figured out that he needed a carriage and horses once he told me he was going for a carriage ride. I wouldn't have even been annoyed by this three days ago, but it was amazing how jealousy could make a perfectly respectable person, such as the prince, suddenly appear to be a vexing brute in my eyes.

"Right away," I replied as respectfully as I could. I quickly readied the horses and hitched them to an open carriage. It was a nice day and I figured that they would get a better view not having to look through windows.

"Would you like to tour the town, Your Majesty?" the driver asked.

I tried not to roll my eyes. This was the prince of our kingdom and he had spent so much of his life away from the people he ruled over, he didn't even know anything about his subjects. This had never bothered me before, but maybe it did now because he was trying to marry one of them.

"No, no. I would like to drive through the countryside to see the grand estates out that way. I saw enough of the towns during the procession." They climbed into the carriage and drove away.

They were going to the countryside, and closer to Ella. I tried to calm myself, knowing that Ella rarely, if ever, had time for long walks along the road.

I climbed the hill toward the upper stables and almost walked in, but I stopped short when I heard some giggling coming from one of the stalls and a lower voice talking. It was Grant's, and unless I was mistaken, the woman's voice belonged to Lady Gwen. I didn't want to intrude, so I cleaned up some things and made sure everything was put away where it should be.

I tried to act surprised when Grant and Lady Gwen emerged from the stable, but Grant didn't have to act. As soon as he saw that someone else was there, his eyes bulged and he barely contained his gasp of shock. When he saw that it was me, he quietly sighed in relief, but was still a little shaken.

It was forbidden for the stable workers to ever be in the company of any lady alone. The rule was invented for the ladies' protection, but I saw it as a way of protecting us men, too. At least when you weren't alone, there were witnesses and you couldn't be accused of something you didn't do. Grant had taken a very big risk being alone with Lady Gwen. If she had been any less kind—or fond of him—I would have been very worried for Grant. Whenever a stable worker was accused of less than the most professional and proper behavior, he would lose his job at the least, and be imprisoned at the most. Most often when this occurred, it wasn't because the man had done anything with or to any lady, but that he *hadn't*, and that was her way of punishing him. Over the years, as we had lost three or four of the men to such a circumstance, we kept our eye out for those types of ladies, secretly referring to them as "Mrs. Potiphar."

But Lady Gwen and Grant both seemed genuinely happy to be in each other's company, so I decided not to worry. Lady Gwen continued walking toward the palace after saying good-bye to both of us, and once she was gone, I nudged Grant in the ribs. He looked over at me sheepishly, and I knew it wasn't the time to reprimand him. Besides, hadn't I just walked home alone with Ella?

Without a word, but with a smile on his face, Grant finished cleaning the stall he had been working in.

Perhaps I wasn't going to reprimand him, but I decided to have a little fun. "Grant, what was Lady Gwen doing here, and on a Sunday?" I asked, trying not to laugh at his guilty expression.

"She just wanted to go for a ride, that's all."

"Did she go?"

"Um, no."

I chuckled. "She looked very beautiful."

Grant's head shot up and he looked like he wanted to punch me in the eye.

"Don't worry, Grant. I wasn't looking. I just wanted to see how you'd react if you thought I had been." I laughed. He didn't even smile. Apparently, Grant didn't like my joke.

"Keep your eyes on your own girl," he muttered.

"Grant, I'm just teasing you. I know how you feel about Lady Gwen. I'm the one who encouraged you to pursue her. Remember?"

His face softened and he seemed a little penitent. "I know, I know. I guess I'm just sensitive when it comes to her. I barely feel worthy of her as it is, and the thought of someone else wanting her just . . ." He stopped talking then and flexed his hands.

"Here," I said, shoving a rake into his tense hand. "Work. It helps. I promise."

Just as the rest of the grooms began gathering outside the stables, a shrill voice demanded our attention. It was a voice I had heard coming from inside the palace many times. It never yelled like this when the royal family was at home, but once they were gone, this voice had free reign. It pierced through the entire palace grounds, making the horses jump and waking sleeping grooms who liked to relax after morning chores were finished. This was none other than Mrs. Hammond, the head housekeeper of the palace.

Mrs. Hammond marched down to the stables from the palace, carefully avoiding any spots of mud and dirt as she weaved through the garden and across the lawn. She was a plump woman with gray hair so wild that it looked like a bird had taken up residence in it. Her cheeks were flushed from exertion and she gasped for breath as if she had run miles, and not walked yards.

"Listen up, you boys. Follow me." She spun around with surprising agility and we all looked at each other. She walked in the direction of the palace, a place we had never been invited to before. They probably would have preferred that our unworthy eyes had never even looked upon it, and now we were supposed to follow her there.

After a moment of hesitation, I trudged behind her, and the other men followed me, wary of what could lie in store for us in that direction. I wasn't afraid of work, but if they were going to make us clean linens or polish mirrors or arrange flowers in preparation for the ball, I was going to put up a fight. I would rather shovel manure all day than iron some doily for a ball.

We reached the front steps of the palace and I worried that we would actually have to go inside. I looked down at my muddy boots and filthy hands, feeling more common than usual. Fortunately, Mrs. Hammond spun back around to face us and we all bumped into each other as we stopped abruptly.

"No, no. You're not going in there. You are absolutely filthy. Only the cleanest and best-behaved . . . and best-*looking*," she added, surveying our faces with scrutiny, "of you will be allowed into the palace." I was tempted to go roll around in the mud. Why would we want to enter the palace anyway?

I looked at Grant and Paul. They looked like they had the same idea and laughed out loud. Mrs. Hammond's eyes narrowed to little slits and almost disappeared in the folds of skin surrounding them.

"You. Big one! You can go straight back to the stables if I hear one more sound out of you!" Mrs. Hammond bellowed at Paul.

"Do you promise?" Paul whispered. I glanced up at Mrs. Hammond, but she didn't seem to hear as she continued with her speech.

"As you know, there will be a ball at the palace on Friday night, five days from today." I was glad she did the math for us, since we were *clearly* too dumb and dirty to figure it out. "Since this ball is unlike any other—not just for royalty—the palace will be full of people, more than there ever have been inside these walls. The whole kingdom, in fact. The prince is aware of the hardships that this is placing on us more civilized and refined indoor servants and has suggested that we recruit some extra help. Of course, I suggested bringing in professionals, but he insisted that we have plenty of help right here within the palace gates. You." Her face scrunched up. "And so, we must train you stable workers to be inside workers. Mind you, this is only for one night. You will return to your regular, lowly duties immediately after the ball is over. But, until then, we need more waiters, ushers, cooks, and dish washers."

I had already begun my descent down the hill back to the stables when I heard her next words. "Whoever helps in the preparation and success of the ball will receive an extra month's wages." I froze. For a moment, I was the Will before the ball was announced—the one that looked for any way to earn an extra penny so that I could ask Ella to marry me. Besides that, I realized an extra month's pay could buy Ella some new shoes. It could buy her some food and desperately needed supplies. I might even be able to buy her a dress, or even a violin if Mr. Wilde from town ever had one to sell. I had returned to the group before I finished that thought. I would iron a hundred doilies if it meant I could buy Ella at the very least some new shoes. Maybe I could even buy them for her before the ball.

"And, the best part of all," Mrs. Hammond continued, "is that you will all get new suits that you will get to keep."

I had to cover my mouth to keep from bursting with laughter when Paul jumped up and down and clapped his hands like a little girl who had just been offered a new doll. Mrs. Hammond actually smiled, believing his excitement to be sincere.

"First things first. You will all need to be measured for your new suits so that they can be sewn for you by Thursday at the latest. Line up here, please."

As she spoke, a group of grandmotherly seamstresses lined up side by side. They all had measuring tapes and quills and parchment to write down our measurements. Without asking our permission, their hands were all over the place, holding out my arms, wrapping around my waist, measuring me from hip to heel. I had never been measured for anything before and was slightly stunned by all these hands fluttering around my body. Paul's laughter kept getting out of control as he refused to let them wrap their arms around him because he was ticklish.

Once they were all done, we were sent back to the stables to finish our duties. There was really nothing left to do besides wait for the prince to return, so most of the boys returned to the bunkhouse. I sat down under a nearby tree and looked out over the kingdom.

I could make out the very edges of Lytton where I had been only a few days before, selling my foal so that I could be in a better situation to take care of Ella once we were married. I couldn't quite see Milton, but I tried to remember how the sticky, salty air felt on my skin. I could see Maycott and the little grove of trees that surrounded the pond. Our pond. Just above the very tips of the trees, I could make out a tiny cone-shaped roof that was Ella's tower, and wondered what she was doing at that moment.

I didn't even know I had fallen asleep until the wheels from the royal carriage and the jingling from the horses' reins woke me. I stood up in time to see the carriage rounding the corner and coming down the gradual slope that led to the stables.

The little party seemed much more subdued than when they had left. As they came closer, I heard the rare sound of an almost solemn prince.

"Yes, yes. The countryside is beautiful. I was simply unprepared for the forlornness in the people's faces. If I lived free, out in the country, I couldn't imagine being unhappy. That young woman's face will haunt me for as long as I live. I hope she comes to the ball. She needs a little gaiety, I think."

"Would you like me to find her for you if she does come?" asked Sir Thomas, obviously referring to his role of finding the next princess.

"She did have something captivating about her, didn't she? I don't know why I didn't stop to talk to her. Something held me back. I was just stunned, I suppose. I've never seen anyone look so downtrodden. I may regret it for the rest of my life."

I couldn't let myself think that they were talking about Ella. I had to tell myself that she was at home, not anywhere the prince could have seen her, and especially not looking so miserable that the prince would take notice from his carriage. No, I hated the thought of her being that sad. I was stuck here at the palace and couldn't go and help her. Not only that, I didn't have the right to show up at her house and make sure she was happy.

The other thought I hated having was that the prince wasn't a terrible person. I had always known that, but this week I preferred to ignore it. It was so much easier to hate him for ruining everything by coming back into town and throwing a ball with the intention of marrying a common girl from his kingdom. But here he was, concerned about the well-being of his people and worrying about the poor, sad girl he saw on the road.

It was Ella. I could feel it. Just because things were under control a few hours ago meant nothing. If Ella had misspoken or had done or not done something, I knew that Ashfield could become a hostile, hurtful place in an instant. Things had seemed fine, better than fine, when I had left Ella after church. But her stepsisters had not been with her, and she had gone in alone. Not that they would have protected her, but they could have caused a distraction so that Ella might not have had to take the full force of Victoria alone.

Suddenly, I needed to be there. Not here. Prince Kenton and his party returned to the palace and I hurriedly put the horse and carriage away. I made sure everything was in order, remembering that those who were going to be trained to help at the ball had to be back at the palace just after dawn every morning.

I got Charlie and we raced out of the palace gates, down through town, and to the road that led to Ashfield. I didn't know why I was in such a hurry. I knew I was being irrational, assuming that the sad girl had been Ella. On the other hand, if it was Ella he had seen, and she was suffering, I had to see if she was all right.

We rounded the bend and Ashfield came into view. I raced up the front drive and then pulled Charlie to a stop. There was a carriage in front of the house, and unless I was mistaken, it was the doctor's. My first reaction was not what it should have been; it was a selfish reaction.

I had wanted to be the one to help Ella, but someone else had come instead. I couldn't come into the house now. I couldn't see if she was indeed forlorn, or if she was her normal, peaceful self. But, I was glad that if I couldn't be with her that it was the doctor who was there instead. He was a good man. And if it turned out that Victoria was ill and that he was there to help, he definitely was the better person.

I turned Charlie toward home. Ella would be all right. She was safe with the doctor there, not just to have help, but also to act as a buffer between her and Victoria's wrath.

It was completely dark by the time we arrived at home. I took care of the animals and cleaned myself up. Then, I chuckled, remembering that Sundays were supposed to be a day of rest.

Chapter 16

Ella never came.

I fished until my line was heavy and the sky turned from inky black to hazy gray. My eyes ached from watching for her to emerge through the trees; the only living thing I saw was a squirrel gathering acorns for the rapidly approaching winter.

I couldn't help worrying. If Ella had been living Jane's life, I would have just figured she had slept late, or had preferred to take an early breakfast in bed, or was perhaps on a ride or on a walk gathering wildflowers. But this was Ella. I pursed my lips as I stared at the empty space where Ella usually sat, wondering what had kept her inside. Was she the sad girl the prince had seen? Was Victoria more ill than I had supposed? Was Ella locked in the cellar, being punished for some false accusation? It had been a long time since she had been punished so severely, owing to her ability to avoid Victoria almost completely, but it was not unthinkable.

Maybe this is good practice for me, I thought gloomily. Maybe I would have to get used to life without Ella. A thought entered my mind that I had refused to think for the last few days. I had been so concerned about Ella and her life after the ball—whether she stayed at the palace, or returned home to the life she had always known, or if somehow she became mine. But my thoughts unwillingly turned to my own fate.

What would *I* do if Ella never came home?

I knew immediately that I could not stay here. I couldn't come to fish every morning, hoping to hear Ella's gentle humming, hoping to see her face light up when she saw me, hoping to catch one glimpse of the expression that told me things neither of us dared put into words. I couldn't see the smoke that rose from Ashfield's chimneys, knowing that it wasn't Ella who had started the fire. I couldn't bear to walk past her home, knowing the emptiness that permeated inside without her warmth and tenderness to fill it. The emptiness inside me at that thought brought an unexpected lump to my throat. More than any house would be, I would be left desolate without her. Experiencing even one morning without her smile was enough to deaden the beauty of the new day, and this triggered a forlorn feeling that I felt I could not escape.

But I would have to try. If Ella never came back home, I would have to try to escape it. I imagined her as the princess—the queen—at the palace. Who would adjust her stirrups? Who would lift her up onto the saddle? Me?

I wouldn't be allowed to look into her eyes. I wouldn't be allowed to reminisce with her about our mornings at the pond. I wouldn't be allowed to ask her if she was happy, and be glad if she was and comfort her if she wasn't. I would be forced to watch as she grew closer and closer to her charming prince-husband, which was exactly what was supposed to happen.

I would have to leave. Not only would I have to stop working at the palace, but I would have to leave Maycott. No, I would have to leave the kingdom. I couldn't be her subject, not that she would see me that way, but that's what I would be—that's all I would be allowed to be. She wouldn't just be the girl I once knew, but the girl I would always love, whose horse I would saddle and brush, whose carriage I would ready for her Sunday drives. She would be another man's wife. A prince's wife.

Abruptly, I stood and raced home, my line of fish dangling from my hands and my fishing rod clenched tightly in my fingers. Once I reached my stable, I threw some oats in the horses' buckets, feeling guilty for neglecting them over the past few days. I promised myself I would let them out to graze soon. For now, I saddled Charlie as fast as I could, secured the fish behind his saddle, and had him running even while I placed my feet in the stirrups.

Charlie ran until his neck was damp with sweat. We rode through the forest, not passing Ashfield. I couldn't think about what was happening inside. I couldn't worry if Ella were being punished. I had to force myself to let go. I urged Charlie even faster, but my pain followed me.

***

Once I reached the palace and placed Charlie in one of the lower stable stalls, I took a minute to calm myself down. I walked around the stable a few times, pretending to look busy. Returning to his stall, I thoroughly brushed Charlie, hoping he would forgive me for having him run so hard. I gave him some sugar cubes and held the bucket of water to his mouth, which he drank eagerly.

I didn't even recognize myself. I was never this tense or agitated. If anything, I was often accused of being too lighthearted and always joking. I had used that personality trait to cheer up Ella when she needed it. Thinking like this, worrying like this, was exhausting.

I wanted this week to be over, but I also needed it to last forever.

I was grateful for the sounds of boisterous laughter as the men filed out of the bunkhouse and toward the stables. We gutted the fish while Paul started a fire. Then we set the fish to roast until they were brown, the aroma comforting and familiar. We talked and joked and my spirits slowly lifted.

"Men." We all turned to face Grant, who looked as if he had just come from a funeral. "I was just passing by the palace and we have been summoned by Mrs. Hammond." Grant's eyes were downcast and he twirled his hat in his hands like he were informing us that a horse had died in the night.

Chuckling and forcing myself to lighten up as I remembered that extra month's pay, I put the last piece of fish in my mouth. "Come on. Everybody up! It can't be *that* bad." I stood and made my way up the slope to the palace. With groans that sounded like they were in pain or in mourning, the men followed after me. We arrived at the palace doors where Mrs. Hammond stood waiting.

"Follow me, boys. You will not be permitted to enter the palace through these doors. You will enter around the back through the kitchens."

Mrs. Hammond led us to the back of the palace. The farther we got from the pristine front entrance, the more and more weeds grew up through the irregular cracks in the pathway stones. The kitchen door didn't even latch all the way. Once we were inside, the cooks, bakers, and dishwashers looked at us in abhorrence. I tried not to mirror their expressions, but instead smiled back, perhaps a little too broadly.

"Who would like to volunteer to be a dishwasher?" she asked. I considered it for a moment. If I were stuck down here in the kitchens, I wouldn't have to be outside where everyone else was. I didn't mind throwing half-eaten food out and then washing the dishes in a noisy, wet, clanging kitchen that would, perhaps, drown out my thoughts of Kenton and Ella.

I raised my hand, and then a few other hands joined mine.

Mrs. Hammond's eyes squinted in thought, though I couldn't imagine what she could be thinking. She had asked for volunteers, and we had volunteered. It didn't seem complicated to me.

"You, you, and you." She pointed at Paul and two other men and told them to go to the dishwashers to be trained, ignoring my hand still raised in the air.

Confused, though not particularly concerned, I followed Mrs. Hammond with the rest of the men down a long corridor. When we reached the end, the smell of lye and perfume overwhelmed me and made my eyes water.

"Who would like to volunteer as linen washers?" We were even deeper into the bowels of the palace. This would most likely be the farthest I could be from the ball. I raised my hand without hesitation. Not only would I be safe down here from any drama up there, but I also had to admit I was an excellent clothes-washer.

"You, you, you, and you." Mrs. Hammond pointed to four men who were standing all around me, but still not to me. I glanced around to see if she had purposely ignored anyone else, but they were all looking back at me with the same expression of bewilderment on their faces. Grant shrugged, also unsure as to why I hadn't been chosen for the two jobs I had already volunteered for. The four men went to stand with the clothes-washers to be trained.

There were about ten of us left, and we followed Mrs. Hammond out of the laundry room, and through the kitchens, where Paul stood with a pink apron around his waist. I could hear the young woman who was training him.

". . . Yes, wash the plates clockwise. It just seems to get the food off better than counter-clockwise. Trust me. And, you *only* use the yellow cloths for washing. Don't *ever* use the blue cloths. Those are for drying. We can't end up with all wet towels, now can we?" She giggled at the mere idea then became abruptly serious. "But, when we dry, we dry *counter*-clockwise."

Paul looked at me like a horse begging to be put out of its misery.

Mrs. Hammond led us up some stairs that became more and more ornamental with each step. The light filtered in through the windows and I noticed for the first time how dark and damp the basement had been. Soon, we were standing in the grand foyer, and I suddenly felt very dirty. I craned my neck up to look at the ceiling, which was three full stories high, each floor standing at least fifteen feet tall. The stained glass windows threw rainbows of color and light across the gray stones and faintly sparkled in the sunshine. Specks of dust glimmered in the motes of sunlight that flooded through the windows, which had been opened to let in the fresh air.

Everywhere, servants were scrubbing and polishing, dusting and mopping. The familiar aromas of polish and lye floated in the air and it had the smell of industry and cleanliness. I felt unexpectedly comfortable in the presence of these people who worked like I did. I admired their determined faces as they washed and polished, though they never looked in our direction. I always imagined everything in the palace moving in dream-speed—lethargic and unreal. But the sweat that glistened on these faces reminded me that this palace was also a home—a home that required work.

I nodded at a man who was shining a candelabra and he squinted and looked away from me, his nose twitching, and I was brought back down to reality.

"Come on, then!" Mrs. Hammond called.

We continued walking and found ourselves in what could only be the ballroom. The floor was a wide circle, polished and almost seamless. The expertly placed stones had tiny cracks in between them that were as narrow as a horse's hair. Candelabras hung from the ceiling every few feet and I could imagine that once this room was lit, it would look as bright as noonday, no matter what time it was. Past the floor was a large wall, or what used to be a large wall, that had once separated the ballroom from the courtyard. Now, there were large chunks missing from the stones and we could see clearly out to the gardens through the holes. There were loud pounding sounds followed by the crunch of stone crumbling to the ground, and wood being hammered and sawed as the workers created an open space to the outside.

"The prince has ordered that this wall be removed," Mrs. Hammond called over the sounds of deconstruction. "The new walls will be made of lightweight wood and will slide to open and close on large wheels. It will be quite a mechanical marvel. This room will be a gathering area and the actual dancing will take place outside near the courtyard to make room for all the guests."

I was already raising my hand to help with the building of the new sliding walls, but Mrs. Hammond reached out and actually pushed my hand down.

"You men have the most important jobs. I needed the most refined and handsome up here, right in the middle of the excitement. You will be the servers at the ball." Suddenly I cursed my parents for being so beautiful. I could have at least been safe in the kitchen washing clockwise and drying counterclockwise. "You will be the ones who greet the guests as they arrive at the palace. You are here to serve, and to embody the beauty and sophistication that is the kingdom of Claire." She abruptly turned, and behind her a line of servants had entered the ballroom, each holding a glass tray on his hands with napkins folded over their forearms.

"Let the training begin!" she cried. "First, posture!" Mrs. Hammond walked over to Grant and pulled a hair off the top of his head.

"Ouch!" he cried, rubbing the spot where she had pulled out his hair.

"Yes, pain brings perfection. I want you to remember that pulling feeling and lift your body up toward it. Like this . . ."

One month's extra pay. One month's extra pay, I repeated to myself.

Chapter 17

I HAD SPENT MY WHOLE LIFE PERFORMING RIGOROUS AND physically demanding tasks. I had spent hours in the sun, sweating, splitting rails, building my own house and stable, and pulling tree stumps out of the ground. I had repaired my roof with shingles I had cut myself, constructed my own fireplace with stones I had quarried, loaded, and shaped . . . but all of that was nothing compared to the exhaustion I experienced performing mindless and menial tasks at the palace. In just half a day I could almost feel my muscles atrophy and my brain deteriorate. At the end of the first day, I collapsed into bed, not even bothering to take off my boots, drained by the monotony of it all.

On Tuesday morning, a quick wash and shave did much to invigorate me after the tedious training at the palace the day before. I hurried to the pond, not even intending to do any fishing. There wouldn't be time to eat any fish once I arrived anyway. I only wanted to see Ella. I needed to see Ella. I had gone a whole day, and I wouldn't be able to make it through another day of ball training without being revitalized by her smile, uplifted by her insightful conversation, and warmed by her kindness.

With every passing minute, my spirits fell deeper and deeper into the melancholy of the day before. I stared into the pond and watched the fish swim near the edge. It seemed they were mocking me, knowing they were going to live that morning. Eventually, I even crossed the bridge, closer to Ella and Ashfield. I wandered to where Ella usually sat in the morning, looking for any sign that she had already come and gone.

Nothing.

The fear that I hadn't allowed myself to put into words overcame me then. I had scared her. On Sunday, the last time I'd seen her, I had touched her face and looked deeply into her eyes. Now, she was taking a step back from me, just as I knew she would, just as she had always done. I didn't blame her. I blamed myself. The ball was making me insane, doing things that I knew were thoughtless and, though I hated the word, desperate.

Another thought entered my mind that made me have to catch my breath. Ella could also be distancing herself because she wanted to be free to go to the ball and meet the prince—without me following her around like a lost puppy. This was exactly how it was supposed to be, and what I truly wanted for her, but I had never considered that she would take steps to ensure her own freedom.

My heart broke a little as I crossed the bridge back to my side of the pond. Not meeting me here as she always had seemed to be Ella's kind way of telling me that she needed to be free, which might even mean that she had begun to feel something for me. My heart broke even more.

The tasks at the palace were almost too demeaning to endure. They trained us how to stand up straight, how to position our hands on the small of our backs as we stood at attention. They taught us how to balance the tray with our left hand while gathering glasses with our right. We were shown how low to bow without being disrespectful, while not bowing low enough to grovel.

We were taught how to open carriage doors without being seen, and how to treat the women when they arrived: Don't look her in the eye, but also make her feel like she is desired and admired by your mannerisms. Make sure the carriage comes to a complete stop before opening the door and hold your hand out, but don't let her weight push it down as you help her, or you will be insulting both her size and your own strength. She must feel that she is as light as a feather and that you are as strong and immovable as a sculpture.

My brain hummed from the dullness. My feet and back ached from standing like the lifeless statue I was being trained to be. My soul ached for Ella, while I also knew I should be grateful for her foresight and strength in doing what I had so far failed to do—let go.

Thankfully, we ended early on Tuesday. Mrs. Hammond's hair was a ball of wiry lines coming out of her head, and her face was flushed and shiny when she waved us all away to go home.

As we walked away, I saw her bend over out of the corner of my eye, place her hands on the small of her back, and moan quietly. The other men couldn't get out quickly enough, and I didn't blame them, but this poor lady with the shrill voice and exacting commands suddenly had my sympathy. She obviously hadn't signed up for this, and probably hated the ball as much as I did.

I spotted a chair in the corner of the ballroom close to where I stood, which we had practiced sitting on (since we apparently didn't even know how to sit correctly—not that we would even be allowed to sit while at the ball), and I picked it up and carried it over to her.

"Here you are Mrs. Hammond," I said, gently placing a hand on her elbow and lowering her into the chair. "And thank you for everything." I bent over to kiss her cheek.

She gasped and held a pudgy hand up to her face. A slow smile crept onto her lips. "I knew you were my favorite, Mr. Hawkins."

We laughed for a moment. I bowed perfectly and she clapped her hands delightedly. Then I left.

As I passed by Corbin's blacksmith shop, I noticed that the double doors were wide open, but Corbin wasn't inside. I walked through the shop and saw that the back door was ajar; I walked through it to the backyard.

Corbin was at the well, pumping water into his hands and splashing it onto his soot-covered face. He saw me and lifted a hand in greeting. His eyes had a glint in them that had been absent for the last few days.

"Are you going over to the Wallace's tonight?" he asked, walking over to the towel that hung on a hook by the door.

"Me? No. Why?" Then I remembered. Roger's sad little party was tonight. "Oh, that. I really don't think I'm up for it."

"Francine is coming with me." Corbin's smile was so happy it was sad. She was his fiancée and he was delighted that she was actually going somewhere with him . . . instead of planning how she was going to leave him for the prince at the soonest opportunity.

"Great! Well, you two enjoy yourselves."

"Will, isn't there anyone you want to bring? Ella Blakeley, for instance?"

My eyes widened, my face reddened, and I stammered like I had just been caught stealing sweets from Mr. Morris's candy counter when I was seven.

"Will, I've known you my whole life. You've never looked at anyone the way you look at Ella. Why don't you ever take her anywhere? What's wrong with you?"

I couldn't find the words to even try to describe why I never took Ella anywhere, or why she could never say yes if I had.

"I've never known you to be a coward." Though he smiled, my eyes narrowed and my hands clenched. Corbin took a step back and held up his hands, though his grin never faltered.

"Whoa, Will. Sorry. You know I was only joking, right?" He laughed as he walked back into his shop, where he also lived.

I followed him and forced myself to calm down. I could hear the words of Henry Blakeley in my mind, "Courage looks like cowardice to those who don't understand." Corbin simply didn't understand the position I was in. The only thing I hoped at that point was that I truly was being courageous, and not using my situation with Ella and her stepmother as an excuse to be cowardly.

Corbin continued as he changed his shirt. "I'm not going to pretend I know anything about what's going on between you two. I've heard the rumors about Ella's madness, but I seriously doubt them. I do know that her stepmother is a wench, so that might be a hindrance. I also know that with the ball coming up, you might feel a little pressure to back off and let her have her chance with the prince—"

"You need to get a more demanding job. You have too much time to think."

He chuckled. "So, my advice to you, since you're asking," he said with a smirk, "is to make sure you have no regrets. I don't know what that means for you, but I know what it means for me. I was feeling pretty low the other day, but I've decided to do all I can so that I have no regrets, no matter what happens at the ball. Francine and I are still engaged and I'm going to remind her why. She may be caught up in all this ball business, but if I need to re-sweep her off her feet, well, I'm more than willing to do it." Corbin pulled on his suit jacket and smoothed the sleeves. "And judging from what I've seen between Ella and you, she has no idea how you feel, Mr. Subtle. She has to know what she's deciding between, doesn't she? You may think you're being noble by stepping aside, but I think you'll regret it if you don't give it all you have while you can."

I wondered how much longer Corbin could talk. Though I couldn't help feeling a little relieved that he saw things the way I did . . . or had at least considered.

"But, back to the Wallace's party." Corbin continued, though I was positive he had already reached his word quota for the day. "You need to either ask Ella to go, or you need to ask someone else to go, or even just go alone. And get used to the idea of living without her if you're not going to do anything about it. Now, if you'll excuse me, I have to go woo my fiancée."

He said this as he hopped up and down on one foot while pulling on his boot. Once it was on, he raked his fingers through his hair and headed out the front door.

"Corbin!" I called after him. He turned around impatiently. "The fire's still going. I'll put it out."

"Thanks, Will! Good luck!"

Chapter 18

It was dusk by the time Charlie and I arrived at home. I slowed Charlie to a walk, thinking about what Corbin had said. I either had to let Ella know how I felt about her, or get used to the idea of living without her. Only, he wasn't in the position I was, and Francine wasn't in the position Ella was. I still had to do what was best for us, even though there wasn't even an *us*.

I paced my little cabin before finally deciding to go to the Wallace's. I knew I couldn't ask Ella to go with me. I didn't want to think of Victoria's reaction if she knew Ella was out at a party. Ella had never gone to a party or dance in the last ten years, and I doubted she would be allowed to go now. In the years before I became reacquainted with Ella, I had gone to dances without her. But this time it felt different. I wasn't just going to have a good time. I was trying to see what life would be like without her. I was already predicting a miserable evening.

I had washed that morning and hadn't even broken a sweat carrying trays around, so I figured a change of clothes would suffice for the evening. We had laughed when Mrs. Hammond had told us we would get to keep our suits from serving at the ball, but now as I considered spending an evening with some of Maycott's upper class, a new suit might have helped me feel less ridiculous.

Thankfully, my one suit wasn't in bad shape. Just before I went to get Charlie, I changed my mind and decided to walk so I could give myself more time to change my mind about going.

As I walked up the path to the Wallace residence, I realized with dismay that I was one of the first, if not the very first person to arrive. Corbin had left long before I did and I wondered where he was. But then I remembered what he had said about wooing his fiancée, and I decided I didn't want to know.

I did not want to be the first one inside. I didn't want to look like I had nothing better to do than to make Roger look good. And I especially didn't want to talk with my new best friend, Mrs. Wallace, about the good old days before my family came to ruin. So, with my hands in my pockets, I sauntered off the path and into the trees that lined the walk up to the house. I found a stone bench, sat down, and waited for more people to arrive while also half-heartedly convincing myself to stay.

It wasn't long before Mabel and Cecelia Blakeley waltzed up the path. Apparently they had changed their minds about coming, even without my considerable influence, as Mrs. Wallace had suggested. A surge of rebellion shot through me and I quietly emerged from out of my hiding place after they unknowingly passed by me.

As quietly as I could, I followed behind them as they made their way up to the Wallace's front door. They were arguing so loudly they couldn't hear the soft crunching of my footsteps in the dirt.

"We already looked in the drawing room! There's no place to hide anything in there! You know that!" "Well, they're not in Ella's bedroom, that's for sure."

"I even looked under mother's bed!"

"Well, I had to look in the barn! Don't complain to me. I'm going to smell like cow manure for a week."

I didn't know what they had been looking for or why, but

I was glad they didn't find whatever it was . . . unless it was compassion or a sense of humor.

They reached the front door and Mabel, I was pretty sure, reached out a hand to ring the bell. I couldn't suppress the grin that spread across my face.

The butler opened the door, and just behind him stood Mrs. Wallace. She approached us and held out her hands to grasp each of the girls'. All hints of their petty argument were gone and they beamed at the older woman.

"Oh, you darling girls! How lovely you look. Thank you for coming to welcome my dear boy home." She looked past them and straight at me. "And Mr. Hawkins, how good of you to escort the Blakeley girls here!" She reached past them to grasp my hands and pulled me down to her level to kiss my cheek. Mrs. Wallace was turning out to be not so bad.

Mabel and Cecelia whirled toward me, Mabel outraged and Cecelia confused but smiling dimly. "It was nothing, Mrs. Wallace. I was glad to have an evening out with some old friends of mine."

Mabel started to protest. I held out my arms and linked hers and Cecelia's through mine and led them away, before Mrs. Wallace noticed Mabel's incensed expression. These girls could use a little humility by being escorted by a simple stable worker. As we walked, however, I felt Cecelia running her hand over my bicep. I scowled and took a wide step and she stumbled, though it only made her cling more tightly to my arm. Once we were out of earshot of Mrs. Wallace, I dropped my arms and turned to each of them.

"Miss Blakeley. Miss Blakeley," I said while using my newly acquired bowing talents—trying to appear polite, while unable to conceal my contempt.

Cecelia placed her hand over her heart and curtsied so low I had to look away. Before she had risen completely, Mabel grabbed her arm and pulled her to stand up straight.

"Cecelia, you fool. This is no gentleman. This is the brute that drove us into town last week."

"Which I think would qualify me as a gentleman, but no matter." I laughed. "You might have missed the prince's announcement if it weren't for me, come to think of it. You're welcome for that, by the way."

"How dare you speak to us as if you had any place doing so!" Mabel continued.

I looked around me in mock surprise. "Well, I don't know if you noticed, but we happen to be at the same place, invited to the same party."

Mabel scowled and actually stomped her foot.

"Oh, and is this how ladies behave?" I laughed. I wasn't exactly enjoying myself, but I couldn't help being entertained by their arrogance, especially since it meant they were away from Ella and she didn't have to endure it for a little while.

"Don't worry, Cecelia. No one here will recognize him." Mabel seemed comforted by this thought and tossed her head.

"Perhaps," I agreed as I turned to face the group that had just arrived. "Mr. Emerson! A pleasure to see you, sir!" Mabel and Cecelia both hid their faces in their fans as they shielded their identity from one of the most respected men in town.

Mr. Emerson looked insulted that I would be addressing him, but when he saw that I was flanked by two women who were *not* his daughter, he positively beamed at me.

"Mr. Hawkins. The pleasure is all mine, young man." He winked at me as he passed. "Enjoy yourself, son," he added with a chuckle.

"Oh, I'll try, sir!" I tried to smile back, but grimaced instead.

Almost completely hidden behind Mr. Emerson was Jane, looking as stoic as she had at church, obviously not caring about any man who wasn't a prince.

Just then, Corbin and Francine entered the room. Francine didn't scowl like Jane, but her eyes darted around the room as if she were looking for someone more important.

Corbin looked like someone had slammed his fingers in a door or slapped him in the face. As soon as Francine spied Jane and the Blakeley girls, she dropped her arm from Corbin's and fluttered across the room to them. She clasped Mabel's hands in her own, and immediately the giggling began.

Corbin growled and I followed him into the ballroom where the first couples were just beginning to dance.

"Entertaining party, don't you think? I'm really glad I came." My voice was thick with sarcasm. "Thanks for the advice. You're brilliant."

He ignored me. "I'm losing my mind, Will. She wants to postpone the wedding . . . indefinitely. What am I going to do?" The desperation in Corbin's tone echoed the tone of my thoughts about Ella. Normally, I would have no idea the pain he was in. But I had received a powerful lesson in empathy over the past few days that made me realize I couldn't answer with any more sarcasm, nor dismiss his words as being overly dramatic. He was feeling exactly as I was; he was just more open in expressing his pain.

I glanced over my shoulder at Francine and the swarm of girls. She had absolutely lit up since she left Corbin's presence, and Corbin and I knew exactly what she was talking about, even without the words "prince" and "ball" carrying over to us above the minuet being played.

"Corbin, nothing has happened yet. She is still yours. She's just a little . . . confused right now. A little distracted. Put yourself in her shoes. What if some princess came to town and offered you riches and comfort . . . and perhaps love? You might be a little swept off your feet." I cowered a little at his livid expression. It was as if all the heat from his blacksmith forge was in his coal-black eyes. "Or, maybe not." I added quickly.

"Will, I would do nothing of the sort. I love Francine more than anything, and all this is doing is making me doubt—and making *her* doubt—her feelings for me. I don't know how I'm going to get over this."

I fought the urge to tell Corbin that this ball might be the greatest gift he's ever been given. From the first moment I met her, Francine had been the most outrageously flighty girl I had ever known. She showered Corbin with affection that was impossible for him to resist, but from what I saw, that physical affection had overshadowed any deep connection between the two.

They had swept each other off their feet, and now there was no foundation left to land on.

I didn't dare say these things to Corbin. He didn't need an enemy now that his fiancée had pulled away from him.

"Go and ask her to dance, Corbin. Remind her what a great man she already has."

Encouraged by the thought of taking action instead of just talking, Corbin marched back to the parlor, stood behind Francine, and placed his hand tenderly on her waist. She spun around in surprise. When she saw who was standing there, her face fell in dismay. I wouldn't be surprised if she had been truly expecting the prince instead of Corbin. It was as though she thought that if she talked about the prince enough, he would appear out of thin air and whisk her away to his palace forever.

Before Francine could turn back to her friends, Corbin placed a hand softly on her face, gently trying to keep her turned toward him, and whispered in her ear while he wrapped his arm around her. Every face in the group of girls softened into longing mingled with envy at the exchange. Jane placed a hand over her heart and Cecelia sighed. She had never looked more human.

Francine nodded, slid her arm through Corbin's, but instead of walking to the ballroom, he led her out through the back door.

My eyes followed them, my regretful smile not doing much to lighten my mood. I hoped they would work things out—truly—but I almost hoped that Corbin would open his eyes to Francine's capricious nature. I would never admit it out loud, but I was grateful that the ball came just in time . . . for them.

A forceful pat on my shoulder brought my attention back to the room I was in. I looked down and one of the Blakeley girls was smiling up at me in what I could only assume was supposed to be a demure expression.

"May I help you, Mabel?"

She giggled falsely. "It's Cecelia, silly!" and she slapped me on the chest.

This was too much.

"Miss Blakeley, you do know I was only joking earlier, I hope? I didn't actually want to escort you to the party."

"You don't mean that," she said as her hand once again found my arm. "Aren't you going to ask me to dance?"

I glared down at her. There was no way in a million years that I would ever dance with one of the girls who had destroyed Ella's life.

I could see only one way out of this. I marched over to where Jane was standing, leaving Cecelia gaping at me. It seemed that in the presence of all these men, the girls had forgotten who they were really after. Or, perhaps they were securing their back-up plans.

"Miss Emerson, may I have this dance?" I said as I bowed deeply. Out of the corner of my eye I saw Mr. Emerson glaring at me over his cigar. Without waiting for an answer, I grasped Jane's hand and pulled her to the dance floor.

"Will, I must tell you that my girlish obsession I had for you has all but vanished into indifference," Jane said as she trailed behind me.

"Thank you for the warning. We can still be friends, right?" I asked, carefully avoiding the daggers shooting out of Cecelia's eyes across the room.

"Yes. But, Will, you really should dance with Cecelia," Jane said, following my eyes. "She really is a delightful little thing."

Jane had been thoroughly taken in. It was tragic, but not unexpected. Jane had almost no abilities when it came to perception. To be fair, the Blakeley twins and their mother were consummate frauds.

I had no desire or interest to even argue about this with Jane, so I changed the subject. "Are you excited about the ball and the prince and . . . everything?" I asked without really listening for an answer, which I never received anyway.

Jane's eyes became wistful. She was so easily distracted. She didn't even answer, she just went into her own little world, right there in my arms. I didn't complain. I wished I had the ability to disappear. Thankfully, my scheme worked. Cecelia rejoined her group and began talking loudly, looking toward a group of men close by to make sure they heard whatever she said.

The song ended and I thanked Jane for the dance, though she walked off without a word and practically floated over to Mabel and Cecelia, a dreamy smile on her face.

"Hawkins!" a slurred voice called. "That's your name, am I right? I think you used to take care of my horse when I would go to the Blakeley's for dance lessons."

Roger Wallace turned back to his group of friends who laughed at his comment. As drunk as he had been, he apparently remembered our little encounter in town after he had offended Ella. Roger stumbled over to me as he spoke. When he reached me, I could see that his eyes were bloodshot and his face was puffy and red. In one hand he held a drink and in the other was a half-smoked cigar, its ashes falling all over the rug.

"Roger." I nodded curtly.

"Don't 'Roger' me. It's Mr. Wallace. And, by the way, I don't recall inviting you, especially after your conduct towards me in town the other day." He glanced around at his friends and received nods and grunts of approval.

I smiled. "Well, Roger, your mother invited me because that was the only way she could convince any girls to come."

Without looking away from me, Roger placed his drink and cigar into the hands of his nearest friend.

"Yes, I meant to talk to you about that, Hawkins." He sniffed and wiped his nose on his sleeve. Besides the ability to drink copious amounts of liquor, apparently Roger had learned impeccable manners in his travels. "I saw you come into my house with the Blakeley girls. I saw you carrying Francine McClure right in the middle of Main Street. I saw you drive Ella Blakeley home from town that same day. I saw you dancing with Jane Emerson just now. You threatened me in town for no good reason. Well, I have a little warning for *you* this time." I couldn't help laughing a little. He had quite a list of grievances. I was stunned by how much he noticed. *I* had barely even noticed those things. He pushed his sleeves back in what he must have thought was an intimidating gesture, though his laced sleeves fell back down to his wrists. "If you ruin my chances with any of these girls, you'll have to answer to me."

I laughed softly and put my hands in my pockets. "Roger, if your chances are ruined with any of these girls, you'll have accomplished that all on your own."

I knew it was coming, and I was ready. Roger swung a heavy fist at my face, which I easily dodged. After spending years of my life with the men at the stables, Roger's aristocratic attempt at a punch was laughable. Roger continued to spin, following his flinging fist, and he was caught by his group of drunkards. I spun around and headed out the back door.

No one seemed to notice our exchange . . . except Mrs. Wallace. She stood about ten feet away, a glass in her hand, her mouth hanging open. I looked at her apologetically, but she wasn't looking at me. Her glare was fixed on Roger and though I could hardly believe it, there was a subtle hint of disappointment in her eyes.

I knew I didn't fit in with this circle of society—even though I had been born into it—and I knew I shouldn't have come. But at the same time it was extremely enlightening. For the first time, I felt a twinge of gratitude that Ella hadn't grown up mingling with this crowd. But she had enough inherent goodness in her that I was sure she would still have been able to retain it, in spite of the influence of these people on her. But in the space of about an hour, they had brought out the worst in me. And even worse than that—I had allowed it.

I walked out into the night. The fresh air was cleansing and invigorating. I removed my hands from my pockets and ran my fingers through my hair, letting it fall onto my forehead. The Wallace's garden was magnificent, and I found myself wishing that I had come straight out here in the first place. I walked around for a while and found a bench to sit on. I looked up at the stars and wondered what Ella was doing. I doubted she was staring up at the stars. I was sure she was working inside the house. My heart began to ache. I chastised myself for letting Corbin convince me to come to this disastrous party. I knew what I was doing and why, even if no one else understood. I felt the need to apologize to Ella for going out and having what some would consider a good time, though she had no idea where I was, nor did she even wonder.

Hunching over, I rested my elbows on my knees and linked my fingers together. I had never felt more like a fraud than I did at that moment. I never should have come. Corbin had told me that I needed to move on and try to live a life without Ella, but I saw that that was simply an impossibility. I had never kissed her, had never held her in my arms, had never told her how much I loved her; and yet, she was a part of me. Every thought I had led to her. Every hope I had for my future was linked to her. Trying to fight that was like fighting the breath I needed to live.

I pushed my hands on my knees and stood with a sigh. I wanted to stop this charade and return to my little hut as soon as possible. I strode toward the gate, but then I heard the unmistakable sound of sobs approaching from just beyond the hedge behind me. I froze, not knowing what to do. I finally decided that I might be able to sneak silently away, but then the person started talking.

"You don't understand! You're making this all about *you*! Don't you want this for me? Can't I have my chance? We're not even married yet! How can you be so selfish?" Francine finished with a sniffle. Staying bent over, I tiptoed away from their conversation. I prayed that they didn't hear me and then assume that I had been listening the whole time.

"Francine, darling. I'm not making this about me; I'm making this about *us*. The ball is on our wedding day! We've been waiting and planning for months. I have our house all ready for us!"

"House? You call that a house? You want me to give up a palace to live in a shack behind your shop?"

"It didn't bother you a week ago," Corbin said. I grimaced. Did Francine hear his pain? Did she hear her callousness? Did he?

"Corbin, I love you. I do. But, I would hope that you would love *me* enough to want my happiness. You're breaking my heart."

Corbin's answer was so quiet and I was far enough away now that their words were fading behind me, but I heard it as clearly as if I had said it myself.

"You're breaking mine."

Francine made no reply.

As I walked home I loosed my cravat; it had begun to feel like a hangman's noose. As angry as I was at myself for going to that party, I did learn one important thing. I was not ready to imagine a future without Ella.

Chapter 19

It was dark when I arrived at home, but not quite the thick darkness of midnight. I had only been at the Wallace's for about a couple of hours, and I hadn't even gotten there late in the evening.

I walked inside and immediately took off my suit, hung it up, and changed into some normal clothes. I remembered the promise to myself that I would let the horses out to graze and get some air. The moon lit the pasture and the chilling paleness seemed to make the night feel colder than it really was. Judging by the partially shaved-off appearance of the moon, it would be full on the night of the ball. The horses galloped and nickered and stretched their legs as they ran and grazed.

My thoughts wandered to Ella, as usual. Without the distractions of the party, Roger Wallace, the Blakeley girls, Corbin and Francine, the prince, the ball, or work, I could let myself return to the simplicity of a week ago. I thought of Ella's smiles, her blushes, her timid laugh, and the way her eyes often became soft and thoughtful when she looked at me. And as I used to do before the ball was announced, I let myself imagine a future with her, if only for a moment. And as painful as it was, I even allowed myself to imagine her living at the palace, warm and comfortable.

She was clean. She was safe. There was always enough food and everyone treated her with kindness and respect. Her shoes were sturdy, her dress beautiful. Imagining Ella as a princess wasn't as painful as I thought it might be. She already was one to me.

I felt the tension melt off me into the coolness of the night. My shoulders relaxed and I breathed a little deeper, my breath coming in puffs of white as I stood in the middle of a blue, moonlit field.

Once all the horses were back inside the stable, brushed, and fed, I headed toward the house to get some sleep. As I walked to the front door, I noticed a carriage parked outside on the road. Confused that anyone would be here, and at this late hour, I walked out to the carriage. It seemed empty and I wondered if the horse had escaped, pulling a carriage behind it. I peeked inside the window and saw Dr. Clayton half-sitting on the seat, fast asleep.

I cleared my throat quietly and he jumped awake. "Oh, William. Forgive me, I must have dozed. Have you been waiting long?"

"I should be asking you that question. I'm sorry, I just saw you out here," I replied, stifling a yawn.

"No trouble." The doctor sat up and stretched. "Well, William, you're just the man I wanted to see."

"Oh, no. Am I sick?" I asked with a grin.

"Wha . . . Oh . . ." he chuckled with me. "No, I hope you're not sick, but Victoria Blakeley is. She may even be dying." He had grown grave by the time he finished speaking.

He let that sink in for a moment. I knew that Victoria was ill on Sunday, but nothing serious. Slowly, I bowed my head, not in sadness, but in shame. I couldn't imagine what Ella must be going through. I had hoped that things were fine at Ashfield, but I could see it now—Ella making breakfast, Ella feeding Victoria, Ella starting the fire, Ella changing Victoria's clothes, Ella milking the cow. . . . I had left her alone during the worst possible time, trying to give her space, thinking that she was trying to distance herself from me. That may also be happening, but it made sense that keeping Victoria alive would prevent Ella from going to the pond every morning.

"I'll go over right now," I said. I backed up from the carriage, but the doctor reached out an arm to stop me.

"No, William. I'm sure they're all asleep and we wouldn't want to wake them. You just go over when you get a chance." He smiled. "She's a strong girl, that Ella. Stronger than she realizes. The poor thing never has been the same since her father's death." He became thoughtful. "If Widow Blakeley dies, Ella will have no one to take care of her. Though," he paused, "I have wondered if . . ."

"If what, doctor?"

"Oh, I don't mean to speak ill of anyone. I just think that Widow Blakeley's illness has turned her . . . cold. Frightening, even. Pain can do that to people."

Yes, I agreed silently. *Pain and also choices.*

The truth coming from someone else made me feel more confident in my efforts to get Ella to the ball. "I'll go over first thing in the morning," I said.

"Thank you, William. I'm glad she has you." He stepped out of the carriage, climbed up to the driver's seat, flicked his horse's reins, and drove away.

Chapter 20

VICTORIA WAS DYING. I TOSSED AND TURNED ON MY LITTLE mat on the floor, unable to get comfortable. There was no way I could have known that Victoria was so ill, and yet my guilt made me restless. I had been so worried about how Ella felt about me, the prince, and the ball—assuming that she was trying to stay away from me, when all she was doing was most likely working so hard she didn't have time to think about anything else. I lay on my back and rubbed my hands over my face, trying to smother out the shame.

What if Victoria died before the ball? What if Ella were truly free to decide her own fate without any fear or remorse or repercussions? Without Victoria there, I wondered if and hoped that it might be easier for Ella to stay. I had always known that it wasn't obligation that kept Ella at Ashfield. It was honor. It was love for her home and for her parents. Without Victoria there, Ella would be the lady of the house. On the other hand, when I was being realistic and not hopeful, I knew it would also be easier for Ella to leave and live at the palace without any more promises to keep or people to take care of. She could let go of her old life and leave the pain in the past. She would be warm and fed and comfortable, the fear and uncertainty of the last ten years a distant memory.

I must have finally dozed, but it was still a restless sleep. After only a few hours, I awoke to complete darkness. I got up, got dressed, and rode over to Ashfield. I was excited to finally do some of the bigger jobs around the yard that I had wanted to do for years. Ella would know I had helped her, but it would have to be all right . . . just this once.

The house was completely dark, as I had expected. It was still early, but not too early to milk Lucy. I crept into the barn and she looked over her shoulder at me and then turned back to munch on her hay. I grabbed the bucket off the hook on the wall, warmed my hands, and began milking her. I was grateful she didn't care who it was who milked her and she stood calmly. I looked around while I sat on the overturned pale, looking for something I could do once I was finished. Lucy's stall and the entire barn were immaculate. Ella wasn't just a hard worker; she was a good worker. She took pride in her work. You could see it in every swept out corner and in Lucy's fresh hay.

I let Lucy out, grateful that she didn't moo. Ella had the habit of sleeping on the hearth, and I was very aware that she could be only a few feet away. I walked Lucy over to the pasture gate and saw that the hinges were squeaky and rusted and that the gate had to be lifted out of the way and then pushed back into place. I looked around and saw a sturdy-looking stick, grabbed it, and used it to pry the nails out of the wood that held the hinges on. It was easy—too easy—to remove the hinges, since the wood was beginning to rot. With the gate now detached from the fence, I got an old, frayed rope that was hanging in the barn. I tied the gate to the fence to keep Lucy contained, and placed the hinges in my pockets.

I went over to the chicken coop and was surprised to see that there was only one chicken left. I wasn't sure if it was Mary or Martha, but I threw some corn kernels onto the ground from the wooden box next to the coop and replaced the lid. The chicken just looked at me. I wondered if it was too early and too dark for her to see the kernels so I reached into the coop and moved the kernels around in the dirt. Immediately, she pecked my fingers and hopped around nervously, her wings and her feathers flying everywhere. I chuckled quietly at her reaction and pulled my hand out of the coop. She waited until I started to walk away before she pecked at the corn. She definitely loved Ella more than she loved me, and I didn't blame her.

Once the animals were taken care of, I walked around the estate, looking for things that needed to be done that Ella didn't have the time or strength to do. The sun wasn't up yet, but I decided to head into town for a few supplies, hoping that some shops would open early.

By the time I got into town, the sky had turned a pearly gray. I knew that I should soon be at the palace for "ball training," but that would have to wait this morning. Everything was still closed, so I walked from store to store, looking through the shop windows. I lingered the longest at the shoe shop. In the display window on a pedestal sat a pair of clean, black, practical shoes. I imagined them on Ella's tiny feet, protecting them from rocks and thorns. She had told me not to worry about what she would wear to the ball, but I couldn't understand why she was so calm about it. That seemed to be all the other girls cared about or talked about. Ella had only one dress that I knew of, and though I thought she looked beautiful in it, I wanted her to have the full experience of wearing a beautiful dress like all the other girls.

I stopped at Corbin's blacksmith shop. I knew he liked to wake early in the morning to get started on the day's work, so I wasn't surprised when I heard the sounds of him tinkering around inside. I knocked quietly, but the darkness made the sound feel louder. Corbin opened the door.

"Good morning, Corbin. Sorry it's so early."

"Couldn't sleep," he muttered. I wondered how things had gone at the Wallace's after I had left. Based on what I'd heard from Francine just before I sneaked out of the garden, and the dullness in Corbin's eyes this morning, I guessed it wasn't anything good.

I tried to think of something I could say that would help him, but no words came to mind. I felt like a failure of a friend. Then I could hear Henry Blakeley's words in my mind, *Sometimes admitting we don't know something is wise,* and I knew that I should just leave it alone.

"I'm sorry," I repeated awkwardly. He knew my apology wasn't just because I was here at such an early hour.

"Don't worry about it. What can I do for you?" he said, grabbing a broom and sweeping up some metal shavings off the floor.

I pulled the hinges out of my pockets. "Ella's gate hinges are rusty and loose. Can you fix them this morning? I'm hoping to get it put back together before she wakes up."

Corbin's eyes brightened and his normal smile lit his face, apparently grateful for a project to keep him busy and thinking about other things besides Francine. "I'd love to. Come back in half an hour and they'll be good as new."

I gripped his shoulder in thanks and he smiled and turned to reach for his farrier's tongs so he could place the hinges in the heat.

"Thank you, Corbin. You're a good friend."

He grinned and got to work.

I walked over to the dress shop while I waited for the lumber mill to open. I had no idea what a dress cost, but when I saw the little board leaning against a dress in the store window with the price painted on it, my breath whooshed out of my lungs. I had never even bothered looking in this store's direction before today, but I was sure that the dresses on display hadn't been there before. They were shimmering with light, even in the dimness of dawn. They were obviously for the ball and were outrageously expensive, with frills and lace and jewels sewn in everywhere. All I could think was that they didn't look very comfortable. Besides this, they were more like three months' extra pay, not just one. I was grateful that Ella was so confident that she would have something to wear.

Finally, as the sky was just beginning to lighten from gray to orange, the lumber mill opened. I quickly bought what I needed, loaded them onto a wagon that Mr. O'Leary let me borrow, and then hurried back to Corbin's.

On my way to the blacksmith shop, I saw Mr. Wilde setting up his cart in the middle of the street, getting an extra early start on the day. I couldn't help noticing that his merchandise had greatly improved in quality since the last time I saw him before the announcement.

"Business going well?" I said as I passed by.

He perked up and looked up at me. "Tremendously well, thank you. This ball is going to make me a rich man. You wouldn't believe the things people are willing to sell for a pretty dress or a gold necklace."

"Like what?"

"Well, for example. This lute. It once belonged to the queen of Laurel. A woman traded this for a pair of silk slippers!"

As he spoke. I climbed down from the wagon and reached for the lute. It wasn't what I had been looking for, but I couldn't help feeling hopeful looking down at the stringed instrument.

"Interested?" Mr. Wilde asked eagerly. "I know it's not a violin, but honestly, a violin is extremely difficult to play. A lute? Why, even a child could . . ."

"Thank you, but I just need a violin." I climbed back up and flicked the reins before he could say any more.

The hinges were finished and cooling, completely flattened out and just like new by the time I returned to the shop. Corbin said they should be cooled and ready by the time I arrived at Ella's.

I got back to Ashfield, hoping that Ella was still asleep. It didn't look like she had been in the yard, miraculously. I refastened the hinges on the top and bottom of the gate of the pasture fence, avoiding the old holes and using new, longer nails I had bought at the lumber mill. I then replaced the bottom step of the front porch with a new plank. The old step was wobbly and loose and split right down the middle; I pulled it off easily without any tools. I didn't pound the nails in loudly, not wanting to wake anyone up. I tapped and pushed them into place, though this took longer. I wished I had the time and supplies to repair and repaint the pillars that framed the front door.

Carrying my box of shingles over to the stable, I got to work repairing the hole in the roof. This was more of a personal repair for me. I had loved this stable and had learned all I knew about horses in it. It had been my second home for four years. I imagined it once again being filled with beautiful horses.

After every shingle was nailed into place, I looked over my shoulder to make sure Ella hadn't come out yet. I knew she would realize that I had helped her, I just didn't want to be caught in the act.

Once everything was done outside, I saw that there still wasn't any smoke coming from the chimney. I peeked inside the kitchen door window but no figure of a woman slept on the hearth. I pushed the door open and noticed that the fireplace could use a little cleaning out. Quickly, I brushed out the old ashes and cinders and bits of unburned wood into the pail and piled fresh, dry wood into the fireplace. I got the fire started and it was only then that I heard muffled voices from upstairs.

I couldn't help the smile from spreading across my face. I couldn't hear Ella's exact words, but I could almost feel her voice. It was strong and beautiful and confident while also kind and patient. She wasn't yelling, but she wasn't afraid either. I couldn't hear Victoria, which meant that Ella had taken charge and it sounded like she was doing a very good job of it. She wasn't letting herself get walked over.

The sound of angry feet stomping down the stairs told me that one of the stepsisters was on her way down, and she wasn't very happy about it. I didn't want to see either one of them, especially after how I had acted the previous night, which I was suddenly embarrassed about. I didn't know who was about to enter the kitchen, but to be safe, I hid behind a tall shelf in the corner.

I was barely out of sight when Mabel came storming into the kitchen and toward the back door. I caught the words "filthy servant" and "stupid mother," which she mumbled under her breath as she walked out into the backyard. She was carrying a washbasin, and I could tell that she was angry about having to actually do something around here. I stayed in my corner as I heard Mabel struggle with the well pump. "*Why* does this *have* to be so *hard?*" she whined and then growled as the sound of her hitting the wall thumped close to my ear. I grinned.

The door flew open and Mabel returned, sloshing water all over herself angrily, though not having enough self-control to slow down to avoid getting wet. I started to worry about Ella. Why hadn't she come down yet? How was Victoria treating her? Was Ella allowed to leave her? The sun wasn't high, but it was late morning, and Ella still hadn't come down. I worried that I would have to leave soon and would miss seeing her.

I rolled my eyes when I heard some whimpering coming from around the corner, near the stairs, or maybe from the dining room. This could only be Cecelia. Mabel was the angry one; Cecelia was the pouty one. I was getting to know them better every day, whether I wanted to or not. Then, there were quick footsteps coming down the stairs. My heart skipped a beat. I knew they were Ella's because the feet were bare and the steps were light and quick.

"Please go and sit with your mother," Ella said. She didn't shout, but she didn't plead. She was in control. After a tense, quiet moment, Cecelia stomped up the stairs angrily. I waited for a few seconds, wondering if Ella was going to come into the kitchen. I heard her start to run; then, she appeared from behind the corner, shock and bewilderment on her face. Seeing her face again was even more of a relief than I had anticipated. The room became noticeably warmer, my breath coming easier than it had in days.

"Nicely handled," I said, smiling. I stood casually at the fire, warming my hands as she looked from me to the fire and back again. I tried not to examine her reaction too closely. This was the first time I had seen her since I had held her face in my hands on Sunday. I now knew that she had been stuck at home caring for Victoria, but I didn't know if anything had changed between us since then. I knew I shouldn't ask or look too intently.

"What are you doing here? And *when* did you get here?" Her own smile lit her face, mingled with relief and disbelief.

"The doctor dropped by and asked if I'd help out. That cow is the most spoiled cow in the world," I said. "I've never seen a cleaner stall."

"Well, there's just the one cow." She shrugged adorably, like it was nothing at all that she kept the barn looking brand new.

"And that pampered chicken! She doesn't like me much, that's for sure," I laughed, remembering her pecking and her refusal to eat when she saw that I wasn't Ella. "I fixed the gate to the pasture so it can close all the way now, and I repaired that hole in the roof of the stable. I know there aren't any horses in there now, but it might as well be ready for when there are." I smiled at the vision and hoped it would someday come true. "Oh, and I replaced the bottom step of the front porch so I don't have to worry about you twisting your ankle every time you use it."

She gaped at me, her mouth wide and her eyes warm with gratitude, and I realized I shouldn't have told her.

"Will, I don't know how to thank—"

"No, don't thank me, Ella. I wouldn't have told you, except I don't want you to worry about them anymore." My shame returned. "I feel terrible. I had no idea how sick Victoria was. I'm so sorry. I can't imagine what your week as been like. How are you?"

"Wonderful now! I can't thank you enough for coming. I never could have done all those things! And poor Lucy would not have liked me very much this morning."

"I'm happy to help. It's been busy at the palace this week, but I'm glad to see you've enlisted some help in the meantime." I laughed and winked, looking up toward where Cecelia and Mabel were begrudgingly taking care of their mother. I couldn't hide how immensely proud I was of Ella for recruiting the help of her spoiled stepsisters.

"They're not too thrilled about it." She laughed quietly and glanced nervously over her shoulder, apparently afraid of who might overhear.

But I wasn't. "You have done some pretty amazing things in your life, but getting those spoiled rotten, good-for-nothing girls off their lazy behinds tops them all!" I hoped they heard me upstairs.

"They put up quite a fight at first, but I must be pretty convincing when I threaten because they have been quite compliant." I tried to suppress my smile. I couldn't imagine Ella being even a tiny bit convincing if she threatened anyone. Once she finished speaking, she turned toward the flames. She didn't notice me watching her, so I kept my eyes focused on her as her expression became solemn. A sadness crept into her eyes. She pursed her lips thoughtfully while her arms crossed over her chest and she absently curled her hand under her chin. "I just couldn't do it all myself. I couldn't keep up with all of the chores *and* take care of their sick mother." She paused and glanced quickly over her shoulder again, then returned to watching the fire, almost as if she were speaking to it. "I always knew they were heartless and cruel, but to see their lack of concern over Victoria's obviously deteriorating health is beyond my comprehension."

"Of course it is," I said. I grabbed another piece of wood from the small pile I had brought in, placed it on the fire, and brushed off my hands. "You don't know how to not care for people, so when you see that level of callousness, you can't understand it." I stood so close to her I could almost feel her warmth, even as I stood next to the heat of the fire. I placed a hand onto the mantle, leaning as close to the flames as I could without getting burned. "You're so kind, Ella, that you can't comprehend unkindness."

She thought about this for a while. She seemed surprised that I had an answer, and I was surprised that she was.

"You're kind, too, Will. How can you stand it?"

"Because I've been out in the world more than you have. Maybe not very much more, but I've seen people do terrible things and say terrible things." I remembered the ruthless, dishonest, and foul people I had met over the years while working at the palace and traveling to other villages to buy and sell my horses. "But I've never seen or heard anyone more terrible than Victoria. She is vicious. The way she treats you puts every other mean person I have ever met to shame. And yet, you tolerate it day after day. I understand why you do it. I know you promised to take care of them. But that doesn't make it any easier for me to believe." I paused, the reality of Ella's position suddenly heavy on my shoulders. "Or bear."

I needed to lighten the conversation before I left her, though I could barely stand the thought of leaving. What if I went days without seeing her again? The ball was only two days away, and she still hadn't answered me about whether or not

I could take her. Unfortunately, now that the stable workers were going to be helping at the ball all night, I didn't know how I would be able to bring her at all. It was probably for the best that she hadn't accepted my offer, though I still had the monumental task of convincing her that she needed to go in the first place. Perhaps if she knew that I was going to be there, whether I could escort her or not, it might make her feel more comfortable.

"Did you know I'm going be at the ball?" I said.

"Really? Oh, I just knew you had a secret desire to live a life of luxury. You just couldn't stand to stay away," she teased. I loved how well she knew me.

"No, thank you." I laughed. "The prince has asked all the servants to help on the night of the ball. The stable hands will tend to all the horses while the guests arrive, and then we'll be *allowed*," I said as I rolled my eyes, "to enter the palace and serve all the people. I have to walk around with a glass tray and serve the guests drinks and food. They've been training us unrefined stable workers how to properly balance a tray on our hands. It's beyond insulting. I have to wear a ridiculous suit and everything."

"Ridiculous? Impossible. You'll look so handsome!" she said, her voice high with excitement. My heart pounded as I watched her cheeks color.

It was the closest Ella had ever come to being the tiniest bit flirtatious. I smiled down at the brightness of her eyes and the shy smile that touched her lips. "Does that mean you'll be there to see me looking so handsome?" I said softly.

I was pleased to see that she considered this possibility, her eyes dropping to the ground and her smile deepening slightly.

"You really should come. With me looking so handsome and everything, who knows what could happen? I'm quite a catch, you know." I laughed quietly, knowing that jealousy would most likely have no effect on her, but it was worth a try.

I was running out of tactics to convince her to go to the ball. I turned to the fire and pretended to warm my hands, though I already felt like I would burst into flames.

I felt her watching me intently and I wondered if she even knew she was. I forced myself not to look at her, afraid of what I might see . . . or not see.

She took a step toward me, almost unconsciously, and when she spoke her voice was soft and fervent. "Will, I feel like I'm always saying this to you, but thank you. You're the kindest friend I've ever had . . . the kindest friend anyone has ever had."

Finally, I allowed myself to look down at her. She was so small and sweet, her eyes so sincere and trusting, and I loved her so much I could barely stand it. How was I ever going to let her go? The prince didn't see how well she kept up the barn, how well she cared for the animals, how she cared for a sick woman who hated her, how she worked all day without complaint in an old dress and without any shoes. She worked alone all day long, with no one to talk to and only memories for company. I thought of all the evidence I had witnessed this morning of how truly good she was.

She was still my friend—my Ella. She had been busy keeping a horrid woman alive and comfortable. She hadn't been avoiding me and was in fact so genuinely happy to see me it made my heart feel too big for my chest.

Suddenly, without thinking and being glad I didn't, I pulled my hand off the mantle, reached out and gathered her into my arms and held her, the warmth of her body making the fire feel like a cool breeze. I didn't care if it would be seen as improper. I didn't care if she didn't love me as much as I loved her. I didn't even care if she would be a princess in a few days. For today, she was mine and I had to hold her. She gasped, but didn't pull away from me. I knew I was holding her tightly, maybe too tightly, but I couldn't let go.

She didn't wrap her arms around me, but she didn't push me away either. Eventually, she let herself relax. Her shoulders fell and her head rested against my chest and she leaned her weight against me, accepting my strength as her own, if only for a moment. I lowered my head and softly brushed my lips across her hair and closed my eyes.

All too soon, she took a breath and slowly pulled away from me, as I knew she would. Her face was flushed and lovely. Her eyes darted around the room, obviously avoiding mine, though I couldn't look away. I felt slightly selfish for making her feel awkward, but I didn't regret holding her.

Finally, she forced her eyes to meet mine, and for the tiniest instant I saw the hint of longing in her fiery blue eyes. But she blinked and took another breath. The expression disappeared as she looked again around the kitchen. I knew that all she then saw was an endless amount of work she had to get done. My thoughts unwittingly turned to the palace and how late I was.

"I better get back to work," we both murmured.

"Then it must be true," I said.

Chapter 21

I LEFT ELLA STANDING BY THE FIRE, A SWEET SMILE ON her face, but almost in too much pain for me to bear.

After I quickly returned Mr. Lawrence's wagon, Charlie and I hurried to the palace. The guards saw our rapid approach and hastily opened them just before we raced through. I wasn't hurrying because I was late. I was trying, once again, to outrun the pain.

It didn't work. It followed me, mocking me. I had been foolish and was now paying the price. I should have just left after I fixed the roof; I shouldn't have gone inside. She knew how to start fires. I was being selfish. But still, I wanted to see her, even knowing it would cause me more pain. Maybe I thought the more pain I experienced, the more bearable it would become. But it didn't work that way. If anything, I had become even more sensitive to it.

Once again, I remembered Henry Blakeley's words, *Sometimes sacrificing our own happiness for the benefit of others brings us joy.* I had sacrificed sleep. I had sacrificed a few coins to buy supplies. I had sacrificed my time. All I knew was that the more I sacrificed, the more I loved her. And the more I loved her, the more I opened my heart to pain.

But I knew the joy would come. Her joy was my joy. And if I could help her realize that beautiful life I wanted her to have, nothing else mattered much to me.

I reached the stables and took care of a very out of breath Charlie. Then, I hurried up to the palace. Mrs. Hammond was standing on the steps—waiting for me.

"I'm sorry I'm late, Mrs. Hammond. It won't happen again."

Her stern expression softened and she smiled warmly. "It's all right, Mr. Hawkins. You go on in. The seamstresses are just taking their last measurements." She laughed at my relief and I was extremely grateful I had shown her a bit of kindness the day before.

I stayed a little later than everyone else that night, trying to make up for my lateness, and to show my gratitude for Mrs. Hammond's generosity. I couldn't believe how quickly the team of seamstresses had sewn over twenty suits. They looked completely exhausted, their bruised and swollen fingers working day in and day out. The ball seemed to be causing more stress than excitement from what I could see.

As I passed by Ashfield on the way home, I saw that there was smoke coming from the kitchen chimney. Ella was still working on some sewing or cooking probably, but I wouldn't stop. I couldn't stop. The ache that began earlier in the day when I had to tear myself away from her had become sharp and merciless. I continued on home and fell asleep instantly.

Ella wasn't by the pond when Charlie and I rode by the next morning. As she had been all week, she was most likely inside, still taking care of Victoria. It was safe to assume that she had also been caring for her through the night. I considered going and helping with chores again, but I knew I couldn't be late two days in a row. Besides that, Ella was strong—stronger than she'd ever been, so I knew she could do it. Whatever she was going through inside the house, she was using it to make herself even stronger and wiser. I was also acutely aware that she didn't need me as much as I needed her.

For the first time, I saw Ella as a flower, trying to grow, reaching deep into the soil for nourishment and twisting around to absorb the sunlight, much like the last of the wild moss roses that grew by the side of the road. If I had reached down and plucked the flower, it would have died, losing its connection to the things that helped it to grow. Yes, the flower would be safe from trampling feet and stray wagon wheels, but, soon, it would shrivel up and waste away with no hope of blooming again when the spring arrived.

I clicked Charlie forward and we wound through the trees and toward the palace. The ball was tomorrow and I couldn't wait for it to be over. I was tired of worrying and wondering if the prince would want to meet Ella. I was tired of wondering about how much and how fast he would love her if he met her. And most of all, I was tired of wondering if Ella would love him.

I was so tired of only having questions with no answers.

The palace was in absolute chaos. Maids had appeared out of nowhere and were doing the last minute shining, sweeping, polishing, dusting, and washing. It was a little bit of a compliment, knowing that all of this was being done for the common people of the kingdom. No doubt Prince Kenton wanted to give the commoners the royal treatment, which made me admire and loathe him.

Near the end of the day, we were presented with our finished suits by the completely worn out and haggard-looking seamstresses. When one of the ladies gave me my suit, I bent over and kissed her lightly on the cheek. She gasped as she touched a withered hand to her cheek and her eyes lit up.

"Thank you for the suit," I said.

"You're very welcome, dear. It was my pleasure," she said. The other old ladies around her giggled. I beamed. They had all worked so hard; I wanted to thank them, though I was surprised by the effect my little gesture had. All around me the stable workers planted kisses of gratitude on the cheeks of the seamstresses, who giggled like schoolgirls. We all got pinched cheeks and ruffled hair in return before we all had to return to work.

As the sun disappeared behind the hills, everyone seemed to be in good spirits. We had worked hard all week, and now, we were almost ready for the ball. The cooks were still working, making the last of the food that would be served at the ball. The aroma wafted over the palace grounds. I hoped that we'd be allowed a small taste of whatever it was. I was about to leave when I realized I hadn't been able to try on my suit as instructed, though I was sure it would fit perfectly. I was alone in the stable and thought I might as well try it on just in case.

I slung my dirty clothes over Charlie's back and put on the new suit. It was cut very differently from anything I was used to wearing. But based on what the guards at the palace wore, I assumed it fit correctly. The shoulders were wide and stiff; the suit coat was snug against my stomach, forcing me to stand up straighter. As much as I hated to admit it, the suit made me carry myself with a little more respect and confidence. The shirt collar was tight against my throat, but it only forced my head up. I had never thought I slouched before, but with this suit on I suddenly felt six inches taller.

It made more sense to stuff my regular clothes into my sack on the back of Charlie's saddle than to stuff my suit in and wrinkle it, so I kept it on. I decided to walk so it wouldn't get dusty and wrinkled from riding a horse.

I walked through town, avoiding the mud in the forest, and Charlie followed close behind, his reins hanging loose around his neck. Boisterous laughter coming from the direction of the tavern echoed through the streets and I was once again grateful that I had miraculously never been tempted by that way of life. That life had contributed to my father's death and I wanted nothing to do with it. There were too many nights I had left work late, only to see men passed out on the sidewalk; or worse, some husband leaving the pub with some strange woman on his arm. I was filled with more anger when I imagined the face of my own father on the faces of those men.

"Hawkins!" Roger Wallace's voice was becoming irritatingly familiar.

I didn't even stop. I wasn't interested in another lame attempt at a fight with the biggest charlatan in town.

"Hey! I'm talking to you," his voice slurred in the darkness behind me.

He sounded closer now and I sped up, not out of fear of him, but fear of what I would do if he didn't stop.

Even before he touched me, I could smell the foul stench of liquor, but then his hand grabbed the shoulder of my suit coat. I clenched my teeth. The sweet ladies at the palace had spent sleepless nights sewing us our suits. He had no right to touch it.

"Looks like you're trying to work your way up in the world, wearing a get-up like this. Honestly, I think it's a little sad. A suit can't hide your dirty fingernails and the smell of manure that lingers around you like a swarm of flies."

I shrugged his hand off and continued walking, his feeble words rolling off me like water off a duck.

Roger's followers were close behind him now, laughing at what they thought was cleverness.

"But you know what's even sadder? All these poor girls who are chasing the prince are going to end up as old maids. Well, some of them already are. Take Ella Blakeley, for instance." I stopped dead and Roger chuckled. "Yes, poor Ella Blakeley. You know, she and I would probably be married now if her old man hadn't died. Now I wouldn't take that mess of a woman if I were offered all that the prince has."

As he spoke, my hand balled painfully into a fist.

"You wouldn't take her, or she rejected *you*?" I asked evenly, without turning around. I knew he was trying to make me angry, and I wasn't planning on letting him; but once he dishonored Ella, I had no intention of letting him get away with it.

His clammy hand grabbed my shoulder and swung me around. I used the momentum to hit him harder than I had hit any man in my life, my fist coming into contact with his stomach, causing him to double over and gasp for breath. He received the full brunt of my anger and frustration that I had been battling all week. I felt this weight lift off of me the moment my fist made contact. It couldn't have been bestowed upon a more worthy subject. My only regret was that I hadn't given him a black eye just in time for the ball tomorrow night.

I left Roger coughing and gasping on his hands and knees in the middle of the road. I didn't even feel angry. Not just because I had let all my anger out when I hit him, but because some men just needed to be punched every once in a while. Plus, satisfaction usually accompanies justice.

As I walked along the road I felt a cool breeze on one specific spot on my right shoulder. I pulled off my suit coat and saw that I must have ripped a seam when I punched Roger. I stopped and looked up toward the palace, hoping I might be able to ask one of the seamstresses to mend it for me, but I knew that they had gone home long ago, desperate for a rest. They weren't even coming to the palace the next day. Their work was done and there was no need.

I stood debating with myself over what I would do. It was a big enough tear that I couldn't just leave it. I felt along the seam to see if I could figure out how big the tear was and if I could possibly sew it myself, relying on the few lessons I had had the patience to sit through when my mother taught my sisters. I found the tear and knew instantly that I would never be able to fix it. The thread had pulled completely free of the fabric and had even damaged it, creating frayed edges around the seam where the thread had been ripped out. I had sewn on a few buttons over the years, but this rip would require steadier hands and more experience.

I knew the obvious answer was Ella, but the thought tore at my already tattered heart. I also wanted to see her desperately. I had said good-bye so many times this week, why not one more?

Chapter 22

I STOOD OUTSIDE ELLA'S KITCHEN DOOR, PREPARING myself for the inevitable pain, but the knowledge that I was about to see her put a genuine smile on my face. Any potential pain was forgotten as I knocked softly on the door.

Whatever pain I was preparing to feel myself was nothing compared to the pain I felt when I saw it on Ella's face.

"What happened? Is Victoria dead?" I asked, trying not to sound hopeful, and failing.

"No." She left the door open and sat down on the chair in front of the fire.

"I guess I should have known. I don't think you would look so sad if that were the case." I knew my joke was insensitive as soon as I said it. My less than kind feelings toward Victoria often clouded my judgment, making me more callous than I would otherwise be.

Ella didn't even smile; though she normally would have, even if her smile would have been touched with mild reproach.

"Ella?" I said softly. She swallowed, but shook her head, telling me she wasn't ready to talk yet, so I did what I always did—distract her . . . or try to.

I cleared my throat, trying to sound cheerful, but barely hiding my anxiety over what possibly could have happened.

"How do you like my suit?" I asked.

She pulled her gaze away from the flames to look at me. I

saw her sadness melt away, even for a few seconds. It was worth standing there, feeling completely awkward, to see her look a tiny bit happy. A smile slowly lit up her face as her eyes went from my head to my shiny black shoes. She still wasn't saying anything, and the embarrassment became too much.

"All right. That's enough ogling," I said, trying not to sound pleased that she couldn't take her eyes off me. I unbuttoned my top collar button. "I didn't only come to show off how incredible I look." I winked at her and she smiled. The pain abated and then increased, and I ignored it. "I was wondering if you could sew the sleeve for me. I was going to have one of the palace seamstresses do it, but they had left by the time I noticed it. They must have taken my measurements wrong and I tore the seam of the sleeve. Or maybe my muscles have grown since they measured me." *Or maybe I punched Roger so hard for the way he talked about you that I'm surprised the sleeve is even still intact.* I laughed at my own silent joke, light-headed from exhaustion.

She smiled a little and walked across the kitchen to retrieve a little sewing box that sat on top of a pile of clothes that needed mending. She was so quiet. Something terrible had happened, I knew it, but she wasn't ready to talk about it yet. I felt horrible for asking her to do one more thing. I had already taken my suit coat off, but I dropped it down by my side. As she passed me, my hand reached out before I could stop it and grasped her arm gently.

She didn't flinch. She didn't pull away. And when she looked up at me her eyes weren't even questioning. She met my eyes evenly, and now that I was so close to her I could see that the rims of her eyes were red, her eyelashes wet with tears. Her mask was on—the one that protected her from everyone and everything. I had never seen it remain so long once she was in my presence, and I suspected it was because her wound was still fresh; we were standing in the home where she had received it. It held her captive, and she was fighting against the pain with every bit of strength she had left.

My voice was soft and pleading when I spoke to her, but her barely concealed pain made me tremble. "You don't have to, Ella. I know you have a lot to do . . ." She didn't even let me finish before she pulled free of my hand, took the coat from me, and sat down on her chair.

"Yes, and this is the most important. I'm happy to help, Will. It's the least I can do," she said calmly as she began to sew. I had never watched her sew before and it was fascinating. Her slender fingers moved effortlessly. Her eyebrows were furrowed in concentration, and though her face was illuminated by the flames, a shadow of pain hovered around her like a dark fog.

Sooner than I could have thought possible, she was finished. She handed the coat to me. I looked at the sleeve in amazement.

"Thank you," I said as I carefully folded the coat over the back of a chair. "I can't even tell where the tear was. You're amazing, Ella!"

She looked up and smiled at me, the saddest smile I had ever seen. Finally, the mask fell, and her face crumpled and fell into her hands. I darted across the room and knelt in front of her, not even caring about the pain that her closeness would cause me. She needed me and I was grateful that I was here when she did.

I reached up, gently placed my hands over hers, and pulled them away from her face. Tears streaked down her cheeks. I softly brushed them away with my fingers. She leaned her head slightly against my hand and closed her eyes.

"I'm going to get you away from Victoria somehow, Ella." I tried to sound gentle, but the determination I had felt returned with overpowering force. She had to go to the ball. She had to get out of here.

"She told me I can't go to the ball," she whispered. "I had finally decided to go and she took it away from me." Her voice shook and fresh tears rolled down her cheeks. I kept my hands on her face, ready to catch each tear that fell. "Victoria called my father a fool. She said that she hated that she married him and that he left her alone to take care of me." I caught another tear. "Father gave me a gown and slippers for my birthday when I was a child." She looked past me and her eyes became soft. "The slippers were glass and the dress was sky blue. It flowed like water and sparkled like the sun on the snow. They were my mother's." She took an unsteady breath and I brushed away another tear. She continued, an unexpected shame tinting her voice. "I had hidden them for years, which is why I knew I would have something to wear to the ball, but Victoria found them on Sunday when she stayed home from church. I hid them again, but I wanted to look at them today, and Cecelia must have seen what I was doing—I'll never forgive myself. I went to check on Victoria and while I was gone, they stole my things and sold them for their own new dresses." She paused, her trembling voice quiet and small. "I feel like I've lost my father all over again."

I didn't interrupt and I didn't ask questions until she was finished. All I could think was that the people who did this to her were probably upstairs admiring their new dresses, most likely very pleased with themselves, and the anger boiled. "Those two twits stole your dress and shoes? That half-dead wretch is getting up out of her deathbed to keep you from going to the ball? Not if I have anything to say about it."

I didn't know exactly how, but I was going to get Ella to that ball. An idea was starting to form in my head. I was suddenly grateful that I was going to be greeting the guests at the ball.

If I hadn't known her so well, I might have missed the flash of scheming on her own face. I decided I would pretend I didn't see it. If she was as determined as I was, I wasn't going to stand in her way. Whatever she had decided to do had brought a familiar, steely determination to her face.

Her tears instantly stopped, her plan giving her peace and purpose, and I had no excuse to stare at her anymore. Or to touch her. Slowly, I dropped my hands, still wet from her tears. But I continued to kneel in front of her and turned to watch the flames. I kept telling myself that I couldn't make the mistake I had made the day before. I had let myself forget what I was doing this week. I had let myself forget what was best for Ella, and even for myself, and had let her be mine for a moment when I had taken her into my arms. It had torn me apart, and I couldn't make that same mistake again, not with the ball tomorrow. Ella needed to be free.

But it was impossible to ignore how close we had become in just a week. No matter how many times I had told myself that I needed to give her up, we grew closer and closer, and many of those steps, though small, had been taken by Ella. I loved her at the beginning of the week. Now I needed her.

I continued to stare at the fire, but I felt her looking at me with uncharacteristic intensity. Her gaze wasn't just curious or thoughtful. It was piercing. I told myself not to look back at her. I disobeyed, naturally.

I had never seen that expression on her face. Her eyes were wide and almost imploring, still bright from unshed tears. Her blush was obvious, even in the firelight, her lips slightly parted, almost in wonder. She had never looked more beautiful.

She smiled slightly in embarrassment that I had caught her looking at me, but she didn't look away.

"Will, I've been thinking," she said softly. "Why hasn't anything ever happened between us?" That was the last thing I expected to hear her say, but it was what I had hoped to hear for years. Did this mean she was becoming more aware of my feelings, or just her own? I immediately stopped myself from even considering the possibility. "I mean, most of the girls my age are married and many have babies. The men your age are off seeking their fortunes, or are married themselves."

She was speaking like we were discussing the weather. She must have known how deep a question she was really asking and was trying not to scare me off, like most men might have been. But, it was having the complete opposite effect on me.

Her hands were clasped on her lap, almost pleading with me to be honest with her. Before I could stop myself, I placed my hands over hers and felt myself lean closer to her. How could I answer this question honestly without telling her everything? I had to be careful. Both our futures were at stake, not just mine.

"I've never had anything to offer you," I whispered. I thought of my tiny cabin that was barely big enough for one person, let alone two. I pictured my sad little stable that was barely suitable for three horses. And I sensed most profoundly my inability to take her far enough from Victoria so that Ella could at last be free from her.

I couldn't look away from her and I couldn't let go, nor did I have any desire to. Ella was mine again. We had never been so open with each other and I didn't want to be the one to close this door. She looked back at me with that same beseeching look from before.

"Why have you never kissed me?" she whispered. As the word *kiss* escaped her lips, I leaned in even closer to her. I could feel her gentle breath on my face and tried to just focus on her wide, blue eyes, but my eyes glanced down to her lips before I could stop them. I pulled one of my hands away from hers and raised it to touch the soft skin of her cheek. I could feel with my fingers where the tears had dried on her face.

She didn't pull away. She didn't drop her gaze to the floor. It was as if she was looking at me for the first time. She studied my face and didn't flinch or pull back when I touched her. Time stopped. I almost couldn't even remember why I wasn't supposed to kiss her . . . almost.

I had held her in my arms and it had almost destroyed me, knowing that there was a very real possibility that she was going to be taken away from me. If I kissed her now, I couldn't survive if I lost her. And Ella had to be free. She had to live with no regrets. If that meant choosing the prince, then that's the way it had to be.

I dropped my hand from her face and pulled my other hand off of hers clasped in her lap. I turned and grabbed my coat from off the back of the chair.

"You were never mine to kiss," I whispered. I looked at her once more and walked out into the night.

Chapter 23

My hands still burned from holding hers, from touching her face. But the rest of me was freezing, especially my chest where my heart was supposed to be. I stepped out into the cool evening air feeling like I was standing in a blizzard. I had never been so close to Ella. My heart, which had been pounding only a moment before, now felt silent and cold.

I led Charlie home, though he was probably leading me. I would have hurried, but there was an almost physical pull coming from where Ella still sat by the fire. I couldn't think of her there, sitting all alone. I worried that once I left, the melancholy she had been feeling when I first arrived would return. I hoped that whatever made her eyes spark with determination would give her strength.

As I walked, I felt bothered by something. It was as if my mind struggled to see something obvious through the dense fog of fatigue and sadness that consumed me. I was missing something. I looked behind me. I thought I heard a noise. Had I left something at Ella's? I had my suit coat in my hands. I hadn't brought anything else.

When I got home, I pulled off my boots, and sat down on my mat, unable to shake the uneasiness. I put my boots back on and went to go check on the horses. All was well. I returned to the house and looked at the suit coat Ella had sewn for me. I couldn't help smiling a little. If she had only known how it had been torn. Would she be disappointed? Would she smile in subtle reproof? Would she laugh? I flexed my fingers, remembering the satisfying force of the blow against Roger's softening belly.

I knew I was stalling. The unsettling feeling was still there, and I had to fight the bleariness in my mind. I pushed through my sadness back to Ella's, and remembered why she had been so despondent when she had opened the door.

She had nothing to wear to the ball. Victoria had said Ella couldn't go to the ball, but that was inconsequential. Ella was going. I would see to that. Only, she had no shoes, no dress. They had been stolen from her. I knew I had to get them back for her.

I stood up from off my mat on the floor and grabbed all the money I could spare, leaving enough so that I could still feed myself and the horses through the winter. I wouldn't let myself consider that I was taking much of the money I had saved to ask Ella to marry me. Right now, all that mattered was getting Ella to the ball, no matter what the risks. But it wasn't just about the ball this time; it was about giving Ella a part of herself—her father and mother—back to her where they belonged. To anyone else, they were just a dress and a pair of shoes, but to Ella, they were a connection to her past that reminded her of who she was.

I changed into regular clothes, stuffed the money in my pocket and went out to the stable. If Charlie could roll his eyes in annoyance, he would have. I had behaved completely irrationally all week and Charlie had been the unfortunate witness to every bit of it. I looked over at my other two horses and felt guilty for how bored and neglected they had been this week. I realized that I had never taken either of them out to ride to the palace as I usually did. Normally, I would switch horses every couple of days to give the other ones a rest. But, I needed Charlie this week. I needed a connection to the man who had given him to me. It was almost as if I could gain a little more wisdom and understanding by having something that had once belonged to him. That was why I understood Ella's situation better than anyone else could, why it had to be me who helped her get her things back.

"Sorry, boy. But we have to leave again." I saddled him up, urged him into a gallop, and we raced into town.

I hopped off the saddle before Charlie came to a stop. I ran up to the dressmaker's shop door and knocked. I was surprised Mr. Sims answered after only one knock. I was ready to pound down the door to wake him if I had to. He flung the door open, his eyes in tight slits, his mouth cut into a deep frown. His white hair was smashed against his head and his night-dress flapped in the cool breeze. I didn't even know what time it was, but I did know that the shop must have been closed for hours.

"Sir. I'm sorry to bother you so late, but I wouldn't if it wasn't an emergency. I need to buy a dress."

"You need to buy a . . ." He looked me up and down like I was insane. I was a single man, pounding on his door in the middle of the night, demanding a dress.

"Yes," I continued, "and I know exactly what it looks like. It's light blue, um, flowy, I guess, and kind of sparkly. The Blakeley girls came in earlier . . ."

"I know the dress of which you speak, young man," he interrupted.

"Oh, good! There's also a pair of shoes, uh, slippers. They're made of glass. That's all I know, but that's probably all you need to know, I mean, there aren't many . . ."

"Mr. Hawkins. The gown and the slippers are gone. They have been sold."

He started to close the door, but my hand slammed it open. He looked up at me in outrage.

"That's impossible! They were just here. You must have

closed right after you got them. Can you please go and check?"

"They're sold!" he hissed, and he tried to slam the door, but this time I stopped it with my foot.

"I'm not leaving here without a dress." I said evenly. I couldn't believe the dress was gone. It was impossible. I reached into my pocket and pulled out a handful of coins. "I have money."

Mr. Sims tried to hide the glint in his eye, but I could see it. Even as he moved aside to let me in with a false groan of annoyance, he gawked at the money in my hand.

"Thank you," I said pleasantly. "Now, will you direct me to your ball gowns?"

He chuckled sarcastically.

"You mean the night before the ball, I'm supposed to have extra ball gowns for poor procrastinators?" I was growing impatient. "Well, where's the next best thing?"

He glanced down at the money in my hand. With a sigh that was more like a growl, he walked to the back of the room, his nightdress fluttering around his skinny white legs. As I waited, I put my coins back into my pocket and wandered around the shop, noticing that it was indeed almost empty. Every shelf was bare, most likely having once held jewels that would complement the now-sold ball gowns. There were only a few bolts of fabric left that lined the walls in little slots, but they all looked like wool and hemp. In one corner, next to a chair, I saw a pile of snapped and bent needles among hundreds of broken strands of thread of various colors. Mr. Sims must have been sewing frantically all week. I felt guilty for waking him on the last night of a terribly busy week, but it had to be done.

Mr. Sims's shuffling footsteps grew louder as he emerged from the back of the shop, a bundle of fabric in his arms. "This is all I have left that will be even somewhat suitable for the ball. It's a little nicer than an afternoon dress, but certainly not an evening dress. And don't ask if I have any other colors, because I don't!"

"I wasn't going to," I replied. From what I could see, even from the dim light of the candle held in Mr. Sims fingers, this dress was deep blue, almost the exact color of Ella's eyes. "How much?"

He gave me the price, and I pulled the money out of my pocket. I smirked as Mr. Sim's eyes grew enormous and caught the moonlight like two coins. He started to stammer, no doubt trying to tell me the dress was actually worth more than his original price, but I quickly placed the money in his hand and took the dress and tucked it under my arm.

"Pleasure doing business with you," I said.

Placing a hand on my back, he pushed me out onto the street, the pleasantries no longer necessary now that our transaction was finished. The door slammed behind me, echoing in the stillness and the force of it shaking the ground beneath my feet. I held the dress under my arm protectively and ran over to the shoe shop. Smiling, I saw that the pair of black shoes were still in the window. I walked over to the door and knocked but there was no answer. I knocked twice more, getting louder each time, but still no one came. Mr. Boyd must be a deep sleeper. Finally, I tried the latch and the door fell opened. Ironically, I was grateful for his trust. Taking a quick glance around me, I walked into the shop and toward the little black shoes in the display.

The only light came from the moon filtering in through the window. With a trembling hand, I reached down and picked up the black shoes. They were plain and practical, but they were sturdy, the soles thick, the leather supple yet strong. The image of Ella's pink bare feet on the cold ground when I saw her plucking the chicken flashed before my eyes, and the shoes I held in my hands became blurry.

Suddenly it didn't matter if Ella would be a princess by the end of the week. It didn't matter that she could have dozens of warm shoes to protect her feet, each pair more beautiful than the next. I had hoped and imagined for years that I could someday buy Ella some shoes. I had saved every penny so that I would be able to take care of her and I was going to do just that, whether she ended up in a palace or remained a peasant.

I tucked the shoes under my arm with the dress and walked over to the counter. Mr. Boyd's quill and parchment were on the counter and I wrote him a quick note, letting him know it was me who had taken the shoes, and placed the amount, plus a little extra, on top of the paper. I closed the door behind me. After I was seated in the saddle, I carefully placed the shoes in my saddlebag. But I held the dress on my lap to protect it from getting too wrinkled.

Once we were home, I unfolded the dress and hung it up so that it would be ready for the ball tomorrow—or today—depending on the hour, and placed the shoes on the floor. I kicked off my boots and lay down on my mat, my fingers laced under my head and I dozed as I looked at the dress. It wasn't the same dress and slippers Ella had lost, but I couldn't let myself worry about that right now. It wasn't an extravagant ball gown, but it was a beautiful dress that would bring out the bright blueness of her eyes and the rosiness of her cheeks. The shoes weren't ball-worthy, but they were warm and new. I also couldn't consider the fact that it was an almost scandalously intimate gift and I couldn't quite imagine how I would offer it to her. I yawned. None of those things mattered now.

Ella could go to the ball.

Chapter 24

As I rode to the palace the next morning, I felt lighter than I had all week. But the whistle on my lips died as my mind returned to last night and Ella's tragically vacant face when she opened the door. It was the first time since I had met her four years earlier that her pain had almost turned her to stone. Thankfully, it hadn't lasted. I was also very grateful I had needed her just when she needed me. Her pain told me she was only one tragedy away from returning to the poor, frightened creature that ran away from me when I saw her from the road. For years I had known that Ella was a person of almost limitless optimism and resilience, but I was given a glimpse last night that Ella may be beginning to lose that battle. She needed relief and I was going to help her get it.

I almost took a detour to Ashfield on my way to work, just to show her that she did indeed have a dress to wear and that she really could go to the ball. But I knew I had to wait. I knew she would be up cooking, cleaning, and preparing her family for the ball. I could just imagine the look on her face when I told her she would get to go, too.

After an endless week of preparation, anticipation, and dread, I rode up the hill to the palace. The ball was tonight.

"Good morning, Simon. Good morning, Hugh," I said as I approached the gates.

"Morning, Will," they replied in lethargic unison. I was sure that Simon and Hugh had opened those gates more times this week than over all the years of their service there.

The palace was almost ready, with just a few finishing touches that we all helped with. The ballroom looked like a place out of a fairy tale—flowers and ribbons draped across every chair and table, hanging from every window. It would be a full moon tonight, so there were not many lights placed outside, just a candelabra placed exactly every twenty feet apart in a large circle. I had been in charge of spacing and lighting. I was just grateful I wasn't in charge of floral decorations. Grant and Paul, along with three other stable workers had that fortunate responsibility.

"No, no. The orchids need to take prominence over the lilies. Lilies are understated," Grant said as his rough fingers gingerly placed a white lily behind a lavender orchid. "Orchids are exotic. They need the lilies to soften them."

Paul puckered his brow thoughtfully and nodded in agreement as he carefully readjusted the arrangement, his big hands uncharacteristically gentle.

"Just make sure they don't soften you," I teased as I walked by. I flexed, knowing that would earn me a punch in the arm, which it did. Grant's hit was half-hearted, though.

"Don't tell anyone, but I really have an eye for this kind of thing! Who knew?" he said as he returned to his flowers.

I never would have imagined a week ago that five of my toughest grooms would be arranging flowers at the palace. I couldn't wait for things to go back to normal, while at the same time knowing that they never would.

Mrs. Hammond came to inspect our work and clapped her hands in delight at the floral arrangements and decorations.

"Now, men, you need to match the splendor of the evening. You wouldn't want your black fingernails and scruffy faces detracting from the beauty you have created, now would you?

You all need baths and haircuts and you must all be clean-shaven by the time the first guest arrives."

Paul gaped and Grant smiled.

I looked up at the sky, trying to figure out how long I had to finish this last task. I knew I had to hurry. On my way home, I decided to stop at the barber for the first time in my adult life. Once he was done, I had to stop myself from shrugging my shoulders to protect my now exposed neck. After a quick but thorough bath at home, I gave myself the closest shave I ever had.

We all returned to the palace—clean and shaven, and feeling extra cold and raw—to change into our suits. Then, some of us went down to the kitchens and the laundry, including Paul. The rest of us lined up in front of the palace, unrecognizable as the men who shoveled the manure out of the stables every day. We actually looked as if we belonged there. I wasn't sure how I felt about that.

About an hour before the ball was supposed to start, the first guests began to line up outside the gates. I realized that exactly one week, one day, and two hours ago I had met Corbin on the road on my way home from Lytton and he had told me how long it would be until his wedding. Francine had run up to him and kissed him in front of everyone in town and Corbin had smiled. It seemed like a lifetime ago. Tonight, instead of witnessing their wedding, I was working at the palace. Francine had postponed their wedding and would most likely be near the front of the line of people waiting for the gates to be opened.

The horses were getting anxious as they waited outside the gates and their whinnies traveled up the hill to the palace. The grooms-turned-greeters lined up along the drive by the front steps to welcome the guests. More and more carriages and horses joined the eager crowd, their excited voices growing in anticipation.

The sound of the door opening behind me and footsteps on the stones made me turn around. Prince Kenton stood there, looking slightly overwhelmed, as he pulled his gloves on.

"They're already here," he mumbled to himself. Though there was at least half an hour before the ball was actually supposed to start, Prince Kenton mercifully raised his hand, motioning for Simon and Hugh to open the gates. "Let them in," Prince Kenton said, though only those closest to him actually heard him say it. I glanced down at the waiting crowd and when I turned around again, Kenton had already disappeared inside the palace.

The gates opened with synchronized groans and despite waiting for so long, the guests filed through almost regally. They approached the palace and I recognized some as being from Maycott, but others must have traveled a day or two or more to get here from other villages. As we opened the doors of the carriages, each guest's face looked up at the palace in awe, their mouths gaping, their eyes wide, their faces illuminated by the setting sun and the hundreds of candles that lined the entrance.

I was third in line and watched as Grant and Clive took over the role of driver as the drivers each exited their carriages. They were obviously thrilled to be invited to such an event as this, where they usually would have to wait outside. Then, the ladies emerged out of their carriages, escorted by the next usher up to the palace, and followed closely by the men who had brought them.

I didn't envy the men who had the role of usher, though they had fought vehemently for that job from the beginning. There was only one lady I wanted to escort into the ball. I just had to wait for my chance.

Francine was indeed one of the first to arrive, but she had come with Corbin, so I decided to be encouraged by that. He didn't smile in recognition when he saw me, his eyes only on her. He didn't look as distraught as he had at the Wallace's party, or even as hopeless as he had the next day when I saw him in his shop. Instead, there was a resignation in his eyes that was almost worse than either one.

About fifteen minutes after the first carriage arrived, I looked down the row of carriages waiting to reach the front of the line and saw Mabel and Cecelia Blakeley's heads sticking out of the open window of Jane Emerson's carriage. I couldn't see into the carriage on account of their heads, but I assumed Jane was inside too, just as excited about the ball, but having the tact to wait until the carriage arrived.

When the Emerson's carriage moved up to the front, Cecelia opened the door before the usher arrived to open it. Grant bent over to pull the step down, but Cecelia jumped down first, knocking him off balance and causing him to fall over and land in the dirt. As Grant stood up, I jumped forward and quickly lowered the step before Mabel could knock him over again. I held out my hand and she was about to accept my help, until she looked down and saw it was me. With her face scrunched up, she withdrew her hand and I grinned up at her mockingly.

"Don't worry, I won't let anyone know that we're old friends, Mabel Blakeley of Ashfield," I said loudly, causing the men around me to chuckle. We were forbidden to interact with the guests, but I knew this wasn't the only time I was going to break the rules that evening, and I couldn't resist making her scowl. I continued to hold my hand out for her and she finally placed hers on mine, putting as much weight as she could on me so that my arm trembled as she pretentiously descended out of the carriage. I handed her off gratefully to Clive who took her the rest of the way.

"After tonight, it will be Princess Mabel of Claire, and don't you forget it," she hissed as she placed her arm on Clive's. Grant was still dusting of his pants so I put my hand out for the next lady. Jane looked lovely, though a wild determination glowed in her eyes that gave her an almost fanatical expression. She looked down at me and smiled as she placed her hand in mine.

"Thank you, Mr. Hawkins," she said, her eyes now focused on the palace. Calling me "Mr. Hawkins" was her final farewell to her girlish fascination with me. It had finally happened. Someone better had come along.

I grinned and bowed as she took the arm of the man waiting for her. He looked extremely pleased to be walking her into the palace.

I remained at the carriage, resigned to the fact that it would be me who would have to help Victoria out of the carriage. When no one immediately exited, my heart dropped into my stomach and my neck felt especially cold. What if Victoria was too ill to come? What if she stayed home out of spite, making sure Ella didn't sneak out somehow? It would make perfect sense, except that Victoria couldn't stand to miss a party, and this would undoubtedly be the biggest—and last—one of her wretched life.

I couldn't help peeking into the carriage and could barely contain my gasp. Victoria sat against the seat, her eyes closed, her face pale as death. Indeed, it looked as if she had died on the carriage ride over.

"Widow Blakeley. Are you unwell? Would you like me to take you home?" Mr. Emerson asked.

Victoria took a labored breath. I looked down the long row of carriages and saw that other heads were now sticking out of windows, wondering what was causing the delay. Victoria shook her head and the action looked like it would cause her head to fall right off her frail neck. She pursed her lips to hold in the groan of pain that made her face become impossibly whiter. Rising from her seat, she hobbled, hunched over, to the door.

If she hadn't ruined the life of the woman I loved more than my own life, I would have felt so much pity it might have even brought tears to my eyes. It almost looked as if she were doing something noble; that she was fighting back the pain to experience something beautiful, or even to witness her daughters experience something life-changing. But I knew the truth. She knew Ella's determination. Perhaps she knew that Ella would very likely find a way to make it to the ball, and she wanted to be here to witness Ella's open rebellion so that she could punish her to the fullest degree. Victoria could have simply locked Ella up in the cellar before she left, but that wouldn't have been as satisfying.

Victoria's head emerged from the carriage and the dimming sunlight threw hideous shadows across every wrinkle in her face, aging her thirty more years in an instant. I felt completely foolish for planning to sneak Ella to the ball so that Victoria didn't know. What could she possibly do? She was a walking skeleton. Once I got Ella here, I planned to walk Ella right in front of her just so I could witness the helpless fury on Victoria's face.

But then I looked in her eyes and froze. My plan altered in a moment and any vindictiveness I felt evaporated. I was reminded in that moment that the pain that she could inflict on Ella was not only physical. Victoria had a way of stripping Ella's hope and confidence. She diminished Ella's value and spirit. Ella had withstood her for years, but last night I had been given an even deeper glimpse into just how much Victoria had weakened Ella. So now, instead of displaying Ella to Victoria when she came to the ball, I would do all I could to make sure Ella never had to be near her again.

With her eyes fixed on the palace, Victoria placed her frighteningly frail fingers on mine. She placed a foot on the step and she wavered dangerously and closed her eyes. I shivered as my fingers closed around hers, feeling like they would crumble to dust in my grasp. She clutched my hand with surprising vigor and stepped down onto the ground. I didn't let go of her until the other usher took her from me.

Mr. Emerson emerged last, a look of absolute bewilderment on his round face. Without his usual grimace in my direction, he followed Victoria up the palace steps, his arms slightly outstretched, ready to catch her should she fall.

The next carriage was the village doctor's. He jumped out of his carriage before it even came to a stop.

"Excuse me, dear. I must go and check on Widow Blakeley," he said over his shoulder.

The doctor's wife smiled and nodded from the carriage and waved a hand of permission at him. By now, Grant was cleaned up and was able to continue with his duties. He and I took turns helping the doctor's wife and his multiple daughters to the palace. Once they were out of the two carriages they had ridden in, the sisters all linked arms and laughed as they walked up the stairs to the front doors. The guards stood there helplessly, not knowing how to separate them to escort them individually into the palace. The girls didn't seem to notice. They only needed each other. It was one of the sweetest displays of genuine familial affection I had ever seen. They weren't competing with each other. They were linked together—equals—excited to experience this night in each other's company. It was very refreshing.

It was my turn to drive a carriage away from the palace to join the long line of carriages with their bored horses as they waited for the end of the ball. Once it was parked, I ran up the drive and took my place at the end of the line. In the row of carriages, something caught my eye. About ten carriages down the line was a gleaming white carriage. The sun was just going down and it cast a warm, pink hue on it, making it look like a cloud that caught the sunlight and softened it. I counted up the row of men waiting to drive the carriages away and saw that Grant would be the one to drive the white carriage.

"Grant," I whispered out of the corner of my mouth, "If you let me drive the white carriage I promise I'll make it up to you."

"That carriage is a little feminine for you, isn't it?" He said with a straight face, though his lip twitched.

"I'm not the one who has a fetish for orchids."

"I would be nicer to me if I were you."

"You're right. I'm sorry. Your manly floral arranging skills are a supernal gift from heaven to please the eyes and delight the noses of all humankind."

He laughed out of his nose, keeping his face smooth. He nodded once and I knew we had made an agreement.

As the white carriage drew near, I could see that it was even more elaborate up close. Pearls lined the seams and something told me they were real. The white horse's reins were actually long ropes of lace, and its mane was weaved into tiny braids with pink bows at the ends. Its tail was not braided, but I could see the glint of pearls that had been attached to some of the hairs. The worst thing about it was that it was a male. I shook my head in pity.

It approached the front of the line and I waited for the guard to escort whoever was inside. He opened the door and this time I could not contain the gasp that escaped my lips. It was Princess Rose. Known affectionately to a select few as The Beast.

Grant coughed quietly, but it was obvious to me that he was disguising a laugh.

Princess Rose glided out of her carriage and practically floated up the steps to the palace doors, her escort having quite a difficult time keeping up with her royal pace.

"All yours," Grant whispered. I stepped forward and took the reins from the driver who happily entered the same ball his employer was entering.

I grinned back at Grant, rebellion making my heart pound recklessly. He nodded, having an idea of what I was about to do. I climbed up onto the driver's seat and politely followed the carriage in front of me, though my foot tapped impatiently. Clive didn't seem to be in a hurry to rejoin the line of drivers as he parked the carriage and slowly sauntered back up the hill toward the palace, his hands in his pockets. He already looked tired and the evening was just beginning. There were only about five carriages after this white one, which was why I didn't feel too guilty when I drove right past the row of parked carriages and casually continued down the hill.

I approached the gates and reluctantly slowed the horse to a walk. Simon and Hugh eyed me suspiciously.

"The horse needs some air," I said, my lip twitching. "I'll bring it right back, I promise."

Hugh's eyes tightened, but a small smile crept onto Simon's face. Simon opened his gate, and Hugh followed, seeming to catch on. Once the gates were open, I snapped the lacy reins of Princess Rose's spoiled, bejeweled horse and raced down the hill.

Chapter 25

I BOLTED INTO MY CABIN, RAN TO THE FAR CORNER OF THE room where Ella's dress hung, and carried it out into the darkening night with her shoes. I considered holding the dress on my lap again, but thought it best to put them both in the storage compartment on the back of the carriage so I could bring them in to show her later. It wouldn't be very prudent to show up at her door, holding the clothes she would be wearing.

The sun was down and the moon was rising steadily by the time I reached Ella's house. So far, the plan was working, but now that I was here, riding up her front drive, my heart started pounding and my hands began to sweat. I was finally taking Ella out for an evening. And even though she may not be going home with me, or even spending any time with me there at all, I decided to live in this moment, right now, and be grateful for it.

I gently pulled on the lacy reins and the horse stopped. I gulped, feeling more nervous than I could ever remember and jumped off the seat before I lost my nerve. The house looked utterly dark and empty. Cold even. But the smoke rising out of the chimney made me smile. There was something comforting about that smoke. It meant Ella was there. I realized how often I looked in the direction of Ashfield, my eyes searching for something comforting and familiar. I found it there, in the smoke that rose from Ella's fire.

Straightening my cravat and smoothing my hair, I climbed up the steps two at a time and reached the front door. I considered knocking, but everything was so silent; the noise might break the spell that enveloped the night. Slowly, I pushed the great oak door open. The ominous creaking of the hinges reminded me to oil them the next chance I got.

The soft glow of a fire came from the kitchen down the hall past the dining room. I could almost feel the heat from where I stood. I tried not to imagine Ella all alone, sitting in front of the fire in her sad, gray dress, mourning her stolen gown and slippers as well as the opportunity to attend the ball. I smiled a little, knowing that if she were sad, it wouldn't last much longer.

"Ella. Are you here?" My voice was so quiet, I could barely hear it myself. I tried again, a whisper louder this time. "Ella?"

Thankfully, I was looking toward the faint glow of the fire so I was able to see Ella's silhouetted figure emerge from behind the dining room wall. Before my mind could even grasp what I was seeing and before I could catch my breath, she spoke.

"I'm sorry. I was hiding. I thought you were Victoria and I'm a coward." Ella's voice was quiet but composed. Her lips were turned up in a demure smile and she dropped her head, but not out of shame or defeat.

"N-No," I stuttered and my face burned. I gained control of my voice before I continued. "You're an angel."

She laughed, so freely and so full of joy that the sound pricked my heart. I realized my mouth was hanging open and I did nothing to close it.

"Thank you. You look very handsome yourself." Her poise and tranquility were almost overwhelming. Her direct gaze, with eyes that were both soft and admiring, made me realize I had been holding my breath for too long. The floor beneath my feet began to feel unstable. I raised my fingers to run them through my short hair in embarrassment, all while I forced myself to breathe.

My eyes had been fixed on hers until then. For the first time that I could remember, I had to drop my eyes from her steady gaze. That was when I noticed what she was wearing. My mind went back to when she described her mother's dress that her stepsisters had stolen: light blue like a cloud-covered sky, flowing like water, sparkling like snow in the sunlight. There was no sun at the moment, but there was a moon and Ella sparkled like a star. This dress she was wearing had to be the same one she had described. How could this be? I had gone to the dress shop in the middle of the night and it was gone. Was it really Ella who had gotten there before me? How did she afford to get it back if it had been her?

"Ella, I was planning on taking you to the ball in your old gray dress whether you wanted to or not." I was joking, even if she didn't know it. It definitely was not the time to tell her I had a dress waiting for her outside. "Is this your stolen gown? How did you get it back?"

There was a hint of defensiveness as she answered, but not sadness. "Will, I had to do it." I could tell she was trying to comfort me, or even shield me from whatever she wasn't quite saying. I stepped closer, admiring how graceful her bare neck was. Even when her hair was bundled in a scarf, there had always been so much of it that it still hung past her shoulders. But now, there was nothing where her hair used to be. I couldn't put the words together. I knew what she had done, but forming them into a sentence in my mind would make them true. She had done something drastic. She sacrificed something of herself to buy back what had belonged to her in the first place.

I couldn't imagine what expression was on my face, but I was even more shocked when I heard her soft laughter. She slowly turned around and I took in a sharp breath, my fears confirmed. Ella had cut and sold her hair. I loved her hair. But I wasn't just distressed that it was gone. Her things were stolen. That was heartbreaking enough. But she had had to suffer even more because of it.

"It will grow back, Will," she reassured me as she turned back around to face me. "I don't want you to be sad, because I'm not. I had to do something and I have no regrets. Please don't worry."

I was astounded by her. She was smiling. She was empowered. It *had* been her who had gotten to the dress shop before me. It had been her who had seen a solution before I could figure one out and she had acted on it without any regrets. If I had hurried to the dress shop first, she would have arrived right behind me and it would have destroyed her—knowing that her stolen things had been sold, and she most likely would have already cut her hair. She had to be the one to see the solution first and act before I did. She had to be the one to take her fate into her own hands, without waiting to be rescued. She had always been this way, but I had thought that surely this last trial would be the one where she would finally need a rescuer. Only this time, in her hour of deepest desperation, when I had come to save her, she had already saved herself.

I was in complete awe of her, but I chose the simplest, truest thing that came into my mind before she thought I had lost the power of speech.

"I like it," I said truthfully. Her short hair emphasized the fineness of her cheekbones, the smooth grace of her neck, the wide innocence of her eyes. I looked back on all the times that she had left her hair down. Her hair was so beautiful, I hadn't thought of it at the time, but I could now see that she had often used her hair as a barrier against the world and its harshness, against Victoria and her cruelty.

Now as she stood before me, beaming and proud, there was no hint of a desire to hide away. She was utterly vulnerable, yet majestic in her grace and poise. Her shyness had been and would always be sweet and captivating, but her confidence was breathtaking.

She laughed again. I had never heard her laugh so much. "I need help with my shoes. I can't reach my feet." Suddenly, she ran in the opposite direction, her bare feet patting against the stones, to something bright and shiny at the bottom of the stairs. Her glass slippers.

I followed behind her, admiring the way her skirts swirled and swayed as she ran. "Allow me," I said. She smiled down at me gratefully as I knelt down on one knee. I forced myself from asking her to marry me, though it was very difficult in this decidedly proposing position. I picked up one of the slippers in my hand. They were so tiny. They looked so delicate, but their quality belied their fragility. There was strength in them.

"I don't know much about shoes, except if they fit or if they hurt my feet, but I can't imagine that there's another pair of shoes like these in the world. Where did they come from?"

"All I know is that they were my mother's." Her voice was gentle and trembling.

I held out the first slipper and she offered me her tiny foot. She slid her foot in and hesitated before setting it down; most likely worried she would crush it, as if that were possible. It would be like a feather crushing a diamond. I slid the other one on her foot and she placed both feet on the ground, sighing a little in relief that the shoes were indeed stronger than they seemed.

"Will, do you mind if I do something I've wanted to do ever since I put this dress on?" Her voice was so high and excited, it was almost unrecognizable.

"Not at all," I said, eager to discover what she was about to do.

Gracefully, angelically, Ella raised her arms out to her side. Time stopped. My breath stopped. My heart stopped. The only thing that moved in the world was Ella. The only thing that breathed in the world was Ella. She spun around and around, her arms floating, her white neck elegant, her slippers clinking softly against the stones. She looked down at her gently rippling skirts and smiled, her lashes brushing against her cheek. Suddenly, she reached a hand out and grasped my arm to steady herself. It took all my strength not to reach out and hold her. Once she was steady she dropped her hand.

"That was the most fun I've ever had!" She laughed.

"Me too." We laughed together and the sound was like a song, our voices blending together in an effortless harmony. I couldn't look away from her and this perfect moment. She looked up at me with the same imploring, searching expression as she had the night before in front of the fire, her eyes wide, her lips slightly parted. Abruptly, she looked down, pink coloring her cheeks.

"So, am I recognizable without a torn dress and a dirty face?" she asked, her eyes still on the floor.

I stepped closer to her, only this time it was because she was pulling me. She looked up at me and I reached down to brush her cheek with the back of my fingers. It was warm and she smiled and ducked her head.

"I have always seen you this way," I whispered as I placed my finger under her chin, gently pulling her face up to look at me.

"Then why are you staring at me like that?" She lowered her eyes timidly, though her face was still upturned.

"Because for the first time, you see yourself clearly," I said softly. "You are beautiful, Ella. Inside and out. Your father and mother would be proud."

I had never seen Ella look so content. She had almost always carried a sense of serenity and quiet grace about her, but there were times when she had forgotten who she was. Now, looking at this pillar of fortitude and joy before me, I knew Ella would never, could never go back to those days. I had been so angry that she had been forced to sacrifice and suffer for this dress and these shoes that were so dear to her. I had grieved for years knowing that she chose to stay at Ashfield, and that I was powerless to save her. But I now saw that she had been saving herself all along. It wasn't just this time with the dress. It was her whole life, caring for this house, working until her hands were raw. Those millions of acts of sacrifice had molded her and shaped her into someone magnificent; someone who valued herself, and not just the things she had accomplished.

The flower—roots deep in the ground, her face turned toward the sunlight—had bloomed.

Chapter 26

We stepped out into the moonlight and I reached behind me to close the door. Ella stood frozen on the porch, carefully surveying the yard to make sure she wasn't being watched. I knew we were safe, but I let her discover it herself. While she was preoccupied, I slipped on the white gloves I had put in my pockets.

"Will, where did this come from?" Ella said so suddenly it made me jump. Had she somehow seen the dress I had brought? Thankfully, she was gaping at the beautiful white carriage, which made me smile with satisfaction.

"I told you I was tending to the horses tonight. Our assignment was to take the carriages and circle them around so that they would be ready to pick up the guests when the ball ended. This carriage's circle was a little wider than the others," I said innocently. I still thought it was a brilliant plan, even though she shook her head in half-hearted rebuke, a reluctant smile on her lips. "Did you think I would let you walk to the ball?"

"That was my plan."

"No, Miss Blakeley. No walking tonight."

When we reached the carriage, I opened the door for her and she grasped my hand as I helped her inside. I wondered if I would ever get used to touching her; or if I would ever get the chance to. Her slender hand trembled as it traced the red velvet walls.

Her tender eyes glistened with tears as she turned to look at me. "I don't know what to say, Will. Besides my father, no one has ever done anything this nice for me." She blinked a few times and took a steadying breath. "I'm overwhelmed."

"You deserve this, Ella. I just wish you could have this every day." I swallowed hard against the tremor in my voice and Ella placed a gentle hand on my arm. An image of Ella riding in a carriage just like this one filled my mind. The only difference was she had a crown on her head.

Ella was looking at me and I forced myself to focus on what needed to happen now. "I think we'd better know the plan before we get there." She nodded, instantly serious. "I will drive you up to the front entrance of the palace. A guard will be there to escort you in. I will have to drive the carriage away, but that will be the last time I'll leave you." It was hard to concentrate with Ella's hand resting lightly on my arm. "I won't exactly be right by your side, but I'll always know where you are and where Victoria is. She will be watching for you."

Ella shivered and I continued. "The other thing we have to worry about, besides Victoria seeing you, is making sure anyone else who might mention you to her doesn't see you. We also have to make sure you are home before she is. I saw her pull up tonight in Jane's carriage. Victoria looks awful, well, more awful than usual. I don't know how long she's going to last. So make the most of the time you have at the ball."

It made me tremendously happy, knowing that Ella was going to have an unforgettable night of dancing and delight. If nothing else happened, I wanted her to enjoy herself.

I was about to close the door, but paused, still feeling the gentle pressure of her hand on my arm. "One last thing." Tentatively, I reached out for her hand and held it in both of mine. "May I?" I asked. I looked up into her eyes for the briefest of moments. It truly was a question I was asking, not just a formality. Her eyes gave me the answer.

I bent over her sweet hand I loved so much and pressed it to my lips.

***

I URGED THE HORSE INTO A GALLOP AND WE HURRIED BACK to the palace, my heart racing to the rhythm of the horse's brisk pace. When we arrived at the gates, Hugh looked relieved; Simon looked amused. As the carriage passed by, Simon glanced inside the window and looked up at me with a shrewd smile and a wink.

We drove up the wide, curving front drive of the palace and I pulled the horse to a stop. I hopped down off the seat and opened the door for Ella. The guards at the doors watched me warily. I hadn't expected this. They must have known I had left, and I hoped that they didn't care. They weren't stable workers dressed as guards; these were the actual palace guards who were on the lookout for any improper behavior. I hadn't warned Ella about what I had to do next—that I had to pretend I didn't know her so that I wasn't accused of leaving the ball to go get a girl. I had to be especially careful with the guards' eyes on me.

I looked stoic and almost bored as I helped Ella out of the carriage. She looked at me questioningly, but seemed to immediately grasp what was happening and went along. As Ella took in the grandeur of the palace, I wondered if she noticed the silent argument the guards were having over who would get to escort the loveliest lady they had seen all night into the palace. I watched as I hurried back to the driver's seat and nudged the horse to a slow walk.

The bigger guard punched his own hand as a warning to the smaller guard. The smaller guard only smiled and began walking down the steps, but then the bigger guard caught up and nudged him angrily with his elbow. The smaller guard grimaced and only ran down the steps faster, the bigger one struggling to keep up. The smaller guard reached Ella first and offered her his arm while the bigger one glowered. I hoped the smaller one wouldn't have to pay for beating the bigger one. But from what I knew of Ella's beauty, she was well worth the fight.

I smiled with pride as she walked into the palace, her head held high, her back straight, her steps steady.

I parked the carriage in the endless row of horses and carriages. Picking up everyone after the ball was going to take as long as the ball itself, I thought with dread. I wouldn't worry about that now. I had to get back to the palace.

After I climbed down from the seat, I walked around to the back of the carriage, and lifted the lid to the storage compartment. I gathered up Ella's dress and shoes into my arms and hurried to the stable, placing them carefully in Charlie's saddle pack.

I ran to the palace, only I didn't go in the front doors the guests had just entered. I went in through the little side door that led to the kitchens. I flung it open, smoothing my hair, and tugging on my coat to straighten it. I blended in seamlessly in the utter chaos that the guests would never get a glimpse of. I couldn't help being amazed by the precision in which everyone worked. The food was arranged on some trays, the drinks poured into sparkling glasses and placed onto others. They were then handed to the men who had lined up for them. It was a steady stream of productivity and I had to admit that we had all been well-trained.

I jumped into the server line and held out my hand for a tray filled with drinks. The trick with balancing was to not think about it. I hurried out of the kitchen, through the underground corridors, up the stone steps, then emerged undetected out a side door that was thankfully propped open by a stone.

My first task was to find Ella. I assumed she would be near the entrance doors, so I headed that way. People immediately started taking glasses from my tray as I maneuvered through the throng. The closer I got to the doors the quieter the crowd became and soon, when the entrance was finally within sight, there was absolute silence. I looked down at everyone around me and saw that they all stared in the same direction—toward the doors.

I finally emerged from the crowd and was delighted, but not at all shocked, to see that standing all by herself, her eyes looking from face to face with a look of extreme discomfort, was Ella. As I made my way toward her, I noted the expressions of wonder, jealousy, and desire on the faces of everyone else, and I felt an urgent need to protect Ella. I pushed past the gawkers and rushed to her side.

"May I offer you a drink?"

She turned to me with a look of relief and gratitude. With my free hand I led her away into a quiet corner as the noise of the crowd returned to normal volume. Ella gasped a thank you as if she hadn't taken a breath since I'd left her.

"I didn't want to be noticed," she whispered, her lips so close to my ear I could feel her breath.

I looked down at her loveliness and almost laughed at her naïveté. "Impossible."

She blushed and her gaze returned to the crowd. I hadn't been able to look away from her yet, but when I saw her duck her head, I immediately scanned the crowd for Victoria.

Who I saw instead was the only person who could have been worse.

When I saw Sir Thomas notice Ella, all my concerns about finding Victoria fled. Worrying about seeing Victoria was suddenly like worrying about a raindrop when a hurricane was coming. He must have heard about Ella's unintentionally magnificent entrance and had come to investigate. I wondered how many emissaries he had working for him, helping him in his duty to find the woman who would be the prince's bride. My heart sank as he strode off, purpose in each definitive step.

"Do you know who he is?" Ella's soft lips were at my ear again, dissolving my previous frustration. "He looks important."

"That's Sir Thomas. He's one of the prince's most trusted advisors." She was looking at me with a fearful expression, so I tried my best to lighten the mood. "He's an excellent horseman. He prefers a dressage saddle."

She laughed and then gazed up at me with unexpected surprise, and even a hint of adoration, though I couldn't imagine why. I could barely even remember what I had just said.

"Relax. I'll be watching as best I can." I reassured her as I looked down at my now empty tray. "I better go refill this. If you stay in this corner, you should be safe for a few minutes until I get back."

Once I reached the kitchen, I returned my empty tray and was handed a new one, this time filled with little sandwiches. My stomach grumbled and I realized I hadn't eaten since breakfast.

"Go ahead, honey," Mrs. Hammond said as she saw me lick my lips. Looking around me guiltily, I grabbed a sandwich with my free hand and put it in my mouth. It was a very small, royal sandwich, not really used to make people full. Eating it only made me hungrier, but I was grateful to have something in my stomach. Mrs. Hammond looked around and motioned for me to bend down as she whispered, "I've been eating them all night. But don't tell anyone, dear." She laughed heartily and I wondered if she had been taking little drinks all night too. With a little something in my stomach, and after my comical exchange with the more-than-likely-drunk Mrs. Hammond, I felt ready to handle whatever was out there.

I was about to leave when Sir Fitzpatrick, who introduced the prince in the procession, came and whispered something to Mrs. Hammond. As he spoke, she held up a hand in my direction, indicating that she wanted me to stay. The man left and Mrs. Hammond motioned for me to come to her.

"Dear, the prince is in need of nourishment. Will you take this tray up to him?" She bent over a tray and arranged a few sandwiches and glasses on it.

"Me?"

She turned around and placed the tray in my hand. "I only send my best," she said like she was congratulating me. "You'll want to stay away from the crowds, or you'll have nothing left to bring the prince."

"Where is he?"

"In the garden by the balcony."

I would have to hurry. I took a detour on my way to the gardens and first went to the wall where I had left Ella. It was empty. Before I could be happy that she was out enjoying herself, or worry that she had been seen by Victoria or taken by Sir Thomas, I had to leave. Eager, hungry fingers were reaching for the contents of the prince's tray.

Trying to appear composed after my race across the palace grounds, I arrived at the gardens. Two voices, a man's voice and a woman's, were talking. I walked toward the sound, but not close enough to disturb them.

As soon as they came into view, I jumped back behind a bush. I accidently dropped one of the sandwiches into the dirt, and nonchalantly kicked it out of sight. Francine was the woman talking to the prince. My mouth went dry and I couldn't swallow. I hadn't seen Corbin at all tonight. Where was he now? Did he know that Francine was with the prince?

"Oh, Your Majesty, how brilliant you are!" Francine sighed.

"Oh, it's nothing. Just a little trick I learned in Laurel."

"So there wasn't an actual coin hidden behind my ear?" she asked in amazement, her voice piercingly high.

He chuckled, but I knew that laugh. He wasn't amused.

"So, Miss . . . uh . . ."

"McClure. Francine McClure."

"Miss McClure. Tell me about yourself."

"Well, I am eighteen years old. I play the harp and the piano-forte. My parents are very well-respected in the kingdom. I know all about how to be a princess. I have been taught by private tutors my entire life. I know all about diplomacy, customs, laws . . ."

"Miss McClure. This isn't an interview. I would just like to talk. You can relax."

"Relax. Of course." She giggled so nervously it sounded like she was about to cry. "I-I'm just so happy to meet you. I really want you to know how happy I am to be here. This is the happiest day of my life."

"Good." I could hear the smile in his voice. "I'm happy that you're happy. So, tell me. What would Francine McClure be doing on a night like tonight if she weren't at a ball . . . being so happy?"

Tension filled the air . . . despite all the happiness. I knew exactly what Francine McClure would be doing tonight. She would be getting married to my best friend.

"Oh, um . . ." She couldn't speak. I could hear her shuffle her feet and then clear her throat. It was true that Francine's family was well respected and she had been taught by private tutors. But, she was also in love with the blacksmith, or had been. And though she had fought vehemently to have him, someone even more irresistible had come along and she was now fighting for him.

I stepped out from behind the bush and approached them. I couldn't say what made me do it. I wasn't trying to make her uncomfortable, though I was angry. I wasn't trying to relieve the awkwardness, though it was quite pitiable. I just couldn't stand listening to them anymore. She was too infuriating. He was too kind and it made me like him, which made me detest him. And I needed to get back to Ella.

I didn't look in Francine's direction.

"Please forgive me for interrupting, Prince Kenton," I said.

The look of relief on Kenton's face was comical. "No, no, Hawkins. Please don't apologize."

He took the tray from me and placed it on a nearby bench. I nodded and began walking away.

"Oh, Hawkins, would you please escort Miss, uh, McClear back to the ball?"

I nodded again and held out my arm for Francine *McClear*. "My pleasure."

Francine looked from the prince to me and back again, her eyes widened and her face went white, even with the pale moonlight shining on it.

"No, thank you. I am quite capable of escorting myself." A sheen of tears moistened her eyes. She turned back to Kenton. "Your Majesty, if I said anything to offend you, I am so . . ."

"No, on the contrary. It was nice to meet you." Though not nice enough to ask her to stay, apparently. He bowed to her and there was nothing left for her to do. She started out walking, but quickly began to run, her sobs echoing through the empty garden.

"This may be the worst idea I've ever had," Kenton said as he picked up a glass. "I don't want the women to feel like they're on trial. I just want to meet them. They're all putting on a show. I don't want to know how rich they are. I have enough money. I want . . . depth. I want someone real."

He seemed to be talking to himself, so I made no answer. I smiled at him, though sympathy, hope, and fear warred inside me. He turned to look over the balcony, his hands clasped behind him.

"Good night, Prince Kenton," I said.

"Good night, Hawkins."

Just then, soft footsteps approached. I passed by the next woman who was coming to meet the prince. I had never seen her before. She bit her lip and pinched her cheeks before she saw me.

"Oh, Your Highness! It's so lovely to meet you." She bowed to me and I laughed quietly.

"I'm sorry. I'm not a prince. He's over there." I pointed in the prince's direction and hurried away.

***

I HAD BEEN GONE FAR TOO LONG. I TOOK A SHORTCUT TO the kitchens, and quickly grabbed a tray of sandwiches. Ella was nowhere in sight. But I did see a large group of Maycott's upper class in the courtyard. They were all laughing and talking together—the Wallaces, McClures, Cornwalls, Claytons, and Marshes. Mabel and Cecelia were there, too, though they were slightly separated from the crowd. Their mahogany heads were bent close together, and they had identical, cunning expressions on their faces. I thought they would be trying to get their chance with the prince. But, as I got closer, I realized they had already met him.

"I just don't understand it, Mabel! I was funny. The prince laughed at my jokes. I don't think I was anything less than capitating," Cecelia whined.

"Captivating, Cecelia. Captivating!" Mabel growled and rolled her eyes. "Anyway, it doesn't matter. Did you notice he's losing his hair? I couldn't look at that for the rest of my life anyway. He's much less handsome close up." She sniffed haughtily, though her eyes glanced at the floor.

"So, Roger then?" Cecelia said pragmatically.

"We have discussed this! *I* get Roger. You go after someone else."

"What about that Hawkins boy?" Cecelia's eyes brightened frighteningly. "He couldn't keep his eyes off me at Roger's party. And he's not losing his hair at all."

Despite being completely disgusted, I chuckled as I walked by them, shaking my head. Mabel scowled. Cecelia batted her eyes.

Behind Mabel and Cecelia, Victoria was seated on a stone bench.

"Quiet! You failed. Both of you! Now go and fix the mess you made. I've done all I can for you." Her hair quivered as her body shook. Her voice was so weak, but it sounded especially menacing. She looked positively insane as she turned away from Mabel and Cecelia and searched every face in the crowd with a hungry expression. No one else knew what she was looking for, but I did. I would make sure that she would never find Ella.

I noticed that some of the Maycott residents looked down at Victoria in shock and confusion. A few wore expressions of pity. Mrs. Clayton reached out a hand to her, but Victoria shook it off. Where was the dynamic Widow Blakeley tonight? Where were her amusing stories? Where was her charming wit? Were people finally seeing through the façade?

I turned away. Directly in front of me, I saw Lady Gwen and she seemed to be searching, though not with the same fanaticism that Victoria had, and not for the same person. She wandered, looking at the face of each man, and when she turned and saw me, her face lit up, but then fell in dismay. I chuckled and walked toward her.

"I'm sorry I'm not who you're looking for, Lady Gwen."

She ducked her head in embarrassment. "Forgive me, William. I'm . . . I just can't seem to find . . ."

I jumped in to save her from any more embarrassment; besides that, I had a promise to keep. "Do you know that little side door that leads out from the kitchens to the courtyard?" She nodded. "If you stay by that door, the person you're looking for will be coming in or out any minute."

She smiled gratefully up at me and headed in the direction of the little door.

Panic seemed to be ripping me apart from the inside when, finally, I found her. Ella's face was upturned in the middle of a crowd; she was completely at ease, talking with a sweet smile on her face to an exceptionally tall man. I could only imagine how much he was already in love with her.

Relieved, I wandered closer to the enormous dance floor and stood with the ring of people surrounding the dancers. Ella stood at the edge of the crowd, looking onto the dance floor as if she were staring over a bottomless pit. She searched the crowd, no doubt for Victoria, when our eyes met. Quickly, before someone blocked my view of her, I nodded, reassuring her that it was safe for her to dance. And even if Victoria were standing there, there was no way I was going to let that come between Ella and her opportunity to enjoy herself.

Ella beamed back at me and her face relaxed. As Ella took the tall man's arm and let him lead her to the dance floor, I realized that I had never seen her dance. I had seen her pluck chickens. I had seen her chop wood. I had seen her gather cattails, pick berries, and harvest vegetables. She performed each task with a natural, stunning grace, but nothing could have prepared me for the way she danced.

It was as if the floor disappeared. Her dress was long enough and she moved so fluidly that it seemed like she didn't even walk on her feet, but simply floated inches above the ground. Surprisingly, her partner was quite a skilled dancer even though it looked like his arms and legs were a foot longer than the average person's. Ella's eyes caught mine and I didn't even try to hide my wonder. I felt like the most fortunate man in the room, and I wasn't even the one dancing with her. But, I had been there for her when she needed someone to hold her. I had been there for her to wipe away her tears and lift up her chin when she wanted to let it fall. I had seen her blushes and heard her laughter.

She had become this vision of angelic brilliance all on her own, but I had had the privilege of witnessing it.

Their dance was coming to an end, and I knew I would have to refill my empty tray. Ella was safer here than anywhere else—being completely surrounded by people and as far away from Victoria as possible—at least for the time being.

With a sigh, I turned away to head back to the kitchen, but not without one last, fortunately-timed glance at Ella. At that moment, Roger Wallace had also noticed Ella and was making his way over to her, pushing past the men who had been waiting in line to dance with her. Before I knew what I was doing, I began weaving through the onlookers around the dance floor to get to Ella before Roger did.

But the crowd was too dense and my fury too strong. Through the gaps in the crowd, I saw that Roger had made it over to Ella and they had begun to dance. Ella's face was reluctant, yet resigned. She didn't seem very happy, but wasn't distressed either, so I held back. My stomach lurched when I saw how closely Roger was holding her; his arm wrapped so tightly around her that it reached to the other side of her waist.

Ella began pushing against him with all her strength, which I knew was substantial considering her size, because of all the work she did every day. Roger seemed to be putting up a good fight, though. I put my tray on a table and tore my suit coat off. I was about to punch Roger, right in the eye this time, but I wasn't going to damage my coat that Ella had already fixed for me. I also didn't want to lose my job being seen in my uniform punching a guest. Roger wasn't worth it.

The music ended by the time I finally reached them, but Roger hadn't let go of Ella. On the contrary, he was holding her tighter than ever, but this time he was leaning toward her face with his foul lips puckered. As I fought to reach them, I wondered if anyone was going to intervene. No one did, but then I realized it was because Roger looked like someone important. The other men might not dare to confront someone like that. But I would.

My hands shaking and my blood pumping so hard I could hardly see straight, I grabbed Roger by the scruff of his neck and yanked him back. He looked at me with more fear than I could remember on anyone's face before. It was a good thing, too, because some of the anger I felt dissipated into something close to pity. He wasn't so tough without his posse around him.

"That will be quite enough of that." Instead of punching him, I used all my self-control to simply place one hand on Roger's chest and push him back forcefully. He stumbled backward, awkwardly reaching out for anyone to catch him. Once he gained control, he glared back at me, knowing the fight was lost, and strode past Ella and me toward the courtyard.

Ella watched him leave for a moment and then looked up, her eyes brimming with gratitude.

"Thank you, Will." She sounded deeply relieved but with a hint of amusement.

I laughed, trying to shake off the last remnants of rage. "What an obnoxious scoundrel."

She looked stunned. "Do you know Roger well?"

"I don't need to know him to know exactly what he is." We laughed together again, our harmony blending in with the music that had begun to play. As naturally as breathing, and with the same amount of effort, I wrapped my arm around Ella's waist, she placed her hand in mine, and we began to move to the music.

"How did you know it was all right for me to come out and dance?" Ella asked.

"Our dear Victoria and her delightful daughters are talking with some friends in the courtyard. Victoria is sitting on a bench looking like she'll fall over dead any second and the wicked sisters are flirting ostentatiously with any man who looks at them. Don't worry. I wasn't taken in." I winked at her, not in a flirtatious way; well, perhaps a little flirtatiously.

Dancing with Ella was like floating on water. I was grateful that my sisters had insisted I practiced with them before they went to their parties. That was one of the downsides of being the youngest. While my older brothers could refuse all they wanted, I didn't seem to have a choice. But, I couldn't complain now. Instead of focusing on the steps, or counting along to the music, I could notice the comforting pressure of Ella's hand in mine, the feel of her waist beneath my hand, and the exquisite way she beamed up at me.

"Will, I don't want you to take any more risks for me," Ella said suddenly. "I would feel horrible if you were to get in trouble for helping me."

I was not going to let her feel guilty about anything. I brushed off her comment, refusing to let her worry. "How else was I supposed to give you the latest news? It doesn't look like there will be a break in dance partners. There's already a line behind me."

Ella danced up onto her tiptoes to peek over my shoulder, her face coming closer to mine. Her eyes widened and her cheeks flushed when she saw that she did indeed have quite a crowd gathered. I held her a little tighter. Not Roger-tight, but just tight enough that I could reassure her . . . and me.

I tried not to think about the fact that Sir Thomas was now among the crowd of admirers and I knew quite well that he wasn't there for a dance. I resisted the urge to hold Ella closer, knowing that no matter how closely I held her, she was about to be taken away from me. Perhaps forever.

The music ended with a sense of finality that made my throat tighten and my hands shake. I couldn't help it; I wrapped my arm more securely around her. But instead of looking uncomfortable, she grasped my hand tighter and her other hand clutched my shoulder. I pulled our hands closer between us and we stood there, feeling each other's strength and warmth and comfort. For me, I saw in Ella's eyes more than just a fear of being left alone. I saw a longing to remain with me.

The mob of admirers was now pushing against me—and each other—and I knew it was time. I started to pull away, choosing to let go rather than have Ella wrenched from my arms. Her hand tightened around mine, her eyes wistful and beseeching.

I had known this moment would come from the first time I heard about the ball. I had made the decision over and over that Ella had to go to the ball, that she had to have the opportunity to meet the prince, and for him to meet her. I had battled with my selfishness, battled over what was best for her—and for me—and had decided that somehow what was going to tear me apart was also what was best for me . . . because it was best for her.

In her eyes, I saw fear and dread, but I knew that those feelings came from the worry that Victoria was out there, searching for her, and that if she were caught, she would be given the worst punishment of her life. But in that moment, when her eyes were filled with terror at the unknown, for once, I knew what was coming. She was still anxious about Victoria, but with every impatient breath I could hear Sir Thomas take, I knew that her old fears were moments away from ceasing to exist.

With an overwhelming calm, I made the decision—once again—to let her go.

Leaning close, her hair brushing against my cheek and the smell of her rosewater soap enveloping her like a flower, I clasped her hand and whispered, "You're safe."

Almost like a dream, but feeling so terribly real, I pulled back from her, all while she watched me with eyes that had become peaceful.

Before any of the other men could claim her, Sir Thomas stood in front of them, blocking their way. Ella gasped and stepped back from his closeness. I couldn't see Sir Thomas's face, but he held out his arm and Ella placed hers on his.

"Please come with me," Sir Thomas said, and they walked away. I kept waiting to see if Ella would turn around to look at me in farewell. She never did.

Chapter 27

As I watched Ella walk farther and farther away from me, my most powerful fears washed over me, as well as my greatest hopes for her. She was everything the prince had been searching for. She was refined, graceful, and beautiful. After what I had seen of Francine's "interview" with the prince, I could only imagine how much he would love Ella. She wouldn't try to put on a show for him. She would be herself. That was all she knew how to be. The prince wanted depth and sincerity and he was about to get it.

But what did Ella want? Did she even know? Had she even allowed herself to wonder?

The musicians took a break for a few minutes just then and the crowd dispersed into chaos as hundreds of voices took over where the music had left off. Everyone moved in opposite directions and I started moving, too, with no destination in mind until I remembered my coat and tray and went back to retrieve them. Before I pulled my coat on, I looked at the tear that Ella had repaired for me just the night before. I couldn't find it.

Mechanically, I went down to the kitchens and was handed a refilled tray. I didn't hear the bustling of the maids and dishwashers. I didn't even know I was carrying drinks and not sandwiches until Mrs. Hammond called out, "Careful, dear! Don't spill those! We're running low!" I automatically held my hand steadier and made my way out to the ball, though there was no life left in it for me.

I went to refill my tray a few more times, always glancing in the direction that Ella had gone. I found myself in the courtyard about half an hour after she had left, each minute feeling like an hour. The guests seemed to give no hint that they would ever leave and the thought made my eyes droop.

The last drink on my tray was replaced with another empty glass, which queued my lethargic descent to the kitchens. At this point, I knew it wasn't just thirst driving people to drink. The alcohol had gotten to their heads and they couldn't tell if they were thirsty, hungry, bored, tired, lonely, or depressed. So, they drank. It was the easiest option.

I didn't feel like weaving through the throngs, so I took a detour through the smaller gardens near the palace. A sight about twenty feet in front of me made me halt. With the moonlight falling on them like approval from the heavens, Grant was kneeling down on one knee, both hands clasped around one of Lady Gwen's. I tried to duck back into the crowd, but not before I saw Grant jump up to his feet, wrap his arms around Lady Gwen and swing her around in a circle. When the kissing began, I was completely out of sight.

The smile that lit my face seemed to radiate through me. The sight of their happiness was like a balm that seemed to heal a part of my own wound that had been festering. I wasn't sure how this evening would end, but it was encouraging to know that happiness had come somewhere to someone.

I continued toward the castle staying close to the hedges, but I quickly discovered that was a mistake. I should have learned when I witnessed the scene between Grant and his new fiancée that the hedges were the perfect setting for such liaisons. I heard a rustling in the leaves and without thinking, turned in the direction of the new sound.

The hedges were high, but not high enough. Just above the tallest leaves were the unmistakable fused faces of Mabel

Blakeley and Roger Wallace. In disgust, I turned my head and quickened my steps. But almost immediately, I had a peculiar desire to protect that wretched girl from that even more wretched man.

As I marched toward them, a voice distracted me. "Mrs. Wallace, do tell me more about him!" The voice of Cecelia Blakeley shrilly floated over the noise of the hundreds of other people talking.

"Oh dear, you'll just love him. Everyone has always thought that my Roger and his cousin were twins! He's dashingly handsome and every bit as gentlemanly and prosperous as my Roger." Did I detect a hint of hesitation in the voice of my old friend, Mrs. Wallace? "I insist that you come and stay with us as we plan your sister's wedding. There's more than enough room. I'll invite him to come and you can get to know each other." Mrs. Wallace nudged Cecelia with her elbow and they both giggled. Mrs. Wallace sighed. "Imagine! My Roger marrying into the Blakeley family—one of the oldest and richest families in the kingdom." She seemed to be talking to the air.

Cecelia smiled, but ducked her head slightly, almost in shame, and said nothing. She hadn't quite mastered the art of deception as Mabel and Victoria had. I wondered how Mrs. Wallace would react when she discovered the Blakeleys were really destitute, having squandered Henry's fortune. And now they were using the Wallaces to secure their place in society. After the wedding, it would be too late to do anything about it, of course. I predicted a wedding within the month. The blindness of the townspeople amazed me. They had been fooled by fools.

Of course, Mrs. Wallace was doing the same thing, or thinking that she was, without openly admitting it. If she were truly looking at the character of her future daughter-in-law, and not just the assumption that they were still wealthy, she would be hiding her precious son as far away from the Blakeley twins as possible.

I shook my head and returned to the kitchen. Mabel and Roger were enthusiastically celebrating their looming union and Cecelia was as good as engaged. I didn't want to spoil the fun, but I wondered how long it would be before Roger learned that instead of a dowry, he was inheriting a debt.

I forced myself to ignore that it was because Mabel and Cecelia had stolen Ella's dress and slippers, at Victoria's insistence I was sure, that the girls were even noticed tonight. Now that I knew how much dresses cost, seeing the intricate details and fine fabric of Ella's dress made me realize what a treasure it truly was, not to mention the slippers that were made of brilliant and durable glass. Ella had taken care of these people for half of her life and had now secured a prosperous future for them. She had certainly kept her promise.

My vindictive side hoped that the next time they saw Ella, she would be their princess. My charitable side hoped for the strength to see the situation as Ella would see it—as a selfless gift to people who simply didn't appreciate it, but a gift that she would give nonetheless.

My eyelids felt like lead as I was handed what I hoped would be one of my last trays. Mrs. Hammond seemed to be more lethargic now that the effects of the alcohol were wearing off, but I missed her irrational enthusiasm. When she lost her energy, it was as if she took all of ours just so she could hold herself up.

"It's almost over, dear," she said, patting my arm, a sheen of sweat on her creased forehead.

I smiled down at her, hesitated a moment, cleared my throat, and finally made up my mind to ask her. "Mrs. Hammond. When will we know if Prince Kenton has found his—" I swallowed quickly, hoping she wouldn't notice, "bride?"

Mrs. Hammond glanced around conspiratorially and then raised a bent finger, indicating that I should bow down lower to her.

"Dear," her eyes darted around the room, "I have just been informed that the prince just may have found his bride. A beautiful girl—golden hair, stunning dress, glass slippers, if you can imagine that! Graceful, elegant—just what he has been searching for. She was brought to him about an hour ago, and she hasn't left yet."

My stomach twisted in knots. "Who is telling you this?"

She chuckled, a bit of the wine still evident in the loll of her head. "Oh, I have people."

I was sure she did. I hurried out of the room, desperate for fresh air. Foolishly, I actually thought I would find it outside, but that air was all being breathed in and out by the thousands of increasingly drunk guests. Their laughter had taken on a stupid, mindless quality, and what I could catch of the conversations around me was increasingly absurd.

Suddenly, the tray I held was lifted up off my hand. Startled, I looked over and saw Grant standing there.

"Let me take it, Will. It's the least I can do," Grant said.

I blinked. "The least you can do for what?"

"For you giving me hope. Gwen and I are engaged."

"I had a feeling." I smiled genuinely at him, since his smile was infectious. "I'm happy for you both."

"Will," Grant began. "I-I'm sorry . . . about Ella."

"You know, too?"

"Gwen has been getting updates. The royals are all watching closely." He cleared his throat. "I saw you dancing with her earlier tonight. I'm . . . sorry."

I nodded. Grant patted me on the back, while also propelling me toward the castle. I knew Grant was subtly hinting that I had earned the right to go home, but that was the last place I wanted to go. Besides, there was still work to be done.

As I headed in the direction of the palace, I was hopeful that at least some guests were beginning to leave so that I could be of some use out there. But the thought of walking hundreds of feet around the palace to get to the front made my feet want to scream, so I boldly strode right in to cut straight through the palace toward the front doors. This place had unfortunately become a second home to me this week and I didn't even care if anyone would disapprove. My hands were clean today.

The unmistakable sounds of a woman sobbing echoed through the corridors, making me cringe with discomfort. I reconsidered my plan to cut through the palace; I was in no mood to hear some royal drama.

I was about to turn around when I saw that the sobbing woman was Princess Rose and she was surrounded by a group of royals. I decided to continue. They were distracted enough that they wouldn't notice me, and besides that, I needed a little distraction of my own.

"I traveled for three days straight to get here! I got on a boat. I hate boats! I still feel like I haven't dried off completely. I couldn't sleep with all that endless swaying." She looked at each face in the circle that surrounded her, seeming to search for some compassion, but was instead met with awkward downward glances and helplessness. "Prince Kenton and I, we were *betrothed*, do you hear me! We were *promised*!"

Her sobs and desperate pleas continued and instead of chuckling, a tightness gripped my chest. The Beast may have expressed her pain in woefully different ways than I did, but I realized at that moment that she and I were more affected than most by the happenings at the ball.

Her cries haunted me as I escaped to the front exit. I closed the heavy doors behind me, a little too hard, ignoring the guards who were standing ready for that very purpose. It felt good to slam something.

"Oh please, Clive. It's me. I can close a door on my own."

Clive smiled at me, grateful to be addressed so informally after a night of acting like a figurine.

"Where are the real guards?" I asked, realizing I wasn't in trouble for my behavior.

Clive motioned with his thumb toward the back of the palace. "They joined the party about an hour ago."

I nodded, about to say something else, when just then, the heavy doors crashed open behind me. It took me a moment to grasp what I was seeing. Dr. Clayton, older than Victoria herself, had her cradled in his arms, his white hair sticking up wispily around his head, his thin arms trembling from the effort, his breath coming in gasps. I jumped forward and lifted Victoria out of his arms. Her head lolled backward and I adjusted my elbow to hold it up. Her eyes, which had been closed, opened for a tiny instant and held mine before they rolled back in her head.

I saw Clive run behind me, going to fetch the doctor's carriage.

"Clive! The doctor's carriage is parked right under the maple tree on the south side of the stables!" I called after him. He waved a hand, indicating that he heard me as he tore down the hill.

We stood waiting in silence as I fought with my emotions. An unexpected and overwhelming wave of compassion swept over me as I looked down at her ghostly pale, clammy face and the dark circles under her sunken eyes that made it seem like death would be a relief. Her body was wasted away to nothing, even compared to just a week before when I had helped her into the wagon. Her face was twisted in pain and she looked truly helpless.

Next, anger crowded out my more charitable feelings. As I looked down at Victoria's face, I saw in my mind Ella's tear-streaked cheeks, her whipped, raw hands, her downcast eyes. This woman was the reason Ella's confidence had been destroyed, the reason she couldn't look people in the eye, and the reason she doubted her worth. I had never felt less worthy of Ella than in that moment when my hatred for Victoria almost overcame me.

Victoria wanted to die. She needed to die. But she wouldn't let herself. Not without one last statement that although she was diminished to nothing, she could still inspire fear and dread.

Suddenly, I needed to be rid of her. She brought out every mean part of me and I couldn't stand it. Thankfully, at that moment, Clive pulled the carriage up to us and hopped down to open the door. I walked forward and gently lifted her up, carefully laying her on the bench. The doctor followed close behind me and climbed up onto the driver's seat.

I reached out to grasp his arm. "No, please. Let me drive. You can ride in the back."

Before I even finished speaking, he was sitting down and reaching for the reins. He looked down at me with sad, tired eyes. "She has her daughters with her," he said, and we both turned to watch Mabel and Cecelia approach the carriage. Mabel paused for a moment to look back at the palace with longing before climbing in. Cecelia yawned and followed in after her. The doctor's voice lowered as he turned back to look at me. "Besides, son, there's nothing I can do for her now."

I let his words sink in for a moment. "I'll get your family home, sir," I said, and he smiled down at me gratefully. Without another word, he slapped the reins and the horses took off at a gallop. I watched as the carriage descended the slope and approached the iron gates. Once they were gone and I heard the final metallic clang of the gates, I felt like a chapter of my life—and Ella's life—had closed. I just wished the feeling of loathing had gone with it.

The dust settled as I watched the carriage disappear. I couldn't help thinking about what I would be doing now if Ella were not with the prince. Knowing that Victoria had gone home, I would have hurried to find Ella and driven a borrowed carriage through every shortcut to get Ella home first. She would have run to the back entrance, changed into her nightgown, hidden her dress, and lain down on the hearth, pretending to sleep. We would have laughed about it the next day, I was sure.

Right now, I had no need to hurry and find Ella. She was as safe as she could be. She hadn't left the prince's presence and now she would never have to be afraid of Victoria again. She would never have to starve again; never have to worry about being whipped or neglected or manipulated. She would never have to worry about being too cold in the winter or if her garden could sustain them through the long, bitter months. And not just because Victoria would most likely be dead by the time Ella got home, but because by the looks of things, Ella wouldn't be going home at all.

The moonlit night took on a blurry quality and I fought the desire to drop my head into my hands. I blinked and turned back to Clive and Harry.

"Have you two eaten yet?" They both shook their heads sadly. They had been standing out here all night, smelling the food wafting from the kitchens and not had a bite to eat. "Run around to the kitchen and grab a sandwich or . . . ten. They're really small. It's as good a time as any." With grateful smiles, they ran off and disappeared around the corner of the palace.

Taking over the job of guard, I stood by the doors and heard voices approaching from inside. I pulled the doors open and stood silently as a red-faced, hiccupping Princess Rose, accompanied by a guard and her lady-in-waiting, descended the front steps. She had come to win back her prince and she had obviously received her answer. With no one else to retrieve her carriage, I hurried down to the stables. I, of course, knew exactly where this carriage was. Climbing onto the driver's seat, I tried not to think about the last time I had driven this carriage and the excitement

I had over taking Ella to the ball. I returned the carriage to the front steps.

"I'll never love anyone else as long as I live!" she wailed. Again, though she was being overly dramatic to the point of hilarity, her cry made my throat constrict painfully. No one offered to comfort her, and I definitely was in no place to do so. Besides, I had nothing to say.

They drove away and would no doubt be returning to their own kingdom, now that the prince had found his bride.

I walked down to the stables to tend to the horses. The night was eerily quiet, especially after the constant hum of talking, laughter, and excitement of the ball. The only sound was the faint echo of the orchestra, but it only sounded like someone wailing in the distance. I shivered. I needed to do something to fight the gloom. I grabbed a bucket, filled it with oats, and wandered from bored horse to bored horse, offering them something to eat while they continued to wait for their owners.

The creaking of the front doors to the palace made me look up in alarm. I had abandoned my post and should be there to open the door for the guests. Patting the horse I was feeding to reassure him I would be back soon, I set the bucket down and hurried back to the palace. The door was still wide open, the light from inside streaking across the front lawn and garden in an irregular rectangle. Looking around me, I saw that no one was there. Assuming that the door hadn't been properly closed after Princess Rose's hasty exit, I thought nothing more of it, closed it tightly, and returned to the horses.

Once the oats were gone, I removed my suit coat, grabbed the shovel and a new bucket and began cleaning up the messes the horses had made.

I was vaguely aware of a commotion coming from inside the palace and I wondered what catastrophe was going to emerge from the front doors next. The thunderous boom of the front doors crashing open so violently made the horses jump, their heads raised in alarm. I marveled that the doors had even stayed on their hinges, or that the stones hadn't crumbled from the force. Swiftly, at least a dozen guards emerged from the open doors and came racing down the hill toward the stables.

"Stop her! She's getting away!" one of them shouted.

Another guard spotted me and motioned for me to come. "Horses! Now!"

I abandoned the waiting horses and carriages and rushed to the stables. I wasn't sure how many they would need, but none of the horses had saddles and I rushed to get them ready.

"Clive! Harry! Come down here!" I called up the hill. I could see the outlines of Clive and Harry who had just emerged from behind the palace, sandwiches in their hands. They paused in alarm for a moment, then ran down the hill to meet me at the stables. As the guards pulled on their gloves, the three of us hastily threw on the first saddles we could grab, strapped them onto whatever horse was nearest, and then the closest guard jumped on and raced down the hill and toward the gates.

No one spoke as we all worked quickly and instinctively. All I knew was that the guards were after a "she" and we didn't ask questions or even appear to wonder what was going on. Once they had all disappeared in a frantic cloud of dust, I went back into the stables and counted the empty stalls. Fourteen horses were gone.

"What was that all about?" Clive asked.

"I don't know. They were chasing after a girl. That's all I know. I guess someone stole something." I replied. "Or, maybe they needed to talk to Princess Rose," I added. Perhaps the prince had experienced a change of heart. But somehow, I knew that wasn't true. I sighed. It didn't matter anyway. As I walked back up to the palace, I tried to resort to my old habit of not bothering myself with royal matters.

Clive and Harry returned back to the kitchens, their sandwiches having been trampled in the commotion. Once more, the door opened and the doctor's wife and daughters came outside and walked down the stairs, looking around for some assistance.

I hurried up to talk to them. "Good evening, Mrs. Clayton. I promised your husband I would see you home. I'll go get your carriage."

I retrieved their carriage and also tied Charlie to it so I would have a ride back once they were dropped off. Once we arrived at the Clayton home, I helped each young woman out of the carriage and they each thanked me. The doctor's wife was last and she looked up at me with troubled eyes.

"How is Widow Blakeley?" she whispered, her compassion as natural as her husband's.

Slowly, I shook my head. "She probably won't make it through the night," I said, remembering the doctor's words before he had driven Victoria away from the palace.

She nodded and clasped my hand, and not just because I was helping her out of the carriage.

Once they were safely inside, their carriage parked, and their horse put away, Charlie and I rode back to the palace. I went back to work in the stables and noticed that fifteen horses were now gone. Someone else had taken a horse, probably looking for the "she" with the others. I hoped Clive had come down to help whoever it was while I was away.

The quiet, eerie music from the orchestra floated over the night and the lights were still gleaming from inside the palace and from the grounds. When would this wretched ball ever end? I couldn't let myself think anymore. Every part of me was tired. I sat down on the ground next to the maple tree, closed my eyes, and slept.

Chapter 28

"Will. Will. Time to wake up. The guests are starting to leave." Whoever had been shaking my shoulder was gone before I could open my eyes to see who it was. I stood up, brushed my pants, put my coat back on, and went to the nearest carriage to drive it up to the palace. I wished I had something less tedious to do. I tried as hard as I could to ignore the sadness over losing Ella. I wouldn't let myself think about it. I couldn't let myself think about what she was doing at that moment, how charming the prince had been, how soon they would be married, or if they already were.

I just drove.

The last guest left just as the pre-dawn light silhouetted the trees on the distant hills. Everything was put away, every horse accounted for, except for the fifteen that had been used during the night, but we would tend to them when they returned. We all moved wearily in the misty morning, every limb heavy, every eye drooping. I watched as Simon and Hugh closed the gate with one final, satisfying clang, and we all breathed a sigh of relief.

I was just about to go get Charlie when Grant came walking down the hill carrying a bundle of envelopes wrapped in twine.

"Wait, men. Before you go, Mrs. Hammond asked me to give these to you before she, uh, fell asleep." I smiled. I had grown very fond of that lady. She deserved a rest, even if it was an alcohol-induced slumber. "These are your extra months' pay. She also told me to let you know that you could have the day off and, well, that she, uh, loves you all." No one laughed or teased. We all felt very proud of the work we had done and the things we had learned from her. We all seemed to feel a mutual affection for this woman who had become a mother to us—a demanding, affectionate mother.

"Clive. Paul. Harry. . . ." Grant began calling out the names written on the envelopes and each man came to retrieve his.

"Will," he said, and I reached for mine.

"Thank you, Lord . . . uh, Grant," I said with a chuckle and he smiled.

***

There was nowhere else to go but home. The thought of it wasn't welcoming. It just felt like four walls and a door and a leaky roof that would simply provide protection, not warmth or comfort. I took the road; I didn't want to go through the forest like a coward, avoiding Ashfield for the rest of my life. Its towers soon emerged from above the trees in the distance, and out of habit, my heart beat faster and Charlie's pace quickened along with it. The practical side of me overpowered the grieving part of me just in time for me to realize that there was no one there who would or could take care of the animals in Ella's absence.

The sun was a half-circle emerging from behind the hills when I arrived at Ashfield. I let Charlie graze on the grass on the side of the road and I walked to the barn behind the house. There was no sign that anyone had been out to take care of the animals. I didn't even try to be quiet. I milked Lucy and led her to the pasture, securing the newly fixed gate behind her. As I walked over to feed the chickens, I noticed a fresh mound of dirt at the corner of the garden next to Mr. and Mrs. Blakeley's graves.

Victoria had died last night. That meant that the house could be completely empty, especially considering that Mabel and Cecelia had already been invited to live with the Wallaces. There was no reason for them to stay now.

I paused at the mound of dirt, my eyes filling with tears—tears that I didn't know were from anger or sorrow. Perhaps just the sight of a fresh mound of dirt inspired tears. Perhaps I felt guilty for feeling glad that she was gone, and that guilt was mingled with an almost blinding fury. Why couldn't she have died a week ago? Two weeks ago?

I wished I had Ella's strength at that moment. I needed it. I had never felt so hollow, yet so filled with despair. I was lost without her smile to warm me and her tenderness to soften me. Victoria was gone, but now Ella was gone, too.

Turning away from the grave, I headed for the back door that led to the kitchen. I remembered coming here, just two nights before—so excited to see Ella, though apprehensive at the same time, worried I was making yet another mistake—and I felt like I had lived a lifetime between then and now.

Without knocking, I walked into the cold and empty kitchen—empty because Ella wasn't there. I placed the jug of milk on the floor and the egg in a bowl on the counter. I didn't want it to roll off and ruin Ella's spotless floor.

There was nothing left to do. The kitchen was gray and dark, the sun rising on the opposite side of the house. A tub sat in the middle of the kitchen, Ella's old gray dress was carefully folded over a chair. My fingers felt along the frayed edge of the hem and I could see where she had meticulously repaired and stitched it over the years . . . and then I couldn't see anymore.

Ella's rocking chair was where it always was—close to the fire so that she could capture the last of the warmth before it faded into coldness; where she had sat to mend my suit coat; where I had kneeled in front of her, held her hand, and brushed away her tears. It was there that I saw that look in her eyes that made me never want to leave her; the look that told me she never *wanted* me to leave her.

I sat down in the chair, feeling the cool wind from outside blow through the vacant fireplace and make a moaning sound in the chimney. I rested my elbows on my knees and buried my face in my hands.

***

After a while, I stood, walked over to the door, opened it, and closed it softly behind me. I knew I would be back later that evening to bring Lucy in from the pasture, but until then, I couldn't make myself go home. My little cabin had never been Ella's home, but now, nowhere felt like home without her.

With one hand holding onto my coat, which I slung over my shoulder, and one hand in my pocket, I walked toward the center of town. I couldn't even look up at the palace, knowing that Ella was inside it, either sleeping in a grand bed or even being fitted for her wedding gown. I tried to smile, but a hollow aching gripped my chest. Charlie walked lazily next to me, probably grateful for an idle morning. Though, I knew we weren't being lazy. I just didn't know where to go.

Unlike everyone else in town, apparently. People were running frantically in every direction, skirts swirling everywhere, people talking excitedly to one another. I could only guess what they were talking about—the prince had found his princess. I tuned them out as I reluctantly made my way over to Corbin's blacksmith shop. Ella hadn't left the ball, which meant that Francine hadn't been chosen by the prince. But I had a feeling that wouldn't mean that all was well between her and Corbin.

The shop looked and felt abandoned as I stood outside the wide double doors. I pulled one of them open and was dismayed, but not surprised, to see that everything had been packed up. The floor was swept and all of Corbin's tools and supplies were stacked in a corner, ready to be taken with him wherever he was going.

The door to Corbin's living quarters was ajar. I walked toward it, knocked softly, and it slowly fell open. Sitting on the edge of his bed was Corbin, his head bowed over a small white glove he held in his blackened fingers.

"When did you leave last night?" I asked quietly.

"About an hour after I got there," he replied with a husky voice. "She wants nothing to do with me."

I nodded, the gloom in his voice palpable. "Did you sleep?"

"No. I've been packing."

"Where are you going?"

"Far."

I didn't try to dissuade him. Suddenly his plan sounded perfect.

"I might be able to help you carry some of that stuff you have out there."

"I bought a donkey from Mr. Goodman this morning. But thank . . . wait. Are you leaving, too?"

"I don't know what else to do. Ella's marrying the prince. They could be married already, in fact."

Corbin looked at me like I was mad and stood up from his bed. "But Ella left the palace. She ran away. I thought you'd be with her now, come to think of it. What are you doing here?" He tossed the glove aside.

"What do you mean 'left'? She's at the palace. The prince chose her."

"Well, she didn't choose the prince, from the sound of it."

"From the sound of *what*? What are you talking about?"

"Ella ran away last night. I thought you knew. You were right there."

I shook my head, trying to grasp it all. Could Ella really have been the "she" they were chasing after? I tried to think of where I could have been when she ran away, if she actually had. I could have been taking the doctor's family home. I could have been near the stables. She could have run right by me.

The open door. Could that have been her? She wouldn't have known to look for me out at the stables—known that I could have taken her home. She had escaped so quickly, she was out of sight before I reached the palace doors.

But that didn't make any sense. Why would she run?

"How do you know all this?" I asked.

"I was here, packing. I saw the whole thing. Ella ran right into the middle of town, right outside the shop. I called out, but I don't think she heard me. She bolted straight into the woods and just a few minutes later, men from the palace came charging into town, demanding to know if I had seen a girl running. I said no." He finished with a grin.

"Why would she run?"

"I think the correct questions are: 'What was she running from?' and 'Who was she running to?'"

By now, Corbin was standing, a smile lighting up his face, thinking things I wouldn't allow myself to.

I felt myself moving toward the door in a daze. "I have to find her," I said, though my voice didn't come out.

"Wait. If you don't know she escaped, you must not know that the prince is still looking for her." Corbin's hand grasped my shoulder. "He's been searching all night."

Understanding dawned on me. "The fifteenth horse," I murmured. It had been the prince who had taken the last horse while I was taking the doctor's family home.

Corbin continued, ignoring my enigmatic statement. "I guess she lost a shoe and he's planning to find her by trying the shoe on all the maidens in the kingdom."

"What kind of an idiotic plan is that?"

"It sounds like the plan of a man who has been made irrational because he's fallen in—"

"Love," I finished for him. What a ridiculous word.

"But obviously, he hasn't found her yet," Corbin said as he gestured out the door at the hysterical people running around the square. Their hysteria suddenly had new meaning. They weren't excited that the prince had found his princess; they were excited because there was still a chance that they could *be* the princess.

I turned back to Corbin. "Where's Francine?" I asked gently.

"I'm not sure, but I can guess that's she's sitting at home with her foot sticking out, waiting for a prince to slide a shoe on it."

I couldn't help wincing at the pain in his voice and the image of his fiancée waiting, once again, for the prince.

"I'm sorry, Corbin," I said.

"Don't worry about me. There's still hope for you. Ella could be at home with no idea what's happening out here. She may even be waiting for you."

I thought back to that morning when I had gone to Ashfield. There was absolutely no sign that Ella was there. It couldn't be true, but I had to know for sure.

"Go, Will!" Corbin said.

I ran over to where Charlie was drinking from the trough outside Corbin's shop. I was just about to put my foot in the stirrup when I saw two guards walking side by side, coming from the direction of Ella's house.

"Well, that was easier than I thought it would be," one of the guards laughed.

"I thought the prince was insane! Trying the slipper on every single maiden until it fit someone! Luckily, she lived right here in Maycott! I guess he did know what he was doing." The other one chuckled, and then heaved a relieved sigh.

"Wait!" I called and grabbed onto the second one's arms. "He found her? The slipper fit?"

"Yes," he replied, prying my fingers off him, but not as rudely as he would have if I hadn't been wearing the same uniform as he was.

"Where is she now? Is the prince with her?"

"Well, I assume he is. We weren't with him, but we just got word. She just had to gather some belongings. Then he's taking her to the palace . . . any moment now, really."

I looked around frantically. There was no prince and no carriage. Ella could still be at home, though I couldn't imagine it would take her more than a few minutes to gather her few belongings.

Once I was in the saddle, I turned to Corbin.

He walked over and smiled, though it was touched with sadness. "I'll wait a little while. If you don't come back here, I'll assume you're staying," he said.

I didn't know if I should say good-bye to him. I didn't know if I would return in an hour, dejected and defeated, or if I would be staying with Ella, never to leave her side again.

"Thank you, Corbin," was all I could say. "Everything will work out for the best."

Chapter 29

I JUMPED OFF THE SADDLE BEFORE CHARLIE EVEN STOPPED and used the momentum to propel myself up the front steps. I threw the heavy oak door out of my way with a crash.

"Ella!" I cried. There was no sound. No movement. It didn't feel empty, but she was still nowhere to be found. I ran all around the first floor—through the foyer, drawing room, living room, and into the dining room.

"Ella," I said. Panic and desperation were making my heart race and my eyes water. I ran out into the yard. Lucy was still out in the pasture. Mary was sleeping in her house. It still looked like I had been the only one here.

I returned to the kitchen and stopped. I walked closer to the fireplace and could feel a whisper of heat coming from the smoldering ashes. I spun around. The milk was gone, probably taken to the cellar. The egg was gone, nowhere in sight.

Ella had been here. She had come home. But now she was gone. The prince had found her and I had missed her.

Slowly, I returned to the foyer and just stood there.

"Ella," I whispered, just so I could say her name in this house that had once been hers.

In the thick silence, I heard the quiet patting of bare feet and a voice that whispered in the stillness.

"Will?"

It sounded like her voice, but I wouldn't let myself believe it. Forcing my head up toward the sound, I saw her. She stood at the top of the stairs, absently drying her hands on her apron. "What's wrong?" Like an angel descending out of heaven, Ella ran down the stairs. I couldn't move. I couldn't breathe. I couldn't even let myself believe that what my eyes were seeing was real.

She stopped close to me, close enough that I could have reached out and touched her, close enough that I could see the brightness of her eyes and the flush in her cheek.

"You're here?" My voice echoed relief but with a hushed hesitation.

"Of course I'm here. Where else would I be?" She laughed freely, clearly thinking I had lost my mind. It dawned on me that she really had no idea what was happening outside her quiet world, and more than that, she didn't even seem to care. "You need to go home and rest," she continued. "First, let me get you something to eat. I need to thank you for helping me this . . ."

She started to walk away from me toward the kitchen, but I couldn't bear to have her out of my sight. My legs wouldn't move to follow her. I reached out and caught her hand. It was so small and perfect in mine, and so real. Without letting go of her hand, I forced myself to move. I walked over to the stairs with her following me, and sat down on the bottom step, pulling her gently to sit next to me. She looked back up at me, questions in her wondering eyes.

"Ella, I assume you've been home all day?"

"Yes," she sighed, "I have had so much to get done here." She looked around, always seeing work that needed to get done. Then she met my eyes with an almost guarded expression. "Victoria died last night," she murmured.

"Pity," I said. Ella was free, and I couldn't help grinning . . . impertinently.

"Will, something happened to me last night," she started to say, but stopped.

"At the ball?" I hoped she couldn't hear my jealousy as I helped her find the right words for what she was about to tell me, though I already knew.

"No, I mean with Victoria. Will, as she lay dying, I saw her for the first time. Really saw her. All her walls were down, whether she wanted them to be or not. She simply didn't have the strength to keep them up anymore. She was frail and weak and vulnerable, like she finally needed someone to care for her, and could admit it." Her voice trembled and her eyes filled with tears. "Her daughters had said good-bye and didn't shed a tear for her. It . . . it broke my heart. Truly broke it. I forgave her. She squeezed my hand." Unconsciously, her fingers tightened around my hand that still held hers.

Ella had spent the entire evening with the prince, who had fallen in love with her. He had searched for her all night, along with every one of his royal guards. The whole kingdom was in an uproar, talking about this beautiful girl who had stolen the prince's heart. Now here she was, talking about how she had forgiven the woman who had made her life miserable, and not even realizing what a miracle that was.

"The prince doesn't deserve you. No one deserves you." *Including me,* I added to myself.

As soon as I mentioned the prince, Ella's eyes widened slightly and her cheeks flushed. I realized that though I had been thinking about the prince, she was genuinely caught off guard when I mentioned him.

"The prince? What are you talking about?" Ella's voice was high and shaky and she couldn't meet my eyes. "I was just telling you about something that happened to me, that's all."

"That's my point. You *allowed* it to happen to you. You let yourself forgive. That doesn't just happen." She met my eyes and tried to read what she saw there. She seemed to look at me with some new awareness that made me feel a little exposed. As much as I wanted to explore that a little more, there were other things we had to talk about. "Well, Ella. It seems that you made quite an impression on the prince last night."

"Oh? How do you know that?" she said in that same high, tight voice.

"Well, it's all over the kingdom that the prince fell in love last night." I watched her more closely than I ever had, but I couldn't help it. I had to know how she would feel about this revelation, if it was indeed a revelation at all.

"Oh? He fell in love?" The stain in her cheeks spread all over her face and she ducked her head.

"Love." Suddenly I hated that word. Her blushes and her downcast eyes were revealing more than her words were.

"Why were you looking for me?" I could tell she was trying to change the subject, only she didn't know that she had only led us deeper down the same topic.

"Ella, did you lose a slipper last night?" I asked, though I was also answering her own questions . . . in a way.

"Yes!" Her eyes shot up at me and relief made some of her blush fade away. "Did someone find it? I thought I'd never see . . ." My face fell and her expression mirrored mine. Until that moment, I had started to let myself think that it might not have been Ella who had lost her shoe; I'd let myself hope that she may not be the girl the prince was searching for. She wasn't with him. She was here, sitting with me, and the guards had told me that the slipper had fit someone. But I knew it had been her slipper that was lost. She had been the girl with the golden hair, the blue dress, and the glass slippers. Mrs. Hammond had described the girl to me who had spent most of the evening with the prince. It could only be Ella.

"Yes, someone found it. The prince." There was so much I wanted to know that my questions seemed to burn my tongue. Why had she run? Why was she home in her old dress, doing her chores all alone in her house? And most importantly, did she love the prince?

"Yes, I lost my shoe. The prince told me he loved me last night. He . . ." In my mind, I begged her not to say what she was about to say. "He proposed. He . . . he kissed me." The heat from her face seemed to mingle with the heat from mine, only mine came from such overpowering jealousy, it brought tears to my eyes.

He had touched her. He had taken her in his arms and kissed her. His lips had touched hers. I was grateful I hadn't eaten that morning because my stomach became a tight ball and water filled my mouth. I looked down at those lips that had never been mine, that I hadn't allowed myself to claim, and he had casually dropped in and taken them.

And yet, here she sat, next to me, still allowing me to hold her hand. She had run away from the palace—for some reason still unknown to me—and my mood lightened considerably. "Hmm. So, he proposed and your shoe fell off?" I grinned.

"No. I . . . I ran away and his guards chased me and I lost my shoe. I didn't even stop to pick it up." A forlorn expression stole across her face and I knew she hated that she had left her mother's slipper.

"Ella, about your shoe. . . . The prince went looking to find the owner of that glass slipper and when he does . . . he's going to marry her."

"What! How is he going to do that?"

"He is already doing it. He started early this morning, going from house to house, trying the glass slipper on each and every maiden in the kingdom."

"But . . . but what if it fits more than one person?"

"That's a very good question."

She pondered this for a moment and then looked up at me. "Will, is that why you were looking for me? To see if the slipper fit me?"

I nodded slowly and stood, reached out a hand, and pulled her up to face me. She looked at me with so much confusion, imploring me for answers, that I wrapped my arm around her, unsure of how she would take the news I was about to give her. She accepted my support and leaned into me as she waited for my answer.

"Word is out all over the kingdom. The slipper fit someone and the prince is taking her to the palace as we speak. I thought you were gone."

She didn't cry. She didn't faint. She didn't scream at the injustice. She just stared back into my eyes, and after a while, her eyebrows puckered, but that was the only thing that changed in her expression.

Slowly, her eyes dropped, but she simply looked like she was thinking, not hurting. I realized then that her calm reaction must be because I was there, holding her, unable to let go. She was worried about my feelings. She must now have an idea of my feelings for her and didn't want to hurt me. She must be waiting for me to leave so she could freely mourn over her recently found, and even more recently lost, love. I wondered if she was thinking about the palace that could have been her home, the husband that every other woman wanted—the man who had been searching for her but had found someone else. Her composure was unnerving and I couldn't bear her silence any longer.

"Ella, tell me what you're thinking. You don't seem upset. Don't act calm just because I'm here. It won't hurt my feelings if you're disappointed." The words came out and I tried to make them true, giving her permission to feel upset without the worry of hurting me. "He's the prince. I understand that. He could have given you everything."

She looked back up into my face and her blue eyes were fire. Suddenly, there was no prince, no ball, no slipper, just Ella. And me. Just us. I couldn't imagine what had brought this unexpected look of longing to her eyes and my breath caught as she looked from my eyes, to my mouth, and back again.

"Ella," I whispered, and I raised my free hand to seize her arm and pull her closer to me. Everything was happening too fast, everything had changed so quickly, I couldn't fully grasp what was happening. My eyes wandered to her lips and she moved infinitesimally closer to me.

I knew I heard them but I wouldn't acknowledge them. He couldn't have come for her. He had found someone else who fit the slipper. But the thunderous pounding of horses' hooves and carriage wheels seemed to shake me back down to reality.

Prince Kenton had somehow discovered who Ella was and where she lived and he was coming. He was almost here.

Of all the moments this past week that I had thought I was saying good-bye to her for the last time, I knew that this truly was the final time. Last night, for whatever reason, Ella had run, and I doubted she would be able to this time, even if she wanted to. Every other time I had said good-bye, it was before she knew I loved her, or at least, how deeply I loved her. And those good-byes were certainly before she had been free to even wonder how she felt about me. As I looked into her eyes just now, I knew that she knew I loved her. Though I had never said it with words, I knew that she saw it in everything I did—every glance, every gesture.

What was still unknown to me, however, was how she felt about me, and as I heard the carriages and horses come to a stop in her front drive, I knew that this was how it was supposed to be. She was as free as she would ever be. There was no Victoria to manipulate her, no fear to hold her back. She also had all the information to make her decision—the fact that I loved her, and also that the prince loved her.

Just this last time I had to leave her. I leaned down, pressed my lips to her cheek, breathed in the sunshine in her hair, and let her go.

"He's coming for you. It's you he wants."

Chapter 30

BLINKING AGAINST THE PIERCINGLY BRIGHT SUN, I CLOSED the back door quietly behind me. Lucy was in the distance, grazing on the grass and Mary hopped around in her coop, alarmed by the pounding of the hooves that had just come to a stop. The dust from all the horses had drifted to the backyard and I rounded the house to emerge on the opposite side.

There was only one carriage that I could see, though it was lined by two dozen horses and riders. Sir Fitzpatrick was knocking on the front door by the time I could see it and behind him stood Prince Kenton. Blocked by trees and too far to be noticed anyway, I silently continued out toward the road. Kenton shifted his weight between his feet and wrung his hands. He glanced over at the carriage and then ducked his head, as if in shame, though I couldn't imagine why.

He loved her. And it killed me. He loved her, but it was a different kind of love than I was accustomed to. He was consumed by it. It didn't seem to clarify his mind and feelings; it befuddled them and made him nonsensical. He was past all rational thought. His only desire was to find her, not try to figure out why she left. He needed her and would go to any length to get her back.

My love for Ella had a different effect on me. From the moment I knew I loved her, I found myself seeing everything clearly. It forced my thoughts outward, instead of inward. Her happiness was my happiness, her pain my pain. My love for Ella brought me a peace and serenity and sense of contentment that almost purified me. It was strange to see how the love of the same woman had such different effects on the prince and me.

The one thing we had in common was that our love for Ella grew almost from the very first time we saw her.

The difference between us, though, was that he was here to persuade her, to plead with her to come with him. I thought of all the times I could have done that—pleaded with Ella to leave with me, but I hadn't. As quiet and reserved as Ella was, she was fiercely loyal and unapologetically independent. The prince didn't know this. He couldn't know this. But he was persuasive, not to mention rich and charming, and he could convince her to come. He saw what he wanted, and he would stop at nothing to have it.

He was a good man; I could admit that. But I had never once seen him not get something he wanted.

The door opened, but I couldn't see Ella. The prince was announced and he walked into the house . . . alone.

I rounded the bend in the road that led toward home and found Charlie grazing in the woods, most likely scared off by the prince's arrival. I ran my hand along his back and patted his neck, then I reached for the reins and pulled him forward.

As we walked along, I chose to focus on the early evening chirping of the crickets, knowing that soon it would be too cold for them to be out to announce the beginning and ending of each day.

I needed to give myself some time to process everything, to figure out what I was going to do. But I knew I couldn't think in the confines of my little cabin. I needed the woods to give my thoughts space to breathe. Corbin would be leaving soon, and I knew that I should go and pack my few belongings and get the horses ready if I were going with him.

Instead, I sat in my usual spot by the pond. The prince was with Ella now, once again offering her the world. I had lost her for the last time. I had lost her a thousand times this week, but I would be willing to lose her a thousand times over again if it meant that I could love her between, and through, each of those losses. But she wasn't mine to love anymore. I found some peace in knowing that I had been there to be a friend when she needed one.

***

The whole kingdom was invited to meet the prince's new bride. I couldn't bear the thought of going, but I had to know if she was happy in her new life. Thousands of people gathered on the lawn under the balcony of the palace and I weaved my way from the back up toward the front. Ella and Kenton appeared and the crowd erupted in cheers and applause. They stood close together and smiled adoringly at their subjects.

Ella's hair was done perfectly. No one else would even be able to tell how short it was, not to mention why. Her sage green gown fell over her flawlessly. I looked over to my side and saw that Mabel and Cecelia were there, identical expressions of horror and jealousy. But I felt none of the satisfaction I had once daydreamed about, because though I hid it better than they did, my emotions mirrored theirs for once in my life.

Ella's ring glittered in the sunlight, but it was her eyes that I couldn't look away from. She was smiling, but her eyes were blank. Dead. Worse than after a beating from Victoria. Worse than when she was fighting back some emotion she didn't want to feel. It was as if she didn't even have any emotions to fight back.

Prince Kenton reached for her hand with a tentative, questioning look. She smiled back at him like she would at any stranger. Stiffly, she placed her hand in his. I looked around at the crowd, wondering if they perceived the awkwardness. Every face was upturned, beaming with joy at the royal couple. No one seemed to notice Ella's tight, sad smile. No one seemed to notice Kenton's unease.

Ella looked down at me and our eyes met. Suddenly it was just me and her. A thousand memories filled my mind and I smiled. I expected to see her face light up and the blankness disappear like it always had when she saw me. I knew I shouldn't hope it. She wasn't mine, after all. Not now.

I waited. My heart didn't pound in my chest; it lay there silent and cold as I searched for something in her eyes, anything in her eyes. Nothing. Slowly, her gaze left mine and she returned to looking at the crowd, the unfeeling smile on her lips.

Kenton raised their joined hands and the crowd shouted for joy, though there were more than a few young ladies who stood there silently, their chins quivering. Ella didn't look back down at me. Slowly, methodically, I turned away and struggled against the adoring multitude to escape. I didn't remember finally emerging through the crowd or making it into the forest, but suddenly I was alone, and running. Running so hard I thought my heart would burst. I clutched at my chest as I fought for breath. I knew I was in the forest but all I could see were Ella's cold, lost eyes before me. I couldn't see the trees. I couldn't hear the frantic fluttering of the birds' wings when they flew from their nests in fear at my loud approach.

This was what I had wanted for her—marriage to a prince, someone who could provide her with the things I could never give her. I had tried to save her by giving her what I thought she wanted.

I had failed her.

Now she was living a life she didn't love. Living in a place that wasn't home. Holding hands with a man she didn't know.

I could hear the leaves crunching under my feet, but I couldn't feel them. I could hear the wind rushing around me, but I couldn't feel that either. Finally, my heart pounding so hard and the pain in my chest making it impossible to breathe, I stopped running—but the sound of footsteps continued. I stood, silent and motionless, and listened. These footsteps were light; not crashing down angrily on the leaves, but almost floating above them. The footsteps slowed . . . and I opened my eyes.

***

Ella emerged from the clearing in the trees. I immediately knew where I was. I was still at the pond. The prince had come to Ashfield to take Ella to the palace, but she hadn't married him yet. I had been dreaming, though it had been a nightmare.

Perhaps she had come to say good-bye before she left. But she looked too cheerful for a good-bye. She looked radiant, actually. Her eyes glowed with some newly discovered happiness. I had never seen her this happy. I had seen glimpses of what I imagined to be true happiness in her, but seeing this made me realize I never had any idea the happiness she was capable of.

It was more than just the transcendent peace that had come to her since her forgiveness of Victoria. It was more than the way she looked at me that told me she knew I loved her, had always loved her. There was something more.

I couldn't breathe and I didn't want to. It was the prince, not me, who had brought this incandescent light into her eyes.

She looked at me and smiled. She had a peculiar expression that told me she knew something I didn't. She passed right by her usual spot on the other side of the pond and continued to the bridge, without pausing. For the first time I had ever seen, she began to cross to my side.

Her steps were so sure, her head held so high. The confused

girl I had left just moments before was now a strong, confidant woman. I felt myself stand up, and then walk to her. *She's coming to say good-bye. She's coming to say good-bye*, I told myself as I reached the bridge and stopped to stand before her.

She looked up at me with eyes so full of sweetness and joy . . . and something else that looked so much like unabashed adoration that my heart almost broke.

"Have you come to say good-bye?" I tried to keep my voice calm and steady, but when I uttered that final, heartbreaking word, it felt like my world crumbled at my feet, though I couldn't even feel the ground.

Ella looked up sweetly at me as she took a step closer, raised her hands, and placed them tenderly on my face. Her eyes filled with passionate, ardent tears. "Never."

Every pain, every moment of indecision and even agony, blew away like the leaves that were now carried away with the wind. But what was left in their place was a surety and a peace that I never could have felt without them. I closed my eyes, slowly raising my hands to cover hers, and finally opened my eyes to look at her. In her eyes I saw the full depth of feeling and affection that she had only hinted at before. My hands traced her arms, down her back and to her waist, where I encircled her in my arms, holding her close to me. Ella glanced down at my lips as she nodded, answering the question I hadn't asked with words.

"I'm yours," she whispered.

I couldn't help a surprised grin from spreading across my face. It was going to be very enjoyable getting to know this new Ella. There was no fear, no hesitation, and no barriers. She came up onto her bare toes as I tenderly, and for what I knew would be the first of a million times, touched my lips to hers.

Slowly, I pulled away and brushed my lips across her cheek. I pulled her up higher to me so that her feet barely touched the ground, ducked my head to rest on her shoulder, and buried my face in her soft, short hair.

"Ella, I thought I lost you!" I whispered, my lips at her ear. "The prince came to marry you and take you away from me. He has everything to offer you and I have nothing. I can't believe you're standing here. Do you realize that you just said 'no' to a prince?" I shook my head in wonder as my lips traced across her smooth, warm cheek.

"No, I didn't," she whispered fervently as she held me tighter.

I laughed. "Ella, I realize you know this and it's not that I want you to change your mind, but you could have been a princess—a queen—in a palace! The prince obviously loves you and wanted you, and yet here you are. Please explain this to me."

"This wasn't just a choice between two lives. This was a choice between two loves."

"Love?" I wondered if there was a more beautiful word in the world.

"The prince told me he loved me last night. He promised me a life of ease and comfort and luxury. He stayed awake all night and searched for me all day. And I will admit, I was flattered. The prince swept me off my feet, but you planted my feet firmly on the ground." I bent and touched my forehead to hers. She had seen it. She had seen it all. She never needed my feeble words to tell her. "You have sacrificed for me. You have given so much. You have suffered when I've suffered. I saw pain in your eyes for my pain. You have shared my joys and have always been there to give me comfort and friendship. This is the kind of love I need. I don't need someone to take me out of the fire so I don't get burned; I need someone to walk through the flames with me. And I will do the same for you." She blinked up at me through tear-filled eyes. Her fingers wound absently through my hair. "How could I have been so blind?"

"I would have waited forever." It was true. Until the moment she said "I do" to the prince, I knew I never would have left.

That was why I couldn't go home and pack after I had left her; that was why I hadn't left to some distant kingdom to escape the pain. Until there was absolutely no hope for us, I would have waited.

"Ella."

"Yes?" She smiled.

I pulled back so I could see her face. "I want to offer you all I have. I will do all I can to make you safe and comfortable and happy. It won't all happen at once, but we're going to make it. I know it can never compete with a palace and jewels and gold, but . . ."

She pulled my face to hers and stopped me with a kiss. "There's no competition." She must have seen the uncertainty in my eyes. How could that possibly be true? "Will, all I need is you. When you told me that night by the fire that you had nothing to offer me, you were wrong. You are everything to me."

I drew my hands away from her waist and reached up for her hands that were wrapped around me. I pulled them up to my lips, kissing first her delicate fingertips, then the backs of her hands, and then slowly—finally—kissing the angry, red lines of pain and neglect she had endured for half of her life. How many times had I longed to do this, to help her heal and to let her know she was so indescribably loved? I whispered her name and she watched me tenderly as tears welled in her eyes and rolled down her cheeks. I touched my lips to each one that fell as I cradled her face in my hands.

"I love you," we said together, and then laughed quietly.

"Then it must be true," she whispered, her lips brushing my ear.

With one more kiss, I took her hand in mine and we turned toward Ashfield. She placed a hand in her pocket and smiled up at me with more contentment and warmth than I had ever thought possible. We emerged through the trees. Ella's home and haven stood majestic and welcoming in the dimming light of dusk. Suddenly I realized we were in a little predicament. There was no way I was going to leave her, but I also knew I couldn't go inside with her without taking care of a few things first.

"I think we better pay Mr. Grey a little visit," I said, chuckling.

"Can I change first?" she said with a smile.

"I'll wait out here."

After a few minutes, she emerged and closed the door behind her and we walked hand in hand down the road toward the church. She had her ball gown on that would very soon become her wedding gown. She had both of her glass slippers on her feet and an exquisite smile on her face.

We returned home—to our home—where we had both learned to love and discovered who we were. She was my angel and this was our heaven.

We were a perfect fit.

Epilogue

"Is that stirrup too high for you, my lord?" I asked with a smirk on my face. I ducked away from Grant's foot, which was swinging at my head.

"If you call me that again, I'm going to really kick you," Grant threatened with an embarrassed grin. Lady Gwen smiled as she reached out to touch his arm.

"Thank you, Will, dear. Someone needs to teach my husband how to be a gentleman."

Grant turned to Gwen and smiled at her; he reached over and took her hand and kissed it.

"Hurry up, you two. You better not keep the prince and princess waiting." I chuckled. With a nod, Grant and Gwen galloped off behind the hills to meet Jane and Kenton.

Jane and Kenton were still getting used to each other. It had only been a few months since the wedding and they still preferred someone else to accompany them on their rides. It helped to provide a buffer between them and the awkward silences. They were fond of each other from the beginning, but were still navigating through the insecurities of their new relationship.

After Grant and Gwen joined Kenton and Jane, I made sure that all was taken care of in the stables. Then I saddled up Charlie and we headed toward the middle of town. The last few months had been strange without Corbin there, working expertly and steadily in his blacksmith shop. I had been doing a lot of repairs at Ashfield and it would have been nice to have his expertise. The new blacksmith was still learning. He had barely finished his apprenticeship in Lytton before he took over Corbin's job. I decided it was easier to do most of the work myself at home.

"Mr. Hawkins!" a voice called. "A letter for you, sir." I turned to see the postman's son running toward me, a letter in his hand.

"Thank you," I said as I reached down and took the letter from him. I reached into my coat pocket and handed him a little sweet wrapped in paper that Mrs. Hammond had brought the grooms from the kitchens. His eyes widened, "Thank you, sir!" he said as he popped the confection into his mouth and ran off. I looked down at the letter, but I didn't recognize the writing. It wasn't from Margaret or my mother or anyone else in my family. I tucked it in my pocket and decided to read it after I got home.

I steered Charlie to the road, but I had to suddenly pull hard to stop him as Francine McClure walked across our path.

"Good day," I said and nodded to her. Francine looked up at me with the same desolate expression on her face she wore every time she saw anyone who reminded her of Corbin. I wasn't sure if she truly missed Corbin, or if he was just another thing she couldn't have, and that was what made her long for him. I sincerely felt sorry for her, though I thought that things had worked out for the best, even if they would take a little time to heal.

Charlie and I hurried along the road toward home. This was always the longest ride of the day. But today I saw the figure of a woman just ahead of us and my heart leaped in my chest. I pulled Charlie to a stop and jumped down from the saddle.

She had a shawl over her head, holding her short hair back and protecting her neck from the cold. She wore a deep blue dress that fell to her feet, her tiny black shoes poking out with each step. Her head was held high. As I approached her I could hear her soft humming.

I caught up to her, and as I did, her hand reached out as she kept her eyes straight ahead, a sweet smile lighting her face. I grasped one of her hands, which were both covered in a thick, wool mittens, and bent down to kiss her cheek.

"Hello, my Will," Ella said with a warm smile as she looked up at me.

"Hello, my Ella." I wondered for the millionth time if I would ever get used to her being mine.

I looked down at the basket she held in her other hand. It was full of ingredients and kitchen supplies. "Helping your sisters again?"

She nodded and smiled a little wider. "They're coming along."

Mabel and Roger Wallace had been married just a week after the ball. Roger had already squandered his entire inheritance by the time they were married. When it was discovered that Mabel had nothing to offer him, Mrs. Wallace refused to give the couple a penny. She had finally realized that Roger would waste anything she gave him, and that Mabel had been dishonest. Mrs. Wallace even refused to let Cecelia be courted by her nephew, but had agreed to let Cecelia work as a maid in her home.

I was glad I had decided to stay on Mrs. Wallace's good side.

"What did you teach them today?" I asked.

"Bread making," Ella replied. "The loaves turned out more like rocks, but that's how mine used to be, too. We'll keep working at it."

Ella had been going to Mabel's little home every week teaching her how to cook and clean. Cecelia was encouraged by Mrs. Wallace to go learn from Ella, too, since Cecelia knew absolutely nothing besides how to pout. There had been many tears and howls of injustice at first, but Ella was a patient teacher. From Ella's last report, they could now sew on buttons, make butter, and start a fire.

Ella's steps had slowed and she looked a little pale. "Would you like to ride? We have a while to go still." I slid my arm around her waist, ready to help her up onto the saddle.

"No, I'm fine, but thank you. My charming husband bought me a wonderful pair of shoes and I feel like I could walk all day in them."

As we walked along, Ella unconsciously placed a hand over her waist and I pretended not to notice. I wondered when she was ever going to tell me her little secret. She had tried a few times, but had ended up blushing so furiously she had to leave the room.

Finally, the towers of Ashfield appeared in the distance and soon the freshly painted pillars greeted us. There was a piece of paper fluttering in the wind that someone had slid into the crack in the door.

"Jane," we both said.

"Then it must be true," Ella said, smiling.

Jane was a frequent visitor at Ashfield. On the times she came when we weren't at home, she would leave a little note, letting us know she would come back another time. Jane never admitted it, but Ella suspected she was lonely at the palace and wanted to reach out to old friends. Whenever Jane came, she always brought her entourage as was expected of her. This was when I could usually be found tending to the horses or chopping wood. Since we still had no furniture, Ella and Jane often sat on the bottom steps in the house, or Jane would follow Ella to the kitchen as Ella cooked them up something to eat. Jane told Ella what royal life was like—the parties, the food, the servants, the clothes and shoes, the rules and expectations and how overwhelmed she was with it all, but also how exciting and glamorous it was. Ella would listen and smile, and offer a word of encouragement here and there, no hint of jealousy or longing on her face.

Always, after Jane left, Ella would hold me a little tighter than usual and thank me for our simple, quiet life. It was in these moments that I felt reassured that, though we didn't have all the luxuries of life—if any—and it would still be a few years before I could stop working at the palace and raise horses full-time, Ella was content and she had no regrets.

"I'll be right in." I kissed Ella on the cheek as we reached the front yard. She smiled and walked in the front doors while I led Charlie to the stables.

I brushed, fed, and watered each of the horses before placing thick wool blankets across their backs. Snow flurries began to swirl around outside. I was grateful the horses had a warm, safe place to stay. I looked up at the hole I had repaired that week before the ball and grinned. I never would have imagined that life would have ended up like this on that day. I never thought that I would one day be living here with Ella. I had always figured, if we were ever married, that I would have to take her away from Victoria. But, she had been able to stay in her own home. We were able to live in this place we both loved. I shook my head, astounded by how things had turned out.

Before returning to the house, I stopped at the garden. I knelt down and slid my hand over the three headstones, dusting off the snow. There was no malice in my heart as I touched the last one—Victoria's. Ella had invited the entire town to Victoria's funeral that we held a few days after our wedding. Ella spoke kindly of her, sympathy and peace crowding out any other emotions she could have let herself feel.

Forgiveness had taken longer for me than it had for Ella. She recognized the need to rid herself of the hurt before I had. Watching Ella experience pain at Victoria's hand—whether it was physical or emotional—had built up a wall of resentment around my heart. Though I knew Ella's hurt was deep, she told me once that watching another person suffer might even hurt deeper; that the helplessness I felt was another kind of pain entirely.

It wasn't until I grew more accustomed to Ella's happiness and the light in her eyes during those first days and weeks of our marriage that the bitterness began to melt away. It was a slow, painful process. Holding onto that anger had become a habit. Letting go of it was almost like learning how to breathe again. But once I did, the air was sweeter than it had ever been.

The wind swirled around me and I stood and walked over to the pasture. I opened the gate and brought Lucy into the barn. She wasn't producing as much milk these days. She would need to have another calf before spring if we were to have enough milk. I patted her back and latched the door. I didn't go to the chicken coop. There were no more chickens.

I closed the door and smiled at Ella. She was bent over the fire, mixing something in a pot that smelled heavenly. I crossed the room and took her in my arms.

"Can I kiss you properly now?" I asked.

"Please do," she smiled, and I did. Like every time I kissed her, every worry and care faded to nothingness. Every pain became a distant memory. In those moments, there was only beauty in the world. Only peace and contentment. Just Ella and me.

When I held her to me, the letter in my pocket crinkled, reminding me it was there, and I took it out to look at it.

"Oh, a letter!" Ella cried. "Is it from your mother?"

"I don't think so, unless she hired a scribe." I chuckled. "Look at this." We bent over the letter, inspecting it. The paper was thick and expensive and the writing was almost too fancy to be legible.

"You haven't charmed any more princes lately, have you? This could be a love note from one of them." I winked.

She pushed my arm playfully. "No, darling. Those are all addressed to *me*." She laughed, kissed me, and returned to mixing her pot.

Smiling, I pulled the letter out of the envelope and started to read it silently. But after the first couple of sentences, I started over and read out loud so that Ella could hear.

Will-

I hope this letter finds you well. I want to congratulate you again on your recent wedding. I, too, am married and am extending an invitation for you and Ella to come and visit at your earliest convenience. You will find me at the palace in Laurel. I have included sufficient funds for your journey.

Your Friend,

His Royal Highness, Prince Corbin of Laurel

Ella had sat down on the chair in front of the fireplace, her mouth gaping open.

"What does this mean?" she breathed.

"Corbin is married. He . . . he's married to The Beast." I couldn't even laugh. I couldn't find anything funny about the situation. I couldn't even begin to imagine how this could have happened. The last I had seen Princess Rose, she was storming out of the castle, broken-hearted over losing Prince Kenton. The last time I had seen Corbin, he was leaving town, broken-hearted over losing Francine. "He doesn't sound very happy," I said finally.

"No, he doesn't," Ella agreed, her face solemn. Ella had never really known Corbin, but I had told her enough stories that even she could tell that he didn't sound like himself.

"I wonder who wrote this for him. Corbin doesn't read or write. Maybe he couldn't be as open as he wanted to be since he couldn't write it himself." I pondered for a moment, rubbing two of the coins between my fingers. "Well, how would you like to finally go on a wedding trip?" I asked, deliberately trying to lift the melancholy mood and shake the worry I felt over Corbin's detached, formal letter.

Ella's eyes brightened, though she looked nervous. "To a palace? With royalty?"

I laughed and walked over to her, knelt down, and took her hands in mine. "If I recall correctly, you have never had any problems winning over royalty."

Ella laughed suddenly, her cheeks coloring, and she kissed me. "You're never going to let me live that down, are you?"

"No, it's too much fun." I kissed her blushing cheek. "Especially since you chose me."

She laughed as she stood to prepare dinner. "You do realize it's your fault he wanted to meet me, don't you? If I had walked to the ball as I had planned, I would have been covered in twigs and dust and my hair would have looked like a rat's nest."

"You still would have looked irresistible." She shook her head and smiled. I glanced down at the cellar doors and abruptly changed the subject. "I don't know about you, but I am in the mood for potatoes."

"Potatoes? Yes, I suppose it has been a while, hasn't it?"

"Six days," I replied.

"You're keeping track that closely?" she asked. "I suppose I better be more diligent in the variety of meals I serve," she teased. I laughed, but felt a little nervous. "Would you mind going down to the cellar and getting me some?" she asked.

I stammered for a moment. "How about I go get the firewood. It's starting to snow and I don't want you out there in the cold. *And* I'll peel the potatoes."

Ella laughed. "You spoil me," she said as she opened the door and climbed down the ladder.

"Nonsense. I'm just afraid of the cellar. You know, all those spiders and everything." I winked and she looked at me shrewdly before climbing down the ladder.

I pretended to walk toward the door, but stopped once Ella was out of sight. I heard her moving some things around and my heart pounded with anticipation. I lit a few candles so that I could see her face better when she came up from the cellar.

Suddenly, all was quiet. Ella was no longer moving things around. I could almost feel her holding her breath. I closed my eyes and smiled as I heard her gentle gasp from the cellar. I sat down in the chair and waited for her. After a few moments, Ella climbed the ladder and emerged from the cellar. Clutching an object tightly against her chest, Ella walked over to me, sat down in my lap, and wrapped her free arm around me.

I enfolded her in my arms as her tears wet my shirt.

"How, Will? How did you manage this?" she whispered.

I pulled back and caressed the tears from her cheeks and looked down at the violin in her lap. Slowly, I grasped the neck of the violin and turned it around slowly to reveal the name "Henry Blakeley" engraved on the back.

Ella's hand flew to her mouth and her other hand reached out to gently trace the name with her fingers.

"Papa," she whispered.

Her face became indistinct and I blinked to clear my vision. She looked at me, her glistening eyes asking a thousand questions.

"Five days ago I was coming home from the palace," I said. "I saw Mr. Wilde selling things from his cart. As I had done for years, I walked over to see if he had the one thing I had been searching for. He didn't say anything as I approached him, only reached to a hidden compartment on his cart and showed me this. Someone in Milton had traded it for a pearl necklace. He had been saving it for me." I gestured to the violin and Ella held it closer to her. "I could hardly believe he had a violin and I knew I had to have it. I rushed home and got my extra month's pay for working at the ball and I was able to buy the violin right there on the spot."

Ella cradled into my side and rested her head on my chest. Tender tears rolled down her cheeks as she looked at her violin.

"You were helping your sisters that day, so I was able to tighten the strings and fix it up a bit before you got home. It wasn't until I turned it over to polish the back that I saw your father's name." The words caught in my throat and I just held her. I remembered sitting next to Henry Blakeley's deathbed, watching him lovingly hold his violin just hours before his death. I took a breath and smiled. "By the way," I added, "I don't really care if we have potatoes. I just couldn't bear to wait one more day for you to discover this." We laughed. "I wrapped the violin in a cloth and put it down in the cellar and hid it behind the potatoes, exactly where it had been taken from you. I wanted everything that had been lost to be restored. I wanted you to be able to pick up right where you had left off."

Ella watched me with her lips slightly parted, a look of wonder in her eyes. Suddenly, she kissed me so ardently my tears mingled with hers. Her fingers reached up to touch my face. "Will, there's nothing I can give you that can equal this."

"It's not a competition or anything, but you've already given me much more."

Slowly, tentatively, I kept my eyes on her face as I reached out my hand to place it on her belly. Smiling, and blushing even in the dim candlelight, she covered my hand with hers and nodded.

I raised my other hand to touch her short, but growing hair, and gently pulled her head down onto my shoulder. We whispered things to each other in the darkening kitchen—our hopes, our uncertainties, our promises, and our dreams.

In the west, the sun descended. I held in my arms everything I loved in the world and felt the promise of our future grow in that warm kitchen. The seed of our unlikely friendship had quietly blossomed into a rare and beautiful flower. In every decision we made, our roots became deeper, our hurt withering away. Until, at last, the sun broke through the clouds and together, we turned toward its warming rays.

The End

Book Club Questions

1. From the very beginning of the novel, we know that Ella is suffering, but refuses to leave. Will respects her decision, but is tormented as he watches her suffer. Did he do the right thing? Should he have rescued her?

2. How is Corbin a foil for Will? Do you agree with how Corbin handles the news of the ball? Or do you agree with how Will handles it? How might Francine have reacted if Corbin had acted the way Will did? How might Ella have reacted if Will had acted the way Corbin did?

3. It takes longer for Will to forgive Victoria than it took for Ella. Do you think Ella was right in saying that watching someone experience pain might sometimes be harder than experiencing the actual pain? Have you ever seen this in your own life?

4. Will genuinely dislikes Roger Wallace. Does this run deeper than just personality differences? How does Will's family's past influence how he feels about Roger?

5. Describe Will's relationship with Prince Kenton. How can our circumstances, positive or negative, influence how we see others?

6. Was Francine justified in pursuing Prince Kenton? Should she have married Corbin without knowing what could have happened with the prince? Is it always worth the price to live with no regrets? Was Corbin right in his decision to leave?

7. How did Will grow as a man throughout the story, considering Henry's advice in the Prologue. Did he become the man he hoped to be?

Acknowledgments

First, I would like to thank my Heavenly Father who is there for us every minute of every day as we live our own miraculous stories.

Huge and heartfelt appreciation to my sweet Gary and my beautiful boys for your love, support, and encouragement. You can count on me like 1, 2, 3 and I can count on you like 4, 3, 2. Wooo-wooo. You're my favorites.

Thank you to my incredible parents, siblings, friends, and extended family for being the best, biggest group of cheerleaders a gal ever had. You make me cry. And laugh. And cry whilst laughing.

Many thanks to Lyle Mortensen, Christine Wilkins, Emma Parker, and Jessica Romrell for helping me tell Will's story. I am so grateful for your talents, insights, and expertise. Will was in very good hands.

Thank you Rebecca Greenwood for the breathtaking cover. I'm in love! Also, thank you to everyone at Cedar Fort for being the best group of people to work with. You complete me.

Lastly, thank you Gilbert, Fitzwilliam, Rhett, yes, even Hamlet. You're all represented here, fellas.

ABOUT THE *Author*

JESSILYN STEWART PEASLEE WAS BORN THE FOURTH of seven children into a family of avid readers, music lovers, movie quoters, and sports fans. Jessilyn graduated from Brigham Young University with a BA in English. She loves going on dates with her husband and playing with her five adorable, rambunctious boys. Jessilyn grew up in the beautiful high desert of Southern California and now resides in the shadow of the Rocky Mountains. As you read this, she is probably folding laundry . . . or should be.

0 26575 19080 9